INDEPENDENT
LEGIONS
PUBLISHING

Horror Writers
ASSOCIATION
SPECIALTY PRESS AWARD RECIPIENT

SPREE AND OTHER STORIES
by Lucy Taylor

ISBN: 978-88-99569-86-0
Copyright (Edition) ©2018 Independent Legions Publishing
Copyright (Work) ©Lucy Taylor
Cover Art by Wendy Saber Core

SPREE AND OTHER STORIES
by Lucy Taylor

SUMMARY

Wall of Words, originally published in *The Flesh Artist,* Silver Salamander Press,1994

Extremophiles, originally published in *Axes of Evil*, Chuba Cabra House, 2014

How Real Men Die, originally published in *Fatal Journeys*, Overlook Connection Press, 2014

La Señora Blanca, originally published in the anthology *Danse Macabre: Close Encounters with the Reaper* edited by N. Kilpatrick; EDGE Science Fiction and Fantasy Publishing, 2012

Making the Woman, originally published in *Unnatural Acts and Other Stories*, Richard Kasak Books, 1994

Things of Which We Do Not Speak, originally published in *The Flesh Artist*, Silver Salamander Press, 1994

Spree, originally published by Cemetery Dance Publications, 1998

WALL OF WORDS

I BURNED the Wall of Words last night, right before I headed south on Highway 87 toward Colorado.

It torched just like a big old funeral pyre, and I watched till the last ember sizzled and charred and the last vowel crisped and the final consonant became just so much soot.

Pa's famous Wall of Words, the talk of northwest Nebraska that people came all the way from Denver and Sioux Falls and Kansas City to see, now it's only so much blackened kindling.

No more words.

Just silence, except for the breeze whistling through cinders and ash.

Enough silence now even for Pa, I 'spect.

We never talked much around our house in Hay Springs, Nebraska, mostly 'cause Pa forbid what he called "idle gabbing," that is, conversation that wasn't absolutely necessary.

Myself, I guess I wouldn't have minded a bit more talk, but then Pa took up his carving hobby, and I figured we had words to spare, more words than I ever knew existed: long, complicated words like *fornication* and *serendipity* stacked up on the mantel, peculiar words like *quandary* and *abacus* on the coffee table, chunky words like *grunt* and *brood* stoppering the doors.

I never did know what most of 'em meant and Pa, he probably didn't either. He just found 'em in the dictionary and liked their shape and sound, figured they'd look right attractive on

7

somebody's dresser top or what-not shelf.

Pa, you see, was a wordsmith. Not some wuss with nothin' better to do than peck out words on a typewriter or a computer, but a real wordsmith. He *made* words. In the shed back of the house, what I reckon some people would call his studio, Pa carved words out of balsa and pine and cherry and other things besides.

It started soon after Pa came back from prison two years ago, when I'd just started tenth grade for the second time. Pa'd been a champion bull rider and calf roper during the years my older brother Josh and I was little, and he spent the best part of the year on the road. Then he got convicted of attempted murder after knifing a rodeo clown that Pa claimed drove him half-crazy singin' Gene Autry tunes all the time. When Pa got out of the joint after six-and-a-half years, that was the end of his career on the rodeo circuit.

I guess maybe he developed a taste for silence in prison, though, 'cause after he come home, Pa started to complain that Ma talked too much. She was a "jabberjaw," as he put it, and Josh weren't much better; Pa called him a "yakkity-yak." Pa forbid Ma to say anything that wasn't absolutely necessary, which I always figured was why she communed with Jim Beam so often and so long. One night, though, after Ma'd threatened to leave Pa the first time some drinkin' buddy offered her a ticket out of town, she screamed, "If words was money, Ben Foley, you'd be the richest man in Nebraska, the way you miser every syllable away!"

Well, that musta gave Pa an idea. Next day he bought some wood and sharpened up the old carving knife he used for whittlin' back in his rodeo days and he started to carve out words.

At first Pa carved ordinary words—folks' names and a few inspirational words, but he tired of that real quick. He bought a dictionary and browsed in it for longer and more unusual words whose letters lent themselves to squiggles and corkscrews: long words and short ones, adverbs and nouns and adjectives, swear words and sex words (which he always carved small, but with a lot of fancy doodads), even a few foreign words—*Himmel* and *merde* and *Kindertot* are a few I recall.

Pa didn't just carve words, you see, he made works of art. He'd spend all afternoon curlicuing the ends of the L's in *languid* and *lewdly* and *longitude* or turning the B in *betrothed* into a fire-breathing serpent singeing its own tail.

The more Pa carved, the less he talked and the more he enforced the No Idle Chatter and No Speakin' Unless Spoke To rules. And Ma, she took to drinkin' in nearby towns like Rushville and Chadron, and sometimes didn't come home for days at a time. When she did straggle in, Pa wouldn't say nothin' at all, but from the door of his workshop he'd hurl a word at her—*slut* or *bovine* or *perversity*—as she teetered on up the walk with her hair teased like a bird's nest and her clothes rumpled and soiled.

And Ma'd retaliate by letting loose a stream of words fit to shame the devil himself.

"You daft old bastard, you with your goddamn woodcarving, you got woodshavings for brains! Why can't you *talk* to me, holler or curse, like any normal man?"

But Pa'd just glare and pull his silence round him like a cloak and turn his back to her.

By this time, Pa'd bought a router and an assortment of attachable drill bits and cutters, so he could make his words bigger and more complex. Some of the letters stood two or three feet high, and the shed where Pa worked was so full up with words the walls looked like pages out of a dictionary.

Finally, I come in from school one day and saw he'd commenced to building something with the words. At first, I thought it was some kind of sign or joke or pun, but I soon realized the words stacked up in the backyard held no particular significance or sense. *Thimble* and *kissing* and *macaroon* formed part of the base with *slurp* and *bereavement* and a very highly ornamental *clannish* topping these and then some other words, short ones, on the third tier. Pa'd driven nails into the wood to hold the words together. The wall rose maybe four feet high then, at its tallest point, and stretched 'bout ten feet long.

Soon after the wall went up, my older brother Josh, who had a small farm of his own across the highway, stopped by the house one Saturday to ask me would I go with him to talk to Pa about what we referred to as "Ma's pastime."

I agreed to go, but my heart was heavy…havin' a conversation with Pa was about as easy as gettin' milk out of a chicken.

But Josh was always better with words than I was and less afraid of Pa, too, him bein' older and livin' on his own.

"We gotta do somethin' about Ma," Josh said, standing there

in the shed while Pa carved. "Get her into a rehab or something."

Pa was working on the tail of the "y" in *chastity*, and he finished it before he replied, which took a good ten minutes.

"A drunk tank?" he said finally.

"No, sir, I was thinkin' more like a treatment center."

Pa carved on. Five minutes later, he said, "She's like the lot of y'all. You gab too much, fritter away your time. Jabberjaw and yakkity-yak, all day long."

He blew loose wood shavings off the letters.

"But, Pa, I think..."

He looked up, eyes hooded and hawkish, woodchips clinging to his beard like dark beetles. He stared at me, and I felt just like he'd turned the router on me and was drillin' out parts of my gut.

"How 'bout you, Billie-boy? You gonna have your say, too?"

I couldn't have admitted it then, not even to myself, but I was scared of Pa. He wielded silence like a club, and the few words that he ever spoke were more the kind that separate than those that might make bridges.

"No, Pa, I ain't got nothin' to say."

His stare carved me up in sections, and I thought about that rodeo clown back in Denver and how many stitches they said it'd took to put his face back together.

"You goin' into town today?"

"Yessir."

He nodded, concentrating on the wood.

"Be long?"

"Few hours mebbe."

"Bring me back some Copenhagen..."

"Yessir."

"...and your Ma some whiskey."

"But, Pa...I..."

Pa reached for his dictionary and opened it to choose another word. I peered over his shoulder and saw his long fingers pick out *scrumptious*.

"...about Ma, I think...maybe..."

But he wasn't listening anymore, and I knew if Josh and I stood there all day long, we'd get no discussion from him.

NOT LONG after Josh tried to talk to Pa, Ma went out on a drunk, and didn't come back. I figured she'd turn up in a few days, like she always did, but when a week passed, I decided she musta gone and done it, run off with some man who asked her to, like she'd been threaten' to do ever since Pa took up his carving. I didn't say nothin' about it, not even to Josh. I missed Ma, but I felt happy that she'd run away. For a while there, I had dreams of me and Ma together, in a fancy party at a big mansion, where everyone talked and laughed about their hopes and dreams and fantasies, and the words just flowed all over each other, all rainbow-colored and glowing like fireworks in the dark.

I hoped wherever she'd run off to there'd be lots of people she could talk to.

Meantime, with Ma gone, Pa worked even harder.

The Wall of Words, as people had begun to call it, was getting higher, longer. Pa added *elephantine* and *gargoyle* and *parsimonious*, carved vertically like totem poles out of huge beams of wood with smaller words connecting them horizontally like in a crossword puzzle. People started taking notice from the road and dropping by to look around, but Pa wouldn't let them inside the shed no longer. He kept it locked, and hardly ever came out at all 'cept to take a piss and nail another word onto the Wall.

Meantime, the visitors that stopped by took pictures of each other by the Wall and let their kids crawl over it till finally Pa put up a fence around it and a sign saying DO NOT TOUCH and NO TALKING.

Over the next few weeks, dozens of other words were added, *obsequious* and *foreboding* and *juvenile*, *malcontent* and *kindness* and *adroitly*, and the Wall just kept getting higher and longer, and some letters were as big as fireplugs and others fancied up with vines and buds and scrollwork, and Pa kept addin' to it, sometimes two or three words a day.

Josh stopped by my room one afternoon while I was laying there, having me a little sip of Scotch and daydreaming about Ma and me gossiping together at some fancy party. He was all fidgety and nervous and had that clenched jaw look he gets when he's been grindin' his teeth at night.

I stood up and offered Josh a pull from my bottle, but he just sneered and said, "Now that Ma's run off, you gonna be the family lush?"

"Helps me kick back," I said, which was true. With enough

booze in me, I could kinda float in and out of that grand, high society party in the mansion where Ma and I drifted among high class nobility, with Ma chitchatting to her heart's content and me confiding my life story to a beautiful big-bosomed lady in a low-cut red gown like one I saw dancing with Johnny Depp in a pirate movie one time.

"Look, we got to *talk*," Josh said.

That made me uncomfortable. It's one thing to fantasize about something, another thing to do it. Josh knew we didn't talk in our family. That wasn't our way.

I shrugged. "'bout what?"

"The goddamn Wall."

"Yeah?"

"Have you *looked* at it lately? Since Pa put up the fence and started makin' it longer?"

"I glance at it from time to time."

"Some of those words, Billie…"

"Yeah?"

"I think…"

And we stood there, staring at the floor, the windows, everywhere but at each other, till I took another swig and lost my balance and plopped back on the bed, and Josh said, "Ya damn drunk…when you can see straight, just go take a look at the Wall."

"Where you goin'?" I said as he walked out the door.

"To talk to Pa," Josh said.

And that was the last I seen of him.

AFTER THAT, it was hard to gauge how many days passed, cause most nights I'd drink and doze off or pass out maybe, and the sun would be comin' up and I'd haul my ass off to school, but like as not I wouldn't go at all. School was a lot like Pa's Wall…just words on top of words that made no sense, all meaningless and stupid.

But when I went by Josh's place sometime later to see would he lend me a few bucks to buy some Wild Turkey and I seen Josh's truck was there but he wasn't anywheres around, I got a little worried. I knocked on the door of Pa's shed to ask if he'd seen Josh anywhere.

Pa unlocked the door and stood there, his big frame blocking my view of everything but one end of his workbench, where the router lay with a particularly vicious-looking cutter slotted into it.

"Josh?" said Pa. "Ain't seen him."

"Not this week?"

"Naw."

"Last?"

"Yep. He stopped by to talk."

This surprised me. "About what?"

Pa actually smiled, but on him it looked unnatural, the muscles at the corners of his mouth hunched up like the hind end of a rutting hound.

"He come by 'cause he got the idea he'd like to sign up with the rodeo for a spell. I give him the names of some buddies of mine he could call up in Laramie and Denver. Told him they could help to get him started. He was all fired up about it. We sat up till past midnight with me tellin' him my stories. If he ain't been around of late, I reckon he left to join the circuit. Reckon he'll do right fine, too. Takes after me, Josh does."

And Pa shut the door in my face.

It was the most words I'd ever heard Pa speak all at one time.

It got me to wonderin'.

THAT EVENING I studied the Wall, looking at the words that had been added since Ma disappeared. There was *mercenary* and *idolater* and *spinnaker*, and below that *flummery* and *euphonious* and dozens of others, words of all shapes and sizes and different materials, and I noticed it then. The two long, light-colored words. Nearly white. Smaller than most and stuck into spaces between the bigger words that were carved out of pinewood and balsa.

There on the side of the Wall, I saw *jabberjaw* and a little ways from that was *yakkity-yak*. They was half hidden by some bigger words, but their paleness made them stand out real sharp.

I musta stared at them two words half an hour or more, running my fingers over each letter, learning their shape and their feel and trying to realize their meaning.

And when I thought I understood, I wrenched loose a word near the top that was carved out of teak, and I went lookin' for Pa.

WORDS. IN Mexico, where I'm headed, I'll hear them, but I won't understand. They'll fall over me like so much freezing rain.

And if I start to understand, I'll move on. To Japan or Vietnam maybe, anyplace where the words, to me, are nothin' more than decoration—singsong, meaningless sounds like birdcalls on a hot summer morning.

'Cause I can't go back to Hay Springs, Nebraska, not never.

That new length of the Wall, the earth below it had been disturbed, dug up and then repacked before the words were piled on top. And them white words I found—*jabberjaw* and *yakkity-yak*—they was carved from human bones.

And Pa? Well, right before I burned the Wall, I cornered him in that shed of his with all the bloodstains on the floor and I killed the silence-loving, murdering old bastard.

With *kindness*, right between the eyes.

EXTREMOPHILES

THE FIRST time I heard the group Extremophile play, I felt like somebody had sawed open my rib cage and dumped in broken glass. Music without a hint of mercy—demented snares, a brutal double bass and barbaric lyrics screamed out by singer/guitarist Magnus Ochoa that unleashed every nightmarish craving I was ever afraid to admit to or lust after. I felt crazy free and at the same time savagely violated.

Right then I vowed to follow Magnus Ochoa to my grave.

I meant it, too.

I just didn't expect it to be this fucking soon.

AFTER THAT first concert at 48 Hours in Las Vegas, I craved Extremophile's sound like something a junkie would mainline into a vein. I ditched my job at the IHOP in Albuquerque and followed the band around the southwest until finally drummer Pretorius James invited me back to their motel. Eventually, after some wild 'n' wooly sessions of musical beds, I got a shot at Magnus himself.

I don't know why, but we clicked. I'm not the nastiest or the biggest boobed of the metal sluts, but Magnus liked having me around. When he was sober, he'd say I was smart like his brother the research scientist and ought to do more with my life than take drugs and follow the metal bands, but when he was using, which was most of the time, he was like me and just wanted to pop pills and fuck. So for a few sex-and-speed-fueled months, we were close—at least as close as two egomaniacs with inferiority complexes and a more-is-never-enough lifestyle could ever be. The sex basically being the libidinous glue holding the rest of the jerry-rigged mess together.

There was also the fact that Magnus enjoyed ruminating between bouts of no-holds-barred sex, and I didn't mind gazing at his beautiful, mixed-blood face—copper skin from his Navajo mother; knife-blade cheekbones and sensuous mouth from his Mexican/Irish father—while I pretended to listen.

At some point, though—I'm not sure when—I actually started paying attention to what he was saying, became engrossed by what was essentially the same tale recounted with increasingly sinister and farfetched variations.

I'd sip Grey Goose from a beer mug as Magnus rambled about the death of his brother, Hector Frane, who had been a microbiologist working at McMurdo Station near the Dry Valleys of Antarctica. Six months earlier, helicoptered into the Dry Valleys to do research, Hector Frane wandered away from camp and apparently become lost or disoriented—not hard to do in an environment that, according to Magnus, is the driest place on the planet, a region so arid and harsh that scientists use it to study what life might be like on Mars.

The geographical equivalent of death metal, he used to say.

Whatever happened to Hector, it was a fucked-up way to die. Magnus said that when his body was found, it was dried out like twists of beef jerky stretched over fossilized bone and his face looked like next of kin to the carcasses of seals strewn nearby.

Whenever he talked about what happened to Hector, Magnus always came back to those seals, how their presence in the Dry Valleys proved the existence of something ancient and malevolent.

"You don't fucking agree, then explain to me, Lizzy, why would seals drag themselves miles and miles inland? Why would they leave the ocean when there's no food in the Dry Valleys, no water?" We'd been awake for three days, holed up in his house in a tony section of Albuquerque, surviving on Jack Daniels, death metal, and a cornucopia of high-quality pharmaceuticals. In his agitation, Magnus kept twisting the turquoise fetish bracelet he always wore, digging the wire ends into his wrist until his zeal to invoke the protection of spirits more benevolent than those of the Dry Valleys finally drew drops of blood.

I put my hand over his to stop him from hurting himself.

"I'll tell you why," he ranted. "Something called those seals out of the sea, just like it lured my brother away from the camp. Then it leached all the water and blood from their bodies and left nothing but husks, just the bones and the skin. That's how perfectly this thing—whatever it is—has adapted to an environment that's totally hostile to life." His voice rose and his dark eyes were so flat and unblinking, he might have been straining to see through a microscope aimed into hell. "Maybe it hypnotizes its victims, it sings to them, whispers—I don't know what they hear—but they follow."

And when I told him, point blank, that it was a batshit crazy idea and tried to change the subject by talking about Extremophile's upcoming gig at the Goregrind Festival in Los Alamos or the feature on the band that *Decibel Magazine* was doing in the fall, he'd just blow me off and go on describing the bizarreness and uncanny strangeness of the Dry Valleys.

At the time, I didn't believe any of it. I thought his descriptions of the Dry Valleys were just lyrics he was making up in his head, but later, after the YouTube video went viral, when not just the metalheads, but the science geeks, too, were weighing in, I was surprised to find out that what he described was actually real—the hurricane-force winds that sweep down from the higher elevations and scour everything in their path, the Blood Falls that gush like a severed artery from the fractured heart of a glacier, the tiny ferocious worms called nematodes that sustain themselves under the ice for centuries by wicking up every last drop of moisture.

A brutal, merciless place. Just where you'd want to go on your summer vacation, right?

It is if you're Magnus Ochoa and think you've got death metal mojo.

"What the fuck are you thinking?" I said when he told me he was planning to go to McMurdo to see the place where his brother had died. "You need a break, fly to Finland, check out Abhorrence and Deathbound. Book some gigs in Helsinki." I rubbed my titties against him, but he was unmoved. It was like trying to snuggle a statue. I voiced my real fear. "What if you go to this weird-shit place and it kills you, too?"

His full lips curled in a beautiful sneer. "It won't. It can't. You know why?"

I waited for him to explain.

"What does the word *extremophile* mean, Lizzy?" His black eyes bored into mine with a look that could suck out your soul. Then he laughed. "Christ, you're this hardcore metal groupie and you don't even know!"

I wasn't about to admit he was right, so I grabbed a bottle next to the bed and took a long, greedy pull.

He grunted as though I'd just confessed to a crime—which maybe in his eyes, I had. "Hell, where do you think I got the name for the band? Those things that live in the Dry Valleys, the microbes and algae my brother was studying, those are extremophiles. Things that can flourish where nothing else would. Like us. You and me, Lizzy, we're extremophiles. We'll survive in the darkest, the most depraved places. The fucking hardcore hell realms of the planet, that's where we thrive!"

LIKE THE hell realm I'm in now, I think grimly, as I survey the motley assortment of thrashers, headbangers, and fight club wannabes assembled here at the fairgrounds outside Gallup, New Mexico. Toxic Swill, the opening act, has been blasterbating for what feels like hours. Some serious moshing's going on in the pit, beer cans careening through the night sky like miniature UFOs, and way the hell out in the no-man's-land between the parking lot and the bleachers, a half dozen small illegal blazes puncture the dark. The air's thick with the odor of burning plastic, cheap booze, and the pungent, aroma of sweat-drenched bodies and furtive blow jobs.

I'm midway between the field and the bleachers, trying to take it all in, and I get a kind of sick, squirrely excitement, the kind of vibe you get at some death metal concerts when the crowd's just a little too gnarly, too hellbent on blood.

It ought to scare me, but it doesn't, because I know Extremophile will be out any minute, and I'll get to see Magnus again.

Even now, after Magnus cut me off after he returned from McMurdo, I can't help wondering if he'll look for me in the pit. Pathetic, huh? Still, he has to know I'd never miss the first gig in Extremophile's comeback tour—even if said tour kicks off in a (literally) shitty fairground where you can still smell the cow pies from the 4-H show that exhibited here last week.

It's not like I haven't tried to talk to him. Since that last night before he left for McMurdo and disappeared from the metal scene for almost a year, I've tried every way possible to contact him, including tracking down groupies he's slept with and IMing and Facebooking the other band members, including Pretorius James, who always lusted for me, but not enough, evidently, to give me Magnus's new unlisted numbers.

Which pisses me off, but just makes me more determined to see Magnus and find out what the hell's going on.

As Toxic Swill grinds to a death-growling frenzy, I climb the bleachers for a better view of the stage and spot a couple of tatted-up mastodons storming the pit. One's wearing a Lamb of God T-shirt, the other's in leather and camo pants. Slackers who don't move out of their way fast enough get an elbow or knee in a sensitive place. For some reason, the way they work as a team, their steely, military-type stares, make me think they're security. Then the shorter one peels off his shirt—oops, my bad, NOT security—he's got Griffin Street 40 tattooed across his massive shoulders, right above the evil-looking slant eyes and a devil's gaping red maw that extends all the way to the small of his hairy back. Griffin Street 40 is the toughest street gang in Albuquerque; even the biggest dudes glare, but get out of their way.

Word at the clubs where I hang out is that Magnus, after his return from McMurdo, had hired Griffin Street 40 as muscle, so maybe my first impression that they were security wasn't far off. I can't see Magnus doing that, though. Death and mutilation lyrics aside, he's basically a peaceful guy who likes to shed fake blood on stage, but wants everybody to go home more or less in one piece.

At any concert, though, there's always one sicko with a death wish, yours or his own. Tonight's would-be suicide is a goateed dude, his long, sheet-pale face bedecked with piercings, who grins and whips out a Madball that he rotates, first with lazy indifference, then gathering lethal speed, just over eye level. People curse and fling themselves out of range. The Griffin goons, unimpressed, wrench away the guy's play toy and snap his wrist in the process, which I can tell by his howls and the way the hand fish-flops like a dead thing at the end of his arm. Now the shorter, shirtless Griffin Streeter grins like a chimp flinging feces and starts swinging the Madball with vicious intent. I hear the meaty impact of cue ball on flesh and see the Griffin thugs swaggering toward the bleachers with shit-eating smirks. The way they eyeball the crowd, they're definitely looking for someone—to avoid trouble, I head in the opposite direction. I figure I'll circle around the edge of the pit and squeeze in at the security bar.

As I elbow my way through the chaos the Griffin gangsters have left in their wake, a headbanger with ratty blonde dreads wearing an Impaled Nazarene T-shirt eye-fucks my tits and offers me a slug from a flask with a death's head on the side. I get an eye-burning whiff of hundred-proof rum. Sweet! I glug as much as I can, then jam the flask in the back pocket of my leather jacket and slither off into the black sea of metalheads.

"Hey, bitch! Come back!" bellows Nazarene.

I push my way forward, Nazarene barging after me. A section of the crowd, triggered by some fracas I can't yet see, suddenly surges between us. I reflect on this unexpected good fortune until I see the guy that everyone seems to be fleeing is headed my way—an emaciated wraith, baggy shirt flapping across a concave chest, features blotted out by the darkness inside a Catamenia hoodie. He looks old or maybe ravaged by some wasting disease. Strands of grey hair that billow out of the hoodie look like the aftershock of some serious chemo. I can't figure why everyone's running—then I catch a whiff of the guy's odor—urine and B.O. and something so putrid I don't even want to guess at, like a tomb in ancient Egypt just opened up and spewed this freak out across time.

The running man gives a hoarse cry and veers toward me. I fend him off, swinging the flask at his head, then see his pursuers—shit!—it's the Griffin Street bruisers pile-driving through the crowd. Catamenia sees them, too, flails his arms as though willing himself to take flight, changes course, and shambles away.

Seconds later, I hear yelling and see Catamenia go down like he stepped off a roof. I get a glimpse of his legs, swinging limply, as he's dragged away between the beefy shoulders of the two goons.

Leaving me covered in chill bumps and quaking for breath, that bad vibe I felt before now a hundredfold stronger.

But fuck it, because the flesh-ripping, drill-bit-to-bone roar that's Extremophile's signature sound suddenly stabs through the night, making everything that came before it seem washed out and bland.

Blue fog sluices over the stage, writhing into the night sky like cobras uncoiling as Extremophile charges onstage: Pretorius James on the drums, Keith Gonzago on the guitar, Abacus Ferro on bass, finally Magnas Ochoa. The fog obscures everything but their outlines, so I can't tell whether they're wearing corpse makeup or masks, but their blurred features look grotesque, like the cement-colored, asymmetrical slab faces a psychotic preschooler might make with Play Doh.

I slam the last of the booze and pitch the flask as Magnus roars out the opening lyrics to "Sadistic Deity": "Here is Damnation! Earth's most exquisite Hell!"

The image of Catamenia being beaten and manhandled is irrelevant now as I wriggle my way through the bodies, closing in on the stage, pressing deeper into the black wall of sound.

"HEAR THAT?"

In the YouTube video (two-and-a-half million hits and counting), Magnus cocks his head, listens, nods as though in confirmation of some sound that only he hears. Behind him stretches an arid, boulder-strewn limbo, bleak and parched beyond imagining. In this frozen desert, his red parka stands out like a wound, providing a single slash of color in an otherwise monochromatic vista of gray rock, pewter sky, and snowless, gunmetal grey slopes. In the background, the gnarled, toothy peaks of the Transantarctic Mountains gouge the underbellies of funereal clouds. The roar of a chopper can be heard fading away.

Magnus's cracked, feral face fills the screen. "Hey, get this, a guy once sued my band because he said his kid killed himself after listening to too much Extremophile. He said our music was evil and carried subliminal messages like 'Die, fucker!' and 'Disembowel yourself!'"

(I didn't know Magnus then, but I remember reading about the trial online, a kid of fifteen or sixteen who'd hung himself with some Extremophile T-shirts knotted together. His old man either believed his crazy accusations about the music or, more likely, just saw some bucks to be made. Magnus never talked about it.

The case went nowhere, of course.)

"Fucking bullshit!" yells Magnus. "You want to hear what evil sounds like, then come to the Dry Valleys of Antarctica! Go walk off alone and just listen, because sooner or later, you'll hear it—the siren song of annihilation! It's what my brother must've heard before he died."

His eyes clock to the side, and the camera pans in on what at first glance appears to be a shrunken head, eyeless and mutilated. The first time I saw it, I recoiled, because I thought it was an autopsy photo of Hector Frane spliced into the video. Now that I know it's the desiccated corpse of a seal—tragically wayward, miles from the sea—it seems like it shouldn't upset me, but I still cringe and look away every time.

"There!"

Wild, leaping strides propel Magnus uphill, into the battering wind, the skin around his mouth and eyes so cracked and ruddy it looks blistered. He offers the camera a bedlamite's raw, ravaged stare. I try to figure out what he's on, come up blank. Nothing we ever snorted, shot up, or swallowed together made Magnus appear this deranged.

"What sound does death make when there's nothing to die?" Magnus throws out this bizarre koan as the camera sweeps over a terrain pocked and mottled as a leper's skin. Fissures, big enough to roll a tire through, scour the boulders, which appear to have been randomly strewn there, but more likely have been nudged along millimeter by millimeter over eons at the whim of the wind.

Now the camera treats us to a close-up of a mummified penguin. Its eyes have been pecked out by the fierce sea birds called skuas, but the rest of the penguin is preserved to almost creepy, petting zoo perfection. A few feet away, another casualty of the Dry Valleys—the flat, flayed-looking face of another seal, long dead but, like its buddy the penguin, impervious to rot and preserved for eternity.

"Nothing lives here, except bacteria that have spent two million years under the ice with no access to oxygen or light," Magnus says. "Two million years in the primordial ooze and still plugging along, still evolving new ways to survive in a place where nothing else does. My brother spent his life studying these things and—"

At this point in the video, which I must've watched a few

hundred times by now, you get a glimpse of a smudgy blue, tentacle-like shape—the wingtip of a skua, a distant chopper blade, the wandering soul of some ill-fated explorer, or a twenty-six-hundred-year-old dead seal?—that slides across Magnus's features, briefly halving them into light and dark, flesh tone and a murky, cadaverous grey. He stops talking, looks flustered. His expression changes to a grimace of what?—surprise? alarm?—then it's gone, both the minuscule glint of emotion and the flickering shadow that conjured it.

He looks up and to the left as the shadows carve his face into a fractal geometry, a beautiful ice sculpture, before he gulps and goes on, "Wandering off alone here means certain death. My brother wasn't suicidal, but he walked away from camp one night and kept trudging for almost thirty miles. He had a G.P.S. and a satellite phone with him, but he ditched them at mile nine. At mile fourteen he threw away his empty water bottles and three miles after that, he took off his shoes. He kept going for another fourteen miles. The people who found him told me his knees and hands were lacerated, because he crawled the last mile and a half. I want to know what the hell happened. What called him out to die and why did he go?"

He tries for the expression of lip-curling rage that he uses on stage, but manages only to look befuddled and vulnerable, like someone who's wandered a long way from home and just realized they forgot to bring bread crumbs. I want to believe it's all for show, an elaborate P.R. stunt or some weird Goth twist the band's taking—that this isn't about his brother at all. Or maybe Magnus's paranoia has just turned a sharp corner into psychosis. Maybe next time I see him, he'll be sacrificing a live sheep on stage.

No sheep. Not yet anyway.

By this time, I've made it to the edge of the pit, a perilous place for anyone, but more so if you're only five-foot-three and 125 pounds. I'm so focused on Magnus I don't see the asshole who slams into me sideways, bulldozing me into the fray.

A black forest of military boots and shitkicker Doc Martens stomp past my fingers and face, miss me by whispers. Powered by panic, I fight my way to my feet, find my balance, and almost get toppled again, this time by a lard-ass chick in a shredded black bodice who grunts "fuck you" as she lunges away.

All around me, bodies careen and collide. I've slam-danced before but this is way worse—it feels like I've stumbled into a gigantic blender inside a sinkhole as I pinball around the circle. A bald guy with a goatee sees my predicament, grabs me by the waist, and deposits me at the edge of the circle, outside the worst of the carnage.

Just in time, too, because up on stage, Magnus has started counting down to a wall of death, which is un-fucking-believable, since he told me about being at a Lamb of God concert at Ozzfest where a guy taking part in just such a ritual got his skull cracked and people were slipping and skidding on bits of his brain. But now, at Magnus's command, people in the pit are dividing down the middle like warring barbarian tribes in some shlock sci-fi battle scene.

"Five—four—(Motherfuckers, split up!)—three—two—one (Fucking HURT each other!)—GO!"

It feels like the earth opens up and regurgitates hell. Bodies break like cheap vases. Teeth take to the air. I hear the roars of the victors, the bleats of the broken. I can just make out Magnus's hair whipping wildly, his hand raised in a claw, but all else is dense fog and smoke drifting in from the fires the assholes in the back field keep setting.

And Magnus, striding around the stage, orders another charge. ("Fucking KILL each other this time!") I've got maybe two or three seconds, and I do something insane—I sprint between the opposing sides of the wall as the two sides converge, dodging a couple of fistfights and leaping over a guy on the ground, make it to the security bar just in time.

People are getting the shit stomped out of them, and I cling to the security bar for dear life. All I want is for Magnus to see me, to know that I braved a fucking wall of death to get close to him, but how can I get his attention when the stage is so swaddled in smoke and fog that Extremophile looks like they're performing inside a gigantic furnace.

From under the stage, a cage creaks into view.

Shivers like tiny electrical charges jolt up my spine.

A minute ago it was so stifling hot in this warm sea of bodies that I feared I'd pass out; now there's a ripple of cold like something long dead, now thawing, that just wafted over the mosh pit.

Magnus jerks his head and Pretorius James reaches over and slips up the latch.

The wraith in the Catamenia shirt totters out, stricken and bug-eyed, poleaxed by the tumult. His wrists are broomstick thin, the skin over his hatchet cheekbones looks ready to split. He staggers out of the cage and collapses to his knees, grasping hold of Magnus's booted foot like a parody of a jilted lover in an old-fashioned melodrama.

Magnus reaches down and wrenches him up by the remnants of his hair.

"Shall I kill him?" he shrieks. "Shall I e-VIS-cerate him?"

The crowd thunders back with murderous zeal. Only a few stand silent but riveted, confused, apparently wanting to believe this is part of the show, but not entirely sure.

"Shall I kill him, motherfuckers? Shall I rip his guts out?"

Catamenia contorts and twists in Magnus's grasp. The hoodie slides back. I see scabbed lips shriveled like old apple peels, blackened gums crowded with too many teeth, the eyes fixed and sunken, empty of everything except anguish.

Around one bruised, skeletal wrist, a stitchery of pale scars is all that remains of the fetish bracelet Magnus once wore.

My guts turn to soup. No one tries to stop me as I clamber over the security bar and climb onto the stage, reaching for Catamenia's limp, leathery hand.

A steel-toed boot finds my ribs, sends me sprawling.

"Kill him, kill him, e-VIS-cerate him!" shrieks the crowd as Catamenia's throat is punched open, a primitive tracheotomy ripped in the papyrus-thin flesh. I expect a gusher of crimson. Instead, a ghastly stench steams out along with rivulets of a murky, yellowish fluid that might once have been blood and which Magnus—the creature I thought was Magnus—puts its mouth to and greedily sucks.

I get to my feet and claw at the thing's face. My fingernails dig into the seams at the edge of its eyes, a fleshy carapace pocked with moist, suction-cup pores, a mask that isn't a mask at all but some kind of exoskeleton designed to sustain whatever resides underneath the grotesque, lumpen features. In spite of myself, I recoil, because I can feel that the outer layer is about to slough off, and I'm not sure I want to see what's underneath.

As I hesitate, the thing grabs my face, pries open my mouth, and probes for saliva with a gray tube of tongue. I can feel its endless thirst and its terrible patience, and suddenly I know what Hector Frane was following when he walked away from the camp in the Dry Valleys.

I'm wet-kissing it right now.

I don't remember how I get down off the stage, maybe I jump or get pushed. One moment I'm on my knees retching, the next I'm swept along in a stampede of bodies that belch out into the parking lot, where I run on blind instinct, the reptilian part of my brain still grinding along, everything else in my head like mangled leftovers from a botched lobotomy.

THAT WAS four days ago. No, maybe three. Hard to be sure.

Magnus said he and I were extremophiles. He was wrong.

Because even curled on the floor with the door barricaded, all the lights on, and death metal pounding me senseless, I still scream out loud at the memory of what I felt when that thing from the Dry Valleys touched me. Not a sound heard by the ears, but a sensation felt by the flesh, the hum and vibration of a terrible void underlying not just the metal, but a web of holes honeycombing creation. I feel it now in the gaps between the cymbal strikes and the growl of the breakdowns and in the stuttering stops between the beats of my heart. Spaces so big that—if I let myself—I could plunge through them and plummet forever into the deep, throbbing dark.

It's what Magnus and I always wanted—the purest, most primal Oblivion. And it calls to me. Oh fuck, it calls.

HOW REAL MEN DIE

EDDIE PITROWSKI hitched up his jeans in a dingy Patpong hotel room and wondered how he could still enjoy sex so much, knowing that in just a few days, he was going to watch his best friend die.

Worse, that he was going to be the one to kill him.

What kind of cold-hearted bastard could compartmentalize such a thing, he asked himself. A sociopath? A sex addict? A nutcase?

All of the above, his ex-wife Annie would have probably said. Their daughter Margaret, too, who according to her mother had become a lesbian purely to spite Daddy and now piloted a Yellow Cab through sections of Detroit that even the cops avoided. The kind of neighborhoods that Eddie had grown up in.

The plump, poppy-lipped girl he'd spent the last twenty minutes bending over the bed collected her clothes, twirled a sequined thong around her finger, and purred, "For a *farang*, you good fook, Eddie. You ready more boom-boom?"

Eddie thought if he had any more boom-boom right now his heart might torpedo right out of his chest, but he grinned at the compliment, happy to hear he was a *farang who could fook*.

He'd had his fun. Now it was time to get down to business. "Your boyfriend back in Soi Cowboy said you'd bring me something extra. You got it with you?"

The girl wiggled the thong up over her hips and reached for her tote bag, which was festooned with sequins and looked larger

27

than the suitcase Eddie'd brought with him for ten days in Thailand. Carefully, she extracted a baggie, which she passed to him using the tips of her nails, as though whatever was inside might try to bite her. Inside was a smaller bag. Eddie unzipped it and shook a minuscule speck of powder onto his finger. Put it to his mouth and got a humdinger of a jolt.

The girl came around behind him, curled her arms around his waist and slithered against his spine like a cobra. "Farang love Thailand," she cooed. "Best sex in world."

"Not to mention the best China White," Eddie said. He resealed the baggie and counted out the girl's money along with what he owed for the heroin. The girl had worked pretty hard, so he added a few hundred baht as a tip, then ushered her out into the steaming, sexed-up, neon-blinding chaos of the Patpong night. He hailed a *tuk-tuk*, gave the driver some bills, and sent her on her way.

No sooner was she gone than another girl approached, this one a mini-skirted bottle blonde who whispered a menu of obscene suggestions like a hostess proffering a tray of hors d'oeuvres.

Though sorely tempted, Eddie declined.

Ah, true paradise, he thought. Then he did a nimble hop-skip to avoid plunking his foot in a pile of dogshit and almost got nailed by a recklessly swerving *songthaew*, a green pickup truck with two benches in the back that served as a popular form of public transportation. The driver screamed something as he careened past, the passengers in back packed in like toothpicks and holding on for dear life.

*Okay, so not a perfect paradise. But still...*every five feet another beautiful, buyable, fuckable woman.

What the hell could be better than that?

Then he thought about the baggie in his pocket and, even in the sticky swelter of the neon-and-exhaust-fume-saturated night, a mean chill banged through his ribs like he'd been tongue-kissed by the devil himself. His mouth filled with ashes and his stomach twisted like a wounded snake.

I need a goddamn drink. Now.

He dodged his way across the chaotic traffic clogging Surawong Road and ducked into the tingling cool of the Nang-Klao Club. His buddies Danny and Kurt sat at the end of the horseshoe-shaped bar, quaffing Singha beers, while a pair of diminutive, bikini-clad bar girls fluttered around them like brilliantly plumaged parakeets. Kurt Anderson was a beefy, fireplug of a man with a barrel chest, curly grey hair receding off a broad forehead, and a goofy, lopsided grin that women found irresistible. He was an ardent photographer and clung to his Sony HD video camera with the kind of protective reverence some men reserve for the family jewels. Beside him slumped Danny Pinchero, fifty-eight years old, a couple years short of retiring from the Ford plant where he'd put in three decades. He was pole-thin and sinewy, with bloodshot black eyes that flashed like exposed synapses and seemed to recede deeper into his skull every day.

All three of them had grown up on Detroit's tough east side, surviving on guile, guts, and sometimes, sheer meanness. They'd each seen the inside of a cell more than once, although only Eddie had done serious time—two years for possession and assault in '83 and a nickel in the early nineties for impulsively holding up a Party Store while under the influence of Wild Turkey and a grab bag of pharmaceuticals. He'd been more or less clean since then, working off and on in construction, but his temper still got him in trouble—he'd been 86'd from so many bars that Kurt joked the only gathering of drunks where he was still welcome was the AA group that met in the First Baptist Church across the street from the neighborhood tavern.

"Got what you went for?" said Danny, his eyes glued to a spotlighted stage in the center of the room.

"Yep."

"So it's under control?"

"As planned."

He took the stool next to Kurt and ordered a Mekong whiskey, then turned his attention to the stage, where a splay-legged young woman was popping ping-pong balls from between her thighs like a hen laying eggs. The crowd applauded uproariously. The woman looked like she was mentally filling out tax forms.

The Mekong came and he chugged it, floating away on the sweet burn for a moment before he signaled the bartender for another. That one went down smoother than the first, and he called for a third.

Kurt leaned over and whispered, "You're hittin' it pretty hard, don't ya think? When the time comes, you don't wanna be too effed up to…you know…take care of business."

Eddie was always amused by Kurt's persnicketiness when it came to good honest cursing, but he didn't care for the lack of trust the comment implied. He grunted and hoisted the fresh drink the bar girl put in his hand.

Kurt sighed audibly. "Just saying, man."

A ping-pong ball suddenly beelined in Eddie's direction. He plucked it out of the air, stuck out his tongue and slurped it long and obscenely before tossing it back to the girl.

He turned to Kurt. "Who the fuck you think you're talking to? This is me, Eddie! I'll be fine."

THE PHONE call had jolted Eddie awake two weeks earlier, on a teeth-clackingly cold night in the middle of a bitter winter, snow pelting down on the icy slick streets of Detroit, wind keening across frozen Lake St. Clair like a blade scraping steel.

Roused from an inebriated slumber, he fumbled in the recliner cushions for the cell and got it to his ear in time to hear Danny say, "Eddie, you there?"

"Danny? What the hell! You know what time it is!"

"Time to head for Bangkok, that's what time!"

Having consumed most of a fifth of Jack before dozing off, the laugh track from an 80s sitcom clawing for whatever consciousness remained in his benumbed brain, Eddie was in no mood for a rude awakening. His buddy's declaration, uttered without preamble and made more menacing by the fact that the speaker sounded stone cold sober, knocked him sideways and pissed him off, as if a not-at-all-funny Zen monk had just blindsided him with a koan and then kicked him in the shins for good measure.

He lurched awake, spilling the dregs of his drink onto the soiled, crumb-flecked carpet. "Bangkok? What the fuck you talking about?"

"Bangkok," Danny pronounced the word with hearty, desperate zeal. "Hot girls, cheap booze, sex capital of Asia—the place you said every real man oughta party hard before he kicks the bucket."

"I said that?"

"Hell, yeah, you did! Up at Houghton Lake four summers ago.

When we signed the pact? Remember?"

Eddie grabbed the bottle of Jack and glugged back a throat full. "Pact? Can't say I recall any pact."

"Bullshit you don't."

He remembered, all right. Like yesterday. A scorcher of a night, sitting around in folding chairs outside Kurt's RV, three boozed-up, reefer-toking, middle-aged fools philosophizing about good deaths and bad deaths and in what manner they wanted to exit this world. They'd reminisced about guys they knew who'd gone out in a blaze of glory in motorcycle crashes, bar brawls, and drug deals gone haywire—these were the good deaths, the macho ones—and then the other kind, like that poor son of a bitch Big Jim Earl from Gratiot Street, whose very name used to evoke awe, but who ended up at the VA, frail and ridden with tumors, wearing a diaper and hooked up to a feeding tube, and how the fear of being weak and helpless, unmanned, the fear that had probably dogged each of them since the moment the doctor pronounced them male, had struck them all silent, like Death had snuck up and grabbed each one of them by the balls.

That was when they'd cooked up a plan to cheat the cancer ward and the Alzheimer's wing and go out like the two-fisted S.O.B.'s they knew themselves to be.

Real men to the end! they'd shouted, high-fiving and slamming shots like the Red Wings had just aced the Stanley Cup.

"I dunno, there mighta been some damn fool thing we signed," Eddie said finally. "But next day, after we sobered up, we burned it."

"Don't matter. A deal's a deal."

Eddie hoisted the bottle, but thumped it down again without swigging. A question commandeered the silence, but he was afraid to voice it.

"If you're saying what I think you are, then—who's getting the one-way ticket? It ain't me. So who drew the short straw, you or Kurt?"

He shut his eyes. The television blatted mindlessly. In the distance, a dog howled.

"I got throat cancer that's spreading like crabs in a whorehouse," Danny said and Eddie could hear the click of fear in his voice. "Doc says without treatment I got maybe another good month or two before it crawls up my neck and takes a shit in my brain."

"Aw, fuck, Danny. Jesus Christ. I can't believe it."

For some reason, he'd always had this premonition that, of the three of them, it would be Kurt who got done in prematurely by some terrible affliction.

"How long you known?"

"Coupla weeks. I could do chemo and radiation, slow it down for a while, but what the fuck for? I'd rather go wild in Thailand and die with a grin on my face and you and Kurt by my side than hooked up to some fuckin' torture device."

"You told Kurt?"

"He's on the phone with Thai Air even as we speak. Ten days from now, I told him. That give you time to clear your calendar?"

"Danny, look, I'm not sure I can do this."

"Don't worry about the money, this junket's on me."

"It ain't the money."

"What then? The pact was your idea, man! The world's a cold fucking place, you said, and we three gotta watch each other's backs! Right up to death's fucking door!"

On the TV Eddie saw a racing hotrod roar off one end of an opening drawbridge, slam onto the other side, and keep going as it outpaced a frantic soundtrack.

Danny coughed, cleared his throat. When he spoke again all the bravado was stripped away. His voice sounded small, constricted.

"Eddie? You're with me on this, right? I'm scared, man. I don't know how to die. I'm counting on you."

In the silence that followed, he could hear the wild wind keening like a madwoman across Lake St. Clair, and he wished he were out there, plowing along in the dark and the cold, the way he did when life got to be too much, not really caring if the ice held him or not, yelling out drunkenly as the snow pelted his face, just him, Eddie Pitrowski, alone in a black-and-white universe with a bottle of Jack in his hand.

No, I can't do this. I won't do this. No fucking way.

He took a deep breath. "Fuck yeah, Danny, I'll help you. Hell, what are friends for?"

"HOLY SHIT, how did she do that?" Danny said as Ping-Pong Girl winked and undulated offstage.

32

"A ping-pong show ain't nothing," said Kurt. "Wait till we get to Chiang Mai. Then you'll see some effing sights!"

Kurt was always raving about Chiang Mai, a city on the Ping River in the northern part of the country that he'd first visited during his tour in Vietnam. Liked it so much he'd been back a couple of times since. Said Chiang Mai was where the really hot girls were, the hardcore stuff, down 'n' dirty.

"I see a sight I like right now," declared Danny, sliding off his stool and putting his arm around the curvy, foxy-eyed bar girl who'd been caging over-priced drinks from him all evening. "How about it, honey? Ready to show an old man a good time?"

The girl giggled and made the *wai* gesture that was familiar by now, palms pressed together, head tilted. She took Danny's hand and they adjourned upstairs, where rooms could be reserved by the hour.

After Danny left, Eddie and Kurt drank their way through the lesbian show and the dominatrix skit and laughed when a ruckus broke out between a blond, Nordic-looking dude who was loudly contesting his bar bill to a couple of hot little numbers in slinky, Day-Glo dresses and matching, drop-dead red lipstick, who'd been glued to him like he was the last lifeboat leaving the Titanic. The guy threw down some baht, which evidently wasn't enough, because the girls pursued him out of the bar, hurling words at his retreating back like poisoned darts.

About that time Danny came back with his girl, who he introduced as Lek. He was grinning as he explained he'd just paid the mama-san for a "long time" meaning he'd bought Lek's time for the rest of the night and could now take her back to the hotel.

"Isn't she the prettiest little thing you ever seen?" Danny beamed as Lek tee-hee'd and covered her mouth, batting lashes black as squid ink.

When they came out of the club, looking to hail a tuk-tuk, Eddie saw the Nordic guy rolling around on the ground with the two hot little numbers kicking the shit out of him.

"What the hell?" His instinct was to help the poor guy and he started toward them.

Kurt grabbed him. "Leave it alone, man."

"But those bitches are kicking that dude in the nuts!"

"Look at the Adam's apples and the biceps," said Kurt. "Those are *katoeys*—female impersonators—and they're tough sons of bitches. You do *not* want to eff with 'em."

A couple of foot patrol cops pushed through the crowd then, stocky, grim-faced men whose brown uniforms fit their muscular bodies like sausage skins. They wore badges identifying them as "Tourist Police." When the ladyboys saw them, they took off, sprinting into the alleyway behind the bar.

"Goddamn, that's the best show I've seen tonight," said Eddie, watching them race off in their towering high heels.

THE FOLLOWING day, rain was pouring so hard it felt like the entire city of Bangkok lay at the foot of a waterfall. The four of them cabbed over to the Grand Hyatt on Rajdamri Road where, during a liquid brunch of mimosas and bloody marys, it was unanimously decided to follow Kurt's suggestion and travel to Chiang Mai.

Lek didn't want to be left behind, so Danny, against all advice from Eddie and Kurt, opted to bring her along. At the bar where they'd stopped for cocktails on the way to the bus station, Eddie tried to ask her if she'd be able to get her job back at the club in Bangkok, but she just smiled like a Southeast Asian Mona Lisa and snuggled up to Danny.

"You gotta get rid of her," Eddie said, "She thinks she's your girlfriend," but Danny said, "She relaxes me. I like having her around," and Lek, getting up to visit the ladies', lost her balance and dumped her drink into Eddie's lap, which caused Kurt to laugh so uproariously he blew beer out his nose.

The rain and the drinking slowed down the pace of their departure, forcing them to catch the last northbound bus of the day, a local that lurched to a stop at every village and rice paddy and didn't arrive in Chiang Mai until the following day. Lek had been to Chiang Mai and recommended the Lucky Star Hotel, a neon-drenched silver tower across from the Ping River, but Kurt said the place was a firetrap and looked like it had been constructed out of tinfoil. He checked into a seedy-looking low-rise hotel a few blocks away called the Mandarin Orchid.

After the endless bus ride, Eddie wanted to stretch his legs, so he agreed to meet Danny and Lek later at the hotel bar and moseyed up Loi Kroh Road by himself. He stopped in a club for an eye-opener and, several drinks later, found himself in a rent-by-the-hour room with an albino hooker who moved with such lethargy and languor he figured whatever drugs she was on were even better than the shit he'd scored back in Bangkok. Her skin was talcum white, her nipples almost invisible. She ghosted on top of him, weightless as fog, and just as he was going to town, really into it, something shifted and the creamy pallor of her skin, so sensuous at first, began to appear corpse-like and horrifying. His erection flagged and he found himself thinking of the China White and how it would liquify when heated, the cloudy whiteness of it filling the syringe, the prick of the hypo into Danny's vein, liquid death leaking in, his best friend dying in his arms.

He rolled away from the woman and crawled onto the floor, dizzy and hyperventilating. The air conditioner was blasting away, but he felt feverish, delirious, like he might puke. His girl sat back on her haunches, looking peeved at being so unceremoniously unseated. If he was having a heart attack, he got the feeling she might not be in any hurry to call the Thai version of EMTs.

After a few minutes, he revived enough to get dressed and splash some water on his face, pay the woman, and head out to meet Danny and Lek, but he'd forgotten the name of the hotel. The streets all looked identical, as similar as the computer generated byways of some generic Asian city in a video game. He meandered past rows of open-air stalls selling charcoal grilled chicken, fresh flowers, and diamond-shaped dumplings sizzling in grease, and noticed a number of people crunching some insectoid delectable that looked like fried grasshoppers. He passed a bustling arcade full of restaurants and stores and paused to stare in the window of The Numbah One Noodle Shop, where customers hunched before fly-speckled windows, slurping from bowls heaped with tangles of silvery, shoelace-thin noodles.

Unsure which direction to go in, he turned in a circle, feeling like a fool for being so utterly lost.

A stiff drink, he decided, would help clear his head and reorient him.

His hotel might be impossible to locate, but he had no trouble spotting a bar. The nearest one was The Joy Palace, across from the noodle shop. He hurried toward it like a desperado fleeing a posse.

As he ducked inside, a tall, overweight American in his late thirties, wearing baggy shorts and a flamboyantly patterned shirt, was barging out. His red-brown hair was shaved down into flat bristles, and his small, furtive eyes darted back and forth under doughy lids. He stared at Eddie openly and rudely, then leaned toward him and stage-whispered, "I wouldn't bother coming in here, I was you. No action."

Eddie took in the array of skimpily attired young women lounging around the back wall and said, "Well, you ain't me, mister. I think those girls look damn fine."

The guy crowded closer, forcing Eddie to inhale the reek of his garlic lunch. He spoke in a gruff, yet circumspect voice, like he and Eddie were part of the same unsavory conspiracy. "They're not bad—if that's what you're into."

Well, what the hell else would I be into, Eddie thought. Then he remembered the brutal katoeys beating up the guy in Patpong and concluded that this dude must have a predilection for ladyboys. He actually grinned, because the mental image of the pudgy flattop getting it on with some skanky, stiletto-wearing chick impersonator was so hilarious.

"Yeah, well, I'd be careful about that kind of action. Could be dangerous." He started to move on, but the big-bellied dude was now staring at him as though transfixed by some magic words Eddie had unwittingly uttered.

"Yeah, you understand, all right. I can tell. Careful—that's the ticket." He tried to take Eddie's arm. "Let me buy you a drink, and I'll give you the names of some people around here you can trust."

Huh?

Eddie wasn't in the mood for creepy cloak and dagger. He shoved the guy aside—it was like elbowing a Humvee—and rather than proceed into the bar, made a beeline out of it. In his agitation, he glanced upward and suddenly recognized his hotel, the "Tinfoil Tower," jutting up out of the swarm of low-rise establishments surrounding it.

A few minutes later, he found Danny and Lek at a table in the lobby bar, sipping frou-frou strawberry concoctions that looked like something you'd serve to kids after an Easter egg hunt.

"About time you showed up!" Danny said when Eddie lurched in. "I was afraid you got lost!"

"Me? Never! This is me, Eddie Pitrowski you're talking to! I got a G.P.S. hard-wired into my brain." He pulled up a chair. "Where's Kurt?"

Danny pantomimed aiming a camera. "Out trolling for local color. Thinks he's gonna be an I-Reporter for Fox News, go viral on YouTube or some such."

"YouTube!" exclaimed Lek.

Danny said, "I been trying to tell Lek about the good old days in Detroit, like when you and me and Kurt stole that crate of .38 specials from the crew of Angels at the Rocking Horse Inn and that time we almost got shotgunned cartin' off TV sets during the riots in '67."

"Good times, all right," Eddie said, while Lek smiled and nodded. Eddie had the feeling Danny could've said "Lek, this is the guy who came all this way so he could hotshot my ass to kingdom come" and gotten the same enthusiastic response.

Danny had just launched into a story about the time he and Eddie and Kurt were out ice-fishing and Eddie fell through and almost drowned, when he suddenly stopped talking. His face took on an ashen sheen. He began to cough so violently that his head whiplashed back and forth and he gripped his throat like a man trying to strangle himself.

A couple nearby stared at him, then got up and moved away.

Eddie glared at them. "That's right, don't get too close! Swine flu! Highly fucking contagious!"

"You crazy?" Danny gasped.

Eddie felt like an asshole. He offered Danny a glass of water while Lek tried massaging his back, but he shrugged her away. "Quit pawin' me! Go find somebody who ain't dying."

Lek shrank back, looking like she'd been slapped. "Want help you, Danny," she said, the kindness and sadness in her voice making Eddie feel bad for the way he'd urged Danny to ditch her.

Sallow-faced, eyes streaming, Danny rasped, "There's nothing anybody can do for me." He looked at Eddie. "Shit, I thought this last hurrah in Thailand was a great idea, but I'm sick and tired of feeling like a fucking piano's about to drop on my head. How much more time I got, man? When we gonna fuckin' do this thing?"

Eddie gulped, his mouth so dry he felt like he was swallowing nails. "Tomorrow. But hell, nobody's sayin' we can't postpone it."

"Fuck postponing. Let's just get it over with. *Right now.*"

Eddie felt a stab of panic. He lowered his voice. "We can't, Danny. It's too late for me and Kurt to change our tickets. We gotta be in the air before anybody—"

"Yeah, yeah, I know. Before the maid comes to clean the room and finds a stiff with a needle in his arm."

"You gotta hang in there, man. You got enough pain meds, right?"

"Yeah, but they make me feel dopey. That nurse I used to date, LuAnn, scored me some liquid Valium, but the one time I shot some, I slept for a day. Don't have time now for any twenty-four-hour siestas."

"Better be careful with that shit," Eddie said.

"Yeah, don't wanna cut short my promising future."

Eddie gestured to the Pepto-Bismol pink cocktails. "There's the trouble right here, this sissy shit she's got you drinking. You need a man's drink." He stuck his hand in the air and waved it at the bargirl like he was hailing a cab. "Three whiskeys down here!"

"I've had enough," Danny said, with such finality that Eddie wondered if he was talking about more than the drinks.

He took Lek by the hand. "C'mon, honey, let's go back to the room. See if we can have some—what's that word you use?— *sanuk?*"

Her face brightened. "Sanuk!"

"What's sanuk?" Eddie said.

"Means having fun," Danny said. "Least I think it does."

As she passed Eddie, Lek pressed her palms together in the wai gesture and bowed, as though she were expressing gratitude. "*Jai dii,*" she said and touched Eddie's chest.

"Jai dii?" Bewildered, he looked at Danny.

Danny shrugged. "No idea. But she said it to me, too. Probably means dumb white dude."

AFTER DANNY and Lek left, Eddie slammed another whiskey, which tamped down the restlessness and quelled some of the anxiety that clawed inside his chest like a caged rat. He thought about visiting a massage parlor—maybe even getting a massage—but didn't think he was good for another go-round this soon, so he ambled out of the bar and swayed up the street, assaulted by the color and chaos. A half-naked man in a blue-and-green sarong squatted at a table, gutting fish. A flock of dusty children galloped after a soccer ball. An old woman slouched in the shade of the awning next to the Numbah One Noodle Shop, drumming her fingers to the beat of some Thai pop song while a gaggle of winter pale tourists looked over her stock of knock-off Prada handbags and Armani sunglasses.

The heat plus the alcohol he'd consumed left him feeling transparent and floaty, like everything was underwater and he was drifting along on a warm, pungent current of seawater. He thought about finding a songthaew to take him up into the mountains that rose cool-looking and green outside the city, but the need to distract himself with women and booze was too urgent to compete with such a placid indulgence.

Drawn by a cool gust of air conditioning, he wandered into a narrow, bamboo-paneled bar with a dancer gyrating on a small stage and a row of girls slouching against the wall. The place looked oddly familiar. When he realized he was back in The Joy Palace, he started to do an about-face, but then a girl at the bar caught his eye. She wore khaki slacks and a blue cotton shirt, and her curves were pleasingly generous. After so many variations on the theme of straight jet hair and boyish hips, she struck Eddie as uncommonly alluring. He claimed the barstool next to her, proclaiming grandly, "Sanuk, sweetheart, when's your turn to shake that sexy tush?"

The woman turned to him. She was a westerner in her early forties, with piercing blue-grey eyes that appraised him scathingly. "Did you just use the word 'tush'?"

"Hey, I was just funnin' with you," he said, embarrassed by the gaffe. "I knew you weren't a dancer. You're too—uh—too—"

"Old and overweight?"

"—nicely dressed, I was gonna say."

"Right." She sighed in that long-suffering way women often adopted around Eddie and began scribbling in a spiral notebook that lay open on the bar in front of her.

He ordered a beer and made small talk. The woman ignored him and continued to write, which puzzled Eddie, since he thought he was being the epitome of charming. He decided a proper introduction was in order and stuck out his hand. "Name's Eddie Pitrowski. Born and raised in Detroit."

She gave his fingers a gingerly squeeze. "Ilsa Jacobi."

"American?"

"From L.A. I live in Bangkok now."

"I just came from Bangkok—helluva place!" The bartender set a Singha in front of him and he took a thirsty pull. "What're you doing in Chiang Mai?"

"Working."

She turned back to the notebook. Eddie leaned closer. "You writing about Thailand? 'Cause if y'are, maybe I could help you with that. Give you an American guy's perspective."

"I'll bet that would be riveting."

He tried to see the page, but it was at an angle and partially covered by her hand. "So what *are* you writing? A journal? My ex-wife used to journal. Women like that kinda thing."

She put down the pen. When she shifted on the stool to face him, her blouse parted slightly and he could see the swell of a breast, the lacy trim of a black bra strap.

"Not that you'd be interested, but I'm doing an exposé on child trafficking for *The Bangkok Times*."

"A reporter, eh?" said Eddie, barely listening. Had she said her name was Ilsa or Elsa? He was trying to guess her bra size. A hefty chest, probably a 36 or a 38C. Bodacious and blonde. His type of gal.

"So what're you up to later, Elsa? I'm staying over yonder at the Lucky Star Hotel. Maybe we could meet for a nightcap, do some clubbing, take in some sights."

She slammed the notebook shut and faced Eddie—who was wondering what the hell he'd said wrong—with tigerish green eyes.

"You may have somehow overlooked this, but along that wall are fifteen or twenty young women who, for a pittance, will accommodate your every stupid, selfish, egocentric whim. So why the hell are you hitting on me?"

He tried his most ingratiating smile. "I'm not hitting on you, honey. I like talking to you is all. Now this thing you're writing, what's it about?"

"I just told you."

"Don't think you did."

She rolled her eyes. "You don't remember because you're drunk on your ass."

He spread his arms. "It's Chiang Mai. Everybody's drunk on their ass."

"I'm not."

He laughed. "Well, there you go. That's the problem. Let's see if we can fix that." He beckoned the bartender. "Another drink for the lady."

Ilsa rattled off some words in Thai. The bartender glanced at Eddie, sniggered, and strolled away flicking her long hair.

"Hey, what'd you say to her? I was just trying to buy you a drink? Pass the time of day with some conversation? Why do you have to be a bitch?"

She gave him an icy once-over that reminded him of a fifth-grade teacher he used to be scared to death of. "Oh, it's *talking* you want? Okay, let's start with this: what're you *really* doing in Thailand, Eddie Pitrowski?"

The question flummoxed him, seeming to hint at knowledge of something she couldn't possibly possess. What did she mean, *really* doing? Did she suspect something? Was she psychic?

After fumbling for words, he finally blurted, "I'm traveling with a couple of buddies. Here to see the sights."

A smirk jerked her pretty mouth askew. "The sights? You mean like the National Museum and the Wat Chiang Man? Maybe the Elephant Nature Park or the Baan Haw Mosque? All are famous attractions here."

Museums, mosques, nature parks—this was all news to Eddie, who gestured at the crowded room and said, "I'm here for the same reason as the rest of these guys."

"So for you then, taking in the sights, that means the bars and the massage parlors and the brothels?"

He felt trapped. Why was she pestering him? "I like to raise a little hell, sure. That bothers you, lady, go hang out in a tea house, not a bar."

"You're the one who wanted to talk."

"Didn't expect a lecture. All I did was ask what you're writing about."

He felt his shoulders tense, waiting for her anger to descend on him like a blade, but instead her expression slackened with a melancholy so profound and unadorned that he turned away, her sadness too painful to confront because it mirrored back his own.

"I'm telling the story of a little girl named Tran," she said finally.

"What?"

"You asked what I'm writing, and I'm telling you. Again. A story about everything people like you avoid looking at. The places where children are bought and sold and raped."

Eddie could feel the fury radiating off her like a heat lamp. "Well, that's terrible, that's awful," he managed. "That go on much?"

"Thailand's a hub for child traffickers. Especially in the north."

"Jesus," said Eddie, and he thought about Margaret. Not Margaret as she was now with the shitkicker boots and *Dykes Rule* tattoo on her biceps, but Margaret as he actually remembered her, as a smiling toddler and a mischievous ten-year-old. Before his drinking got out of hand. When she still called him Daddy and hugged him around the waist.

He realized Ilsa was still talking. "My brother and his wife adopted a little Thai girl a couple of years ago. Six months ago, she died of AIDS that she'd contracted while being forced to work in a brothel in Chiang Mai. Her name was Tran. She was thirteen years old."

"That kind of thing, it can't be going on right out in the open?" Eddie was wishing he'd never started this conversation. All he'd wanted was to buy the woman a few drinks, get his mind off Danny. Now she'd gotten his mind on something worse.

"Did you notice the noodle shop across from the arcade?"

"Yeah, Numbah One Noodle Shop." He pronounced the word as it appeared on the sign, so that it rhymed with rumba. "These people can't spell worth a damn."

"Have you been inside?"

"No, don't really care for that *khao soi* shit." He couldn't believe he was still trying to impress this woman, showing off the name of a regional dish he'd heard Kurt order a few days earlier. "I'm more of a steak and eggs man myself."

She laughed harshly, looking at him like the word moron was tattooed between his eyebrows. He hated women like her, women who just by existing made him feel like a loser. He wanted to get up and leave, but didn't want her to think she'd run him off.

"The noodle shop? You're telling me it's some kinda kiddy brothel?" When she didn't answer, he blustered, "That's impossible! It's just a bunch of people sucking down soup."

"Not if you know a guy named Toy and not if you get

upstairs."

"Toy? Guy's name is *Toy*? You're kidding me, right?" He saw she was serious and went on, "Well, what about the parents of these kids? Don't they look for them?"

"Sometimes they're the ones who sold their children in the first place."

"They do that?"

"If the family is poor enough or greedy enough, yeah, they do."

Eddie absorbed this. "Okay, if you know so much, call the authorities. Get the cops involved."

"They are involved. In more ways than one. Some of the police are as bad as the traffickers. Short of finding a dead body on the premises, getting the police to organize a raid is tough. My partner and I have a couple of connections in the police force, but it's not enough yet. The legal system here is unbelievably complicated and—"

"Oh, screw the legal system," Eddie snapped. It was a sentiment he'd frequently expressed before—often in more colorful terms—about the court system back home on the occasion of numerous arrests and arraignments. "People like you, reporters, writers, you find something absolutely over-the-fucking top terrible and get your skirts all in a knot, but then what? If what you're saying is true, kids are being held prisoner in that noodle joint right now and all you're doing is sitting here yakking about it."

"Okay, Captain America, I suppose you'd know what to do?"

"Well, hell, when kids are in danger, you don't diddle around crying about how awful it is, you take action. You get your hands dirty, you do whatever it takes!"

"Easy to talk tough when nobody's gonna call you on it. You're too busy being a sex tourist to do anything more challenging than unzipping your pants."

"Hey, I just came here to have a good time."

She leaned back, appraising him. "I'm sorry, Eddie, but for somebody who came all this way to get drunk and buy sex, you don't look like you're having much fun."

"Listen, lady, if I told you why I really came to Thailand—" He stopped himself just in time. *Jesus, what was he thinking?*

Her mouth crinkled disdainfully. "Yeah, I know, you'd have to kill me."

THE SUNLIGHT outside hit Eddie in the face like a blowtorch and he almost staggered as he navigated his way up Loi Kroh Road. Across the street from the Numbah One Noodle Shop, he paused, taking the measure of blank-faced customers who sat at counters in the windows like birds on a line, and watched others—mostly men—come and go. After about ten minutes, a side door opened, and a lean, sinewy man with brilliantly tattooed arms sauntered out. He wore boot-cut black jeans and a red T-shirt and he walked with a hip-rolling, arrogant glide. He didn't seem in a hurry to go anywhere, but shook a cigarette out of a pack and strolled into a passageway between the restaurant and an adjacent shop full of tourist geegaws.

Just for the hell of it—to have a look-see and prove to himself that Ilsa was wrong—Eddie decided to go in and get something to eat. He pointed to a picture on a laminated menu, but the bowl of yellowish, flat noodles the guy behind the counter gave him reminded him of a mound of worms the vet had once extracted from his hound dog's butt. He'd barely paid for the food before he abandoned it and went plunging back into the mid-afternoon furnace.

The intense heat hit him like a brickbat. He lunged to the edge of the pedestrian traffic, ducked into the passageway where the skinny guy had gone to have his smoke, and heaved up a putrid stew of undigested noodles and beer.

When he straightened up, wiping his mouth on the back of his hand, he found himself looking at an incongruous scene. The passage opened into a narrow street, little more than an alley, where vendors had set up a line of booths, hawking the usual assortment of tourist rip-offs and trinkets. Flat Top was standing there with a little Asian girl, looking over a display of DVDs.

If that's the kind of action you're into...

Suddenly, in light of the conversation he'd just had with Ilsa, Flat Top's words seemed to make terrible sense. Eddie was besieged by a mad impulse to do *something* and do it *now*, an act of expiation for all the grief and rage that was percolating in his soul like what had just been disgorged from his stomach.

He stepped out of the passageway and hollered, "Hey you!" but in the general hubbub his voice was drowned out.

Flat Top was leading the little girl into the maze of booths. Eddie followed, staying at a distance until the pair turned onto the crowded street and Flat Top raised his arm to hail a cab. At that point, the decision seemed to make itself. He raced to catch up to them and blocked the way.

"Let go of that kid!"

Flat Top looked up, dumbfounded, and barked, "Who the hell are you?"

"I'm your buddy from The Joy Palace, remember? *This* is the kind of action you meant? A kid, for Christ's sake!"

"Lower your voice, you old coot. Walk away. This isn't your concern."

"I'm making it my concern."

"How about this?" He brushed his shirttail aside, a casual gesture that gave Eddie a glimpse of the lethal-looking knife sheathed next to his waist. "You want to make this your concern, too?"

Big mistake.

Eddie Pitrowski was a man who'd grown up on Detroit's meanest streets, who'd survived gang fights, rogue cops, and five years in prison. In the fight-or-die mentality of Eddie's youth, you never let the enemy see the blade until it's stuck between his ribs.

"Fuck you," Eddie said, and smashed his fist into Flat Top's broad nose. There was a crack like celery snapping, and blood spurted out. Flat Top looked stunned. He threw a sloppy roundhouse, but Eddie parried the blow and banged a hook off his temple. As he moved to throw another punch, he glanced down and saw the little girl cringing in terror. For a second, he felt bad for scaring her, then realized that her reaction wasn't directed at him, but at something behind him. He turned too late—a blow that felt like a mule kick slammed his lower back, a second, harder one pounded his kidney. Pain razored through him. His lungs emptied, and his legs liquified as the ground swooped up to meet him. Above him, backlit by a supernova of diamonds, the wiry, sinew-and-bones man from the noodle shop twirled a retractable metal baton above his head, grinning like a demented majorette. His eyes blazed with crazed, manic energy as he circled Eddie, snorting and jabbering. "You make trouble here, I fooking kill you. I kill you, moothafooka."

"C'mon, Toy, take it easy," Flat Top said, using his shirttail to staunch the flow of blood from his nose. His voice was as amiable and conciliatory as a gent in a fine dining establishment recommending a good Merlot. "He's just some drunk thinks I fucked his little sister. He won't bother us again." To make his point, he stepped back and lobbed a kick into Eddie's side. Eddie rolled away, pain gusting through his body like a gritty wind.

By the time he got to his feet, the little girl had disappeared and Flat Top and Toy were going into the noodle shop, friendly as could be.

RATHER THAN pursue the two men, which was his first inclination, Eddie reluctantly heeded the demands of his aching body and hobbled back to the hotel, where he found Kurt fiddling with his camera in the lobby bar. He looked up in amazement when Eddie limped in.

"Jeez, what the heck happened? You piss off the wrong ladyboy?"

Eddie ordered a whiskey and recounted a heavily edited and embellished version of what had occurred.

"Effin' pervs," Kurt said when he'd finished the account, "oughta be stomped on like roaches."

"Damn straight." Eddie said.

"Man, you can't pull that shit here."

"My sentiments exactly—fuckin' freaks."

"No, Eddie, I mean you can't pull that macho shit, playin' hero and all. You're lucky you didn't get your skull busted open. Don't forget why we came here—to give Danny a smokin' hot send-off, right?"

That rankled Eddie, because Kurt seemed more interested in wandering off to find photo ops than hanging out with Danny, but he didn't say anything. Kurt went on, "This isn't the States, Eddie. You see things don't sit right with you, keep your nose out of it. Walk away."

"Shit, man, you weren't there. I'm telling you, you seen that creep with the little girl, you'da done the same thing."

Kurt stared at him as though trying to read his mind. "No, Eddie. I would not. You know why? Because I control my temper, I'm not a hothead who takes crazy risks. Most of all, I do not screw up in foreign countries with prisons that make our slammers back home look like the effing Four Seasons." He drained his beer. "C'mon, you look like you could use some cheering up. Let's go bang on Danny's door and see if he's ready to ditch that clingy chick and put some variety in his love life."

They paid their tab, rolled out of the bar, and were getting off the elevator when the door to Danny's room burst open and Lek sprinted into the hall. Her eyes were huge and wet and raccooned with goopy rings of mascara.

She latched onto Kurt's arm, spewing a rapid-fire hodgepodge of English and Thai.

"Hey, slow down," said Kurt, trying to peel her off. "What's wrong? Is Danny okay?"

Eddie got a bad feeling in his gut, like a fist constricting. He charged up the hall into the room, barking Danny's name. No Danny, so he tried the bathroom door and found it locked, yelled at Danny to open up. He had lifted his leg to kick the door, when the lock turned and Danny opened the door. He wore a pair of boxer shorts and an expression of weary disgust.

He looked at Eddie with his leg cocked and sighed. "Jesus, look at this. You're worse than she is. I'm surrounded by goddamn drama queens."

"What the fuck is this?" Eddie said, barging past him. On the back of the toilet was a bottle of Stoly and three prescription medicine bottles. The Vicodin and Oxy were in Danny's name, the liquid Valium was made out to an Oleg Rastinov.

"Who the hell's Oleg Rastinov?"

"No idea. My nurse friend swiped it from the hospital pharmacy."

Eddie picked up the vodka. "And what exactly was the plan here, Danny? The way the girl was carrying on, I figured you were standing out on a ledge."

He shrugged. "Mighta been, if I coulda got the damn window open. I told you my plan. Get it over with."

"How much of this shit did you take?"

"None of it—thanks to you and my nosy girlfriend. So you can hold off on the goddamn stomach pump."

Kurt and Lek came to the door. "It's okay, everything's cool," Eddie said. "Kurt, take the girl down to the bar. Danny and I got to talk."

Lek's eyes flashed fire. "You asshole, Eddie. I not girl. My name Lek. I stay here with Danny."

Eddie looked at Danny. "Guess her English is improving."

Lek hissed something in Thai and gave Eddie the finger.

Danny dampened a washcloth and wiped the mascara streaks off Lek's face.

"I'm okay," he said. "Go on down to the bar with Kurt. Please. I'll be there in a few minutes."

As soon as Lek and Kurt left, Eddie started in. "What the fuck, Danny, you were gonna off yourself right in front of her?"

"No! I told her to leave! I gave her a whole bunch of baht, enough for the bus back to Bangkok and a lot more."

"What about me and Kurt? Were you gonna send us back to Bangkok, too, so you could die here alone?"

"Wouldn't it be better that way?"

"What about the pact? Friends to the end? We said we'd be there for each other."

"Oh, screw the damned pact. That shit's for kids." He shuffled over to the bed and sat down heavily. When he looked up, despondency drew his face down like a clay effigy crumbling. He looked like he'd aged fifteen years since that morning. "You and Kurt weren't around, so I decided to man up and just do it myself."

"But what's the rush! Look, Danny, you got a beautiful girl here to spend the night with, why piss it away? You know, carpal deity and all that stuff."

"Carpal what?"

"Never mind."

"Look, man, you don't understand. Lek's the reason I decided to get it over with. Meeting her, being with her the past few days, it just makes it all worse! Makes everything from before look so shitty and small by comparison."

"Then get rid of her!" exclaimed Eddie, waving his arms like he was leading a battlefield charge. "Kurt was right about Chiang Mai, this town's overpopulated with hot babes. Let's go get some!"

Then he fell silent, because what he saw scared him and mortified him and touched something so deeply entombed in his heart that decades had passed without his ever admitting its existence, the alcohol doing its part, of course, in the service of this helpful amnesia. Danny was sobbing. The tears slicked his cheeks unashamedly. And Eddie, who on a few occasions had found himself in situations where he was required to bend over, spread 'em, and cough, while a couple of guards watched to see if any sharp objects or dope or maybe a long-stemmed red rose popped out of his ass, squirmed with an embarrassment more acute than any he'd felt in his life.

"I just can't believe my goddamn luck," Danny said. "First time in years I meet a woman I really like, someone I have fun with, and when do I meet her, but when I'm all set to drop the fuck dead!"

Eddie held up his hands. "Hey, whoa, it don't have to be that way. Jeez, Danny, come on back to Detroit. Do the chemo, the radiation, whatever it takes. Maybe somebody'll come up with a miracle cure. Hell, you never know, earth could get hit with a meteor and kill us all."

Danny gave him a blank stare. "Is that supposed to cheer me up?"

"Well, no, but I'm just saying..." He waved his hand. "Aw, hell, I don't know what I'm saying."

They sat in silence for a minute before Danny said, "You know what I hate most? It's not that I'm scared of dying anymore. It's feeling like I never did anything with my life. It all went by so fast—like a dream—and now it's over and I'm like, wait a sec, this can't be all there is to it. I never did anything important or special or even fucking noteworthy—I never made a difference to anybody."

"That's not true. You raised some great kids—"

Danny rolled his eyes. "Cut the bullshit! My son Jimmy's doing fifteen to twenty for his third felony. Benjamin, he just got another DUI and moved back in with his mother. And Angie—shit, I don't know what the hell Angie's doing and I'm scared to ask!" He gave a sour smile. "Prob'ly make for a drama-filled wake, though. Wonder if any of 'em will show up."

Eddie couldn't come up with a reply. He was thinking about Margaret and her mother, asking the same question about himself.

Kurt stuck his head in the door. "Hey, you two old sad sacks. I thought this was supposed to be a party." He held up the camcorder. "C'mon, boys, let's make some memories."

"Of what?" Danny said. "Me croaking?"

"Shut the fuck up before I kill you myself," Eddie said, shoving

Danny out the door ahead of him with one hand and pocketing the drugs with the other.

AS THEY bar-hopped that evening and into the night, Eddie discovered a terrible truth: no matter how much booze he slugged back, he couldn't get drunk. Since the age of twelve, when he figured out the combination to the lock on his father's liquor cabinet, alcohol had been his reliable life partner and friend, amping him up when he required bravado, mellowing him out when he needed calm. When things got really crazy, sufficient amounts of it delivered him into the promised land of sweet, pain-free Oblivion.

Now he felt betrayed and furious, because the drinks delivered only a gut-wrenching clarity, his thoughts brutally sharp. Danny's words rat-tatted through his head like a drumroll. What had he done with his own life, for Christ's sake? No wonder his daughter hated him—he was a loser, a low-life, a drunk.

So outwardly, for Danny's sake, he joined the party, but inwardly he brooded and fretted and ran himself down in a belittling loop of recrimination.

A little before midnight, Danny, Lek, and Kurt called it a night and cabbed back to their hotels, but Eddie wanted to walk. He headed back up Loi Kroh Road and loitered across the street from the Numbah One Noodle, which was closed up tight, the shades drawn down like sleepy lids over the plate-glass windows.

A strawberry-lipped girl cooed to him from a doorway in the nearby arcade. She might have been an owl serenading the stars for all the interest he felt. A pair of Tourist Police swaggered by, and from long habit in dealing with the law, he turned his face away and briefly fell into step with a group of Europeans carousing past.

Recrossing the street, he slipped into the alleyway, noticing an area behind some garbage bins that was strewn with cigarette butts. He moved deeper into the alley and decided to wait. He was good at waiting. He'd learned how to do that in prison. The night settled around him, cloying and moist, the air marbled with the aroma of hibiscus and wet earth mingled with the sour smell of the garbage. Out on Loi Kroh Road, traffic hummed and horns squealed and The Joy Palace glowed in pink neon, but the alley was submerged in shadow, purplish and still, like deep water.

Presently, a man slouched by, glanced around, and rapped on a side door, which opened to admit him. This pattern was repeated three more times over the next hour. Then Toy strolled outside, ambled around the corner, and lit up a smoke. He began to talk, low and heatedly, which almost rattled Eddie into giving himself away until he realized Toy was speaking into a Bluetooth-type device.

Crouched on aching knees, Eddie fought the urge to grab the pimp by the throat and bash his head to bloody mush against the wall. He argued himself out of it. Still, the arrogance of a man who exploited children, yet felt safe to loiter in the darkness, puffing on a smoke and kibitzing, presented some possibilities.

He was considering this when a taxi pulled up and disgorged Flat Top, who much to Eddie's satisfaction, sported a butterfly bandage across his swollen nose. Toy greeted him, but instead of going into the noodle shop, the two men crossed the street and disappeared into the neon-veiled Joy Palace.

As soon as Toy and Flat Top went inside, Eddie straightened, brushed himself off, and knocked on the side door.

A bulky man with gelled hair and a face as flat and expressionless as a plank opened the door. He wore jeans and a black muscle shirt under a loose sport coat. His prolonged, silent scowl exuded such menace that Eddie figured he must practice it in front of a mirror.

If there was some kind of profile for perverts, he must have passed it with flying colors, because the plank-faced guy gave him the most cursory once-over and admitted him.

Inside, a stairway led to a green-paneled lounge and a dinky bar where a couple of solitary drinkers nursed Klong beers. Pornography featuring western actors played on a big screen TV.

A petite, buxom woman, dimpled and round as a dumpling, perched behind a counter. She stood up when Eddie approached, made the wai gesture, and proposed a few ethnic specialties.

"You want Thai? Cambodian? Vietnamese?"

For a crazy instant, Eddie almost thought she was talking about food.

The woman misread his hesitation. "You want boy? We got boy, too."

"No, no boy." His voice boomed in his ears. Was he shouting? "A girl. Toy told me you have them young." He put his hand down as though patting a child on the head. "Like so."

"You know Toy?"

"Yeah, friends. Guy at a bar introduced us."

The woman cocked her head and considered him like a banker about to turn an undesirable customer down for a loan, then touched a taloned finger to her chin and chuckled softly, a prickly sound that scurried up Eddie's neck like a spider. He shook off his desire to flee and fumbled his wallet out.

"I want her for all night."

"No all night. Two thousand baht, one hour."

"I'll give you ten thousand baht, and I take her with me. Have her back here tomorrow morning. That's a good deal, lady. I'd take it, I was you."

"You not me." A derisive smile gashed the woman's face, but her eyes remained dull and impassive as a freshly swept floor. She must hear this kind of pitch all night, Eddie thought.

"One hour," she said. "Two thousand baht. You have problem with that, talk to your friend Toy."

"No, no problem. An hour's fine."

The woman smiled and nodded enthusiastically. They were buddies again.

She led him behind a gold curtain and up some stairs into a low-ceilinged hallway lined with numbered doors. An air conditioner whirred somewhere, but the air was stagnant and moist, swirling with dust motes and smelling of disinfectant. Thai pop music blatted loudly over tinny speakers.

The woman selected a door, unlocked it using a clutch of keys, and motioned Eddie inside. The room was minimalist sex-club chic—a bamboo floor lamp with a low wattage bulb, a flat screen TV, and a queen-sized bed covered in blue silk sheets with a drip pattern of stains in the center.

"Stay," she said as though addressing a pet.

Eddie waited, wondering if the next person to come to the door would be Toy or maybe the police. He wondered what Ilsa would say if she saw him now and then quashed the thought of her, because he was cat-nervous and needed to focus.

The door opened gradually and the shadow of a child flowed into the room, silent as water. As the girl moved into the light, Eddie could see she wore pajamas with a black-and-red triangular pattern and red rhinestoned sandals. Her hair hung in a long ponytail, and she stared at her pink-painted toenails.

He squatted before her, knowing he reeked of liquor and sour sweat, and tried his best to communicate by his tone of voice that he meant to help her.

"Hi, honey. I'm Eddie. What's your name?"

She didn't answer. The floor riveted her attention.

"I'm not going to hurt you, understand? I'm getting you out of here. Okay? Speak English?"

She looked up at him, her tiny round face so lacking in emotion that she might have been a life-like doll. "You want boom-boom or lick-lick?"

Eddie recoiled. "Jesus, no, nothing like that." He put his finger to his lips. "Shhh. You be quiet, and we'll get out of here, okay?"

He scooped her up and checked the hallway. Empty. The discordant music had stopped, leaving a disquieting silence in which all sounds seemed amplified. His own breathing boomed in his ears. From behind the eggshell-thin walls came the sounds of squeaking bedsprings, shuffling feet, murmured voices.

At the end of the hall, a metal door opened into a stairwell. Descending it, he entered another corridor, narrow and poorly lit, that reeked of grease and cooked vegetables. He thought he must be near the noodle shop kitchen and began searching for a door connecting the two sections of the building. Worst case scenario, he figured he could break a window to get out. He tried a likely looking door. It opened to reveal a small, gloomy room where a half-dozen young girls lay curled on mattresses on the floor.

An older girl, who appeared to be in her midteens, sat up and gaped at him. Eddie started to close the door, then saw the raw fear in her eyes and tried to reassure her.

"I'll send help," he said.

Her eyes flicked to the child in his arms. For a second, there was crystal cold silence. Then she threw back her head and screamed.

From overhead came a staccato burst of voices. Feet trampled the stairs.

Desperate for a means of escape or a place to hide, Eddie raced back down the hall, grabbing at doors along the way, finding them locked. The last door that he tried was poorly latched and gave when he put some muscle into it.

There was a grunt and the banging of bedsprings, then a male voice like a wild beast roared, "Shut the effing door, we're busy in here!"

Eddie reeled, the scene before him stabbing his eyes like ice picks. His mind struggled to process the images—a camera mounted on a tripod, a child's skinny legs, the white, thrusting rump of a man—and something cracked in his chest like a bone breaking.

When he turned around, his face was inches from Toy, who bared his teeth and shoved a baby Glock against the side of Eddie's mouth.

"Put her down," said Toy, and when Eddie did so, bending slightly to lower her, he lifted the gun and hammered the butt into Eddie's skull like a wrecking ball into a wall. The world receded to a pinpoint. A massive roaring filled his ears, and he felt himself sinking into red darkness.

Suddenly Toy yelped and jerked up on his toes. A knife blade scraped so roughly into his neck that blood oozed out in a thin crimson line.

"Drop the gun or I'll cut your fucking throat," Flat Top said.

ILSA PACED back and forth in the living room of the Thai-style wooden bungalow near the Ping River where Flat Top had brought Eddie, piling him into a tuk-tuk, tipping the driver extra because of the blood he left on the seat. She wore a flowered silk robe and slippers and paused only to light another Gauloises from the pack she'd been chain smoking ever since Eddie and Flat Top arrived. Between puffs, she'd furiously explained that Flat Top was her brother, David Abbott. Since the death of his daughter Tran, they'd been working for Child Rescue International, with Abbott trying to win Toy's trust by playing the role of a pedophile attempting to buy a little girl.

"I kept an eye out for pedophile johns and tried to buddy up with them," Abbott interjected into her tirade. "Then I'd send their pictures and data on to Interpol."

"Now wait a minute," Eddie said, wincing as Ilsa pressed a fresh ice pack to his throbbing head. He was lying on a sectional sofa, a painful lump that he tried to ignore jabbing his lower back. "You mean you thought I was one of *them*. I oughta kick your ass."

"Hey, you looked the part," said Abbott. "I saw you staring in the window of the noodle shop like a man trying to come to a decision about something, and whatever it was seemed a lot more important than what you were gonna have for lunch. You looked—I don't know—haunted, freaked out. Sometimes the ones who still have a conscience, that's how they look."

Eddie turned to Ilsa. "What about when you and me met at the bar? Had this guy here told you to bust my balls?"

Ilsa exhaled a thin twist of smoke. "No, that was just me busting your balls. On general principle. I didn't know you and David had already had a magic moment." She paused to crush out her cigarette. "What you did tonight was incredibly stupid, Eddie. Nobody steals a kid from a Thai brothel, and certainly not Toy's! He's obsessed with protecting what he considers his. He doesn't even sleep at night, just wanders around guarding his little house of horrors. He wouldn't've thought twice about killing you."

"She's right," Abbott said. "They'd be fishing your body out of the Ping."

"I still don't get it," Eddie said. "I saw you and Toy waltz into that bar, the two of you thick as thieves. I figured you'd be in there all night. Why'd you come back?"

"Toy got a text from the Dragon Lady," Abbott said. "She told him some weird guy claiming he was Toy's friend wanted a young girl. I had a feeling it might be you, so I followed him back."

"What about the kid you were with yesterday? Toy let you take her?"

"She isn't one of Toy's," Abbott said. "She's a girl Ilsa and I helped free from another brothel a few weeks ago. I wanted Toy to see her with me, then tell him I was making a porn flick and try to persuade him to sell me one of his girls. If he went for it, I'd be taping the whole conversation, which would be enough to get the police to organize a raid." He glared at Eddie in disgust. "But that's not going to happen now. I'll never get near Toy again. In fact, now *I'm* a target. I may have to leave Chiang Mai."

In the silence that followed, the only sound was the tiny whoosh of Ilsa's lighter and the soft scrape of her slippers on the polished wood floor.

"So what do we do now?" he said.

"There is no 'we.' Now David and I try to figure a way to deal with the mess you've created." She lit another cigarette and inhaled so deeply the smoke must have blackened her toenails.

"Best case, Toy thinks you're just a loony crusader on a misguided mission—which I guess pretty much sums it up, doesn't it?—or maybe you were trying to kidnap a child for your own nasty purposes. I might have chosen otherwise, but David felt he couldn't just stand there while Toy pistol-whipped you to death. So as far as infiltrating the brothel, he's useless now."

"But the guy tried to kill me. David here's a witness to that."

"Unfortunately another way to look at it is you're a guy who was trying to run off with a kid, and David pulled a knife on the man who was trying to save her."

"What about the johns? There was a guy—" Eddie gulped and had to pause to collect himself "—a guy in the room right behind me who must've seen or heard what went on."

"You think a man who has sex with children is gonna admit to it?" said Abbott.

"Well, hell, I'll go to the cops myself."

Ilsa sighed and sank down heavily into an arm chair. "Just know that if you go there with some wild story about Toy, odds are better that you'll end up in prison than he does."

"So he just gets away with it?"

"He does for now. Thanks to you getting involved in something you know nothing about."

Eddie figured he'd swallowed his ration of shit and then some. He got up gingerly and aimed his aching body at the door.

"Hey, sorry, lady. Sorry I tried to make a difference." He looked at Abbott. "Too goddamned bad you didn't cut the bastard's throat when you had the chance. If you had, I'da been happy to put my prints on the knife and say it was me done it."

He let himself out into the moist, fragrant night and found himself in a garden fringed with frangipani and hibiscus, redolent of perfume. He heard his name called and Ilsa appeared in the doorframe, a darkly Rubenesque silhouette punctuated by the orange flare of her cigarette.

In the ink-drop darkness of the garden, her low, throaty voice washed over him.

"You tried to do a good thing, Eddie, there's no shame in that. But no more heroics, okay? Go back to your friends. Whatever you saw tonight, let it go. Forget about it."

She had no way of knowing the effect her words had on him, but they acted like kerosene on the fire of his rage. For a second, his vision purpled and he had trouble drawing a breath.

"That's what you don't get," he said finally. He stood facing her so she wouldn't notice the bulge that the gun made under his shirt. In the confusion after Toy dropped it, he'd managed to palm the pistol without Abbott noticing. "You don't know what I saw. You got no idea. And if I don't do something about it, I'm gonna keep on seeing it till the day I die."

A FEW minutes after leaving Ilsa and David's house, a tuk-tuk dropped Eddie at his hotel, where he went to his room, popped a couple of Danny's Vicodin, and collected what he was going to need. Rain had begun to spatter the windows, so he put on a slicker and rain hat, which made it easier to conceal his battered face when he strolled past the snoozing desk clerk at the Mandarin Orchid and took the stairs to Kurt's room.

He banged on the door, and Kurt opened it, clad in boxer shorts and an undershirt. A TV bolted to the ceiling in one corner of the room blared, but Kurt appeared to have been sleeping through the commotion, his eyes sleep-encrusted, pillow marks indenting one cheek.

"What is it?" he said, backpedaling as Eddie shouldered his way past him. "Hey, you're dripping water on the floor!"

Eddie took off his rain slicker and threw it over a chair. He checked the bathroom, the closet, and under the bed, then he started pulling out drawers, throwing Kurt's meticulously folded T-shirts and trousers and underwear every which way.

"What the hell, Eddie? What are you doing?"

"I wanna see your camera."

"Are you blind, you damn fool?" Kurt pointed to the camcorder on the dresser. "It's in front of you."

"The *other* camera. The one you use to film yourself when you rape little girls." He started ransacking the closet, tossing clothes onto the floor. "I *saw* you, asshole. That was *me* opened the door on you tonight. I saw you, I heard your voice, and now I get why you needed to be in a different hotel than Danny and me—you needed privacy."

Cunning and fear flared in Kurt's eyes, twisting his face into something hateful, unrecognizable. Then it vanished as fast as the memory that spawned it and he was Kurt again, with his loose, crooked smile, easy-going, unfazed. "Well, shit, Eddie, you had me going there for a second. I thought this was something serious."

"I find out a man I grew up with, a man I've known all my life, a *real* man, I thought you were—you're out there raping babies and you don't call that serious!"

"That's the second time you've used that word *rape*, and that's effing enough. Nobody's raping anybody. And let me ask you this, what were *you* doing in Toy's joint? Looking for some young stuff yourself?" He made a show of yawning and scratching his ribs. "It's Thailand, Eddie, it's an effing foreign country. Our rules don't apply. So the chicks you've been doing look like they're eighteen—maybe they are, maybe they aren't. Who's to say? I like 'em young, always have. So what? Eighteen or eight years old, man, they're all effin' whores."

The sound that exploded from Eddie's throat was guttural and choked, a combination war cry and moan. He plowed into Kurt, driving punches into his face and gut, pummeling him onto the floor and pounding his face until there was a fine mist of blood on the carpet. He forced Kurt's arms back, whipped off his belt and tied his wrists. With another belt from Kurt's closet, he secured his legs.

Meantime, Kurt's eyes were coming back into focus. Eddie grabbed the gun and jammed the barrel under his chin.

"One chance or I swear, I blow your brains out. The other camera, where is it?"

Kurt's eyes clicked to the TV set bolted to the ceiling. "Up there. On the strut behind the TV."

Eddie pocketed the gun, climbed onto a chair, and retrieved the second camcorder. He didn't watch much, just enough to verify what was on it and that Kurt's face was clearly revealed. After seeing it, he figured he had no choice, hadn't really had one since he opened the door to that room. He fished in the pocket of his slicker and went into the bathroom for a minute or two. When he came out, Kurt had flopped off the bed and was inchworming his way across the floor toward the door. Eddie resisted a powerful urge to kick in his head.

Instead he hauled him upright and threw him onto his back on the bed.

He held up the hypodermic he'd prepared in the bathroom. When Kurt saw it, he started babbling desperate, weepy promises, but Eddie wasn't listening. He stuffed a wash cloth in Kurt's mouth.

"Guess I'll owe Danny an apology for taking this," he said, "but I think he'll understand. Way I recall, we agreed that if one of us was too far gone to be saved, we'd put him out of his misery with a smile on his face. So this is better than you deserve. And this is me, Eddie, putting you out of your misery."

THE RAIN had begun to pour, obscuring his departure, when Eddie descended the fire escape into an alley behind the hotel. A few blocks away, he found a pay phone in a 24-hour convenience shop and called the Tourist Police, using the emergency number he'd seen plastered on posters in touristy sections of town.

There was still a couple hours of darkness left that he prayed he could make use of. He headed off toward the Numbah One Noodle Shop.

IT WAS midmorning by the time Eddie returned to his hotel, after briefly detouring to toss Toy's pistol into the river. He thought how nice a drink would go down right now, but instead fortified himself with a cup of coffee from the pot brewing on a counter in the lobby. When he knocked on Danny's door Lek opened it clad in one of Danny's shirts, her long hair damp and glistening around her shoulders.

Danny was slouched in a chair, watching a kickboxing match on TV. He saw Eddie and scowled, "Where the hell've you been? You forget what day it is? Danny Pinchero's Grand Exit Party!" He took in Eddie's beaten up face. "Holy shit, you look like ten miles of bad road."

"Tough night," Eddie said.

"And where's Kurt?" Danny leaned forward, craning his neck as though Eddie's body was a scrawny shrub Kurt might be hiding behind.

"He's not coming."

Danny's face crumpled like a wadded up tissue. "What the fuck? What kind of friend doesn't show up for a buddy's last day on the planet?"

Eddie swallowed. His hands were twitching so bad he was scared to take them out of his pockets. "Kurt wasn't the man you and I thought."

"You mean he chickened out? He couldn't even come to shake my hand and say good-bye?"

"He can't be here, take my word for it."

Eddie expected a barrage of questions, but Danny absorbed the news with surprising stoicism. He waved his hand. "Fuck him then, fuck Kurt Anderson. Let's get down to business."

"Look, Danny, I..."

"You gotta catch the bus to Bangkok in a couple of hours to make that flight back to the States, don't you? So let's do this. I'm ready, man, I'm so ready. You know why? Cause while you were off paintin' the town, I stayed here and, you know what, I prayed. First time in years. Lek prayed with me. Oh, we couldn't understand each other, but she's got a real soothing presence, know what I mean? Now I'm right with the Lord. I'm ready to haul ass and go."

The shivers weren't confined to Eddie's hands now. They were traveling up his forearms into his shoulders. Pretty soon he was gonna have to pull his hand out of his pockets or Danny was gonna think he was diddling himself.

"Danny, I don't think I can do this."

"What?" Danny stood up and poked a finger into his chest. "You can't back out now, buddy. Man-up, for Christ's sake! We signed a pact!"

Eddie looked down at the finger jabbing his chest. If the offending digit had belonged to anyone but Danny, he'd be swinging at the guy's jaw. But now his throat felt like it was closing, and he had to gather himself to speak.

"Listen, Danny, I did something, okay? Something real bad. And I know we made a deal, but don't ask me to do this—"

"Wait just a damn minute!" Danny gave his forehead a theatrical slap. "I get the picture! The smack's gone, is that it? You snuck off and had yourself a little party last night. Kurt, too, I'll bet. That's why he's ashamed to show his face."

"No, no, Danny, you got it all wrong. Something else happened—just let me explain—"

"Shut the fuck up, you sorry-ass liar!" He stared hard at Eddie and then he started to laugh. The laughter began low in his chest and then deepened, rumbling up from his belly, like a volcano suddenly coming alive after decades of dormancy. His face turned splotchy red and tears spilled from his eyes.

Eddie felt a new kind of terror now. He thought Danny was losing his mind.

"If you could see your face," Danny said finally, still guffawing. "Jesus, Eddie, you look like you're about to keel over. Don't sweat it, bro. I'm just yanking your chain."

When Eddie looked uncomprehending, he went on. "You're the one who said I'm allowed to change my mind, right? Well, I fuckin' changed it. Forget the China White. I don't give a shit what you and Kurt did with it. I got a better plan."

He glanced at Lek and then looked quickly away, as though not wanting her to know she was to be the topic of conversation. "This girl here, Eddie, she tells me she's twenty-two, but I think she's closer to thirty. Over here, kind of life she's living, thirty's like Methuselah. It won't be long before she's used up and worn out and then what's she got? Nothing. Most of the money she makes goes back to her family in the mountains."

"Jesus, they all say that," Eddie said, but Danny silenced him with a look.

"I'm not an idiot, Eddie. I know she's a hooker and practically everything she says is a lie, but what choice does she have? It's a shit life. I just met her, I don't love her and I sure as hell don't think she loves me—but she seems to like me a lot or pretends to, and she's sure given me a good time so far. The thing is, I'm on my way out and she's not. And I've got a little money and not too bad of a house, and I got American citizenship which still means something here and there. So what the fuck, I'm gonna stick it out. I got a translator to discuss it with her and it's all set. She's gonna go back with me to the States and we're gonna get married. I leave her what I got, which isn't much by our standards, but it's a fortune to her. After I kick the bucket, she can stay or she can go, but now she's a little bit ahead of the game and I get to die feeling like I did something good in this world. I think that's important, you know? To feel like before I croaked I made things better for somebody."

"But you don't even know her, Danny. It's not like she's family or anything, she's just a—"

Danny held up a hand. "Don't say it. I want to do this."

Eddie started to stay something, but stopped when he heard footsteps approaching. Someone knocked on the door to his room across the hall from Danny's. Before he could stop her, Lek opened the door and said something in Thai.

The boy from the front desk stood holding a folded piece of paper, which he handed to Eddie. "Lady who called said it was important, to make sure I give you the message in person."

As Eddie read the note, his mind went into overdrive, trying to figure out how fast he could get out of Thailand, what he'd do if cops were waiting for him at the airport, and what kind of alibi he could establish with Danny and Lek to prove he'd been with them in the wee hours of the morning. Then he decided that was the old Eddie's way of thinking. He'd done what he had to do. If Ilsa was planning to turn him over to the police, then so be it.

"I gotta go, Danny." Impulsively he leaned over, bear-hugged Danny, and kissed Lek on the cheek. "If I'm not back in time to catch the bus to Bangkok, you and Lek go on without me. Don't miss that plane."

"Wait a second! What's going on? You didn't tell me what happened to Kurt!"

"He decided to stay in Thailand."

OUTSIDE A light drizzle fell, warm as spittle.

As he got close to the noodle shop, traffic was gridlocked, pedestrians darting every which way, the satellite dishes from a couple of news vans gleaming like giant toadstools in the rain. He pushed his way through the crowd of onlookers until he spotted David Abbott conferring with a squat, stern-faced guy who had the look of a plainclothes detective. Behind the noodle shop, a bus was loading up kids, some crying, others looking blank-faced and stunned. Ilsa was squatting down, saying something to each one as they boarded the bus, a safari hat shielding her face.

Eddie stood to one side, grateful for the rain, which transformed the scene before him into a monochromatic blur of smeary outlines and indistinct faces. The warm rain running down his back felt icy now, as though mere proximity to the noodle shop had caused some kind of thermal shift. In the torrid humidity of the Chiang Mai morning, he realized he was freezing.

Abruptly Ilsa looked up, her gaze uncanny in its accuracy, as Eddie tried to pretend he hadn't seen her. But it was too late now. He held his ground as she stepped under the police tape and strode over.

"Jesus, Eddie. You look like death's leftovers."

"Thanks. Got your message. Can't believe you remembered where I was staying." He tugged down his rain hat as a couple of policemen passed by. "Looks like the police decided to raid the place after all."

"That they did. David got a call from a cop friend at eight this morning telling him it was going down."

He made a show of looking around. "Don't see that son of a bitch Toy. Did they haul his ass off to jail already?"

"No, they hauled it down to the morgue."

"Well. A morning full of happy surprises."

Ilsa said nothing, and Eddie shuffled his feet as the silence expanded uncomfortably.

"I didn't think you'd show up," she said finally.

"Why's that?"

"You had a busy night. I figured you'd either be sleeping in or fleeing the country."

"That some kind of joke?"

"Am I laughing?" She pulled out a pack of cigarettes, shook one out, and ducked her head down to light it. Exhaling, she said, "Aren't you even curious what happened to Toy?"

"Not really. Dead's dead."

They stood watching as the bus pulled away, the rain rat-tatting off the roof, streaming down the windows, obscuring the heads of the children that Eddie imagined must have their faces pressed to the glass, wondering what would come next. Or maybe not. Maybe they were like him, and they stared straight ahead, pretending none of it was happening.

"Amazing the way coincidence works," Ilsa said. "The other day at the bar I told you the police would need to find a dead body on the premises to get motivated to do anything—for the record, I was being sarcastic, not issuing instructions. This morning, a street cleaner finds Toy's body stuffed between the garbage cans behind the shop. Apparently he came outside in the early morning and somebody shot off the top of his head at close range."

Eddie shrugged. "Guess God answers prayers."

"If God's in the vigilante business."

"Cops find the gun?"

"I'm guessing it's in the river. I know that's what I would have done with it."

"Yeah, me, too. Think they'll send divers down?"

"Why? You worried?"

"What would I have to be worried about? After I left your place, I went back to my hotel and conked out. Slept like a baby."

She groaned like he'd told a lame joke. "I'm surprised at you, Eddie. I figured you'd have the lying skills of an accomplished sociopath, but you sound like a little boy explaining how the cat threw up on his schoolwork."

"Don't know what you mean."

"Well, first of all, David's sources with the police said that early this morning someone called in a tip that a pedophile was sleeping off a bender in room 216 at the Mandarin Orchid and that the guy's camcorder was there full of child pornography, a lot of it shot at the Numbah One Noodle. So they go there and find the guy beat up, with ligature marks on his ankles and wrists, sleeping off some kind of tranquilizer."

"Sounds like someone with a guilty conscience."

"So he beat himself up, then shot a needle full of sedatives into his neck?" She flicked rain from her face. "Pretty strange, huh? Just a perv and his camcorder, taking a nap. They said the name on his passport was—"

Her words struck him like a barrage of stones; he felt stunned, annihilated. He whirled on her. "I don't want to hear the asshole's name! I don't need to know the details! A bad guy got what was coming to him, that's not good enough for you? Why you got to keep yapping about it?"

They stood in silence after that, the lights from the police cars shedding streams of color into the slate rain as the remaining children straggled onto the bus. When finally it pulled away, Ilsa tossed down her cigarette and said, "Something's wrong with you, Eddie."

He tried to feign the calm detachment of a man who had nothing to hide, all the while feeling as though his guilt glowed as brightly as bloody hand prints sprayed with luminol.

When he didn't reply, she squinted and tilted her head like someone trying to puzzle out a riddle. "It's almost noon and you're sober. Shouldn't you be shit-faced?"

"Felt like giving my liver a day off."

"Right. And what happened last night, you had nothing to do with any of that?"

"You kidding me? I'm just an old drunk who got his ass kicked trying to play hero."

She studied him and in that gaze Eddie saw sadness and resignation but also something else that might have been a grain of acceptance—or gratitude.

"If you say so, Eddie. But you don't want to be having this conversation with the police. That being said, aren't you getting homesick for Detroit?"

"You got that right. I'm taking the bus back to Bangkok in a few hours and flying home tonight."

"Then you better get going."

He wanted to kiss her, but settled for shaking her hand. "You take care of those kids, Elsa."

"Ilsa," she muttered as he trotted off into the rain.

THE SPRING that Danny Pinchero died was the coldest in seventeen years, and Lake St. Clair remained frozen deep into the spring. A freak snowstorm came in early May, an arctic blast slamming down out of Canada, whiting out the skyline, the lake, the world. Eddie drove down to the ice and stepped off into white nothingness, the snow gusting so heavily that his boot prints filled up almost as fast as he made them. He thought about Danny and Kurt and he let himself rage, cursing and crying out there in the bluster and screech of the wind, his voice drowned out by the storm, his tears frozen.

With Danny gone and Thailand behind him, his whole life felt out of whack and confused, like a jigsaw puzzle missing key pieces. His emotions ran the full spectrum from pissed off to really pissed off to murderous, but he was running out of furniture to smash and slugging walls just bruised his knuckles. He'd tracked down Ilsa's email address through the rescue group she worked for and wrote to ask her what happened to the guy at the Mandarin Orchid. He was hoping to hear that the bastard would be out of prison about the time Detroit ran out of cars, but she never responded, so after some resentment over being ignored, he let it go. He tried to feel good about the fact that he'd chosen to dose Kurt with Danny's liquid Valium instead of the lethal smack, but he still nursed a dangerous fury—Kurt had grown up with him and Danny on Gratiot Street, how could he have turned into a monster and how could he, Eddie, not have known?—so that snowy spring afternoon, all he could do was stomp out onto the ice and scream his rage into the cold, howling white.

After a couple of miles, though, he ran out of steam. Here was where the idea had been to guzzle down the bottle of Jack he carried inside his parka, stretch out on the ice and fall asleep or fall through, whichever came first, but that plan, like everything else in his life, had changed recently. He set the bottle down unopened—a prize for some ice fishermen if they were lucky enough to find it—mumbled a few words to Danny or God or anybody out there who might be listening and trudged back to the safety of the shore. He wondered idly if this failure to follow through on the original plan meant he'd lost his nerve or his cojones, but figured, if Danny could change his mind, so by God could he.

When he got back to his truck, he sat for a while running the heater, getting warmed up and gritting his teeth at his cell phone, which he'd laid out beside him on the passenger seat. It irked him to no end how nervous he felt, because a real man ought not to be scared to call his own daughter any more than a real man ought to need those damned fool AA meetings he'd dragged his ass to a couple of times.

Then again, he was starting to wonder if he had any idea what a real man really was.

What the hell, he thought, and picked up the phone.

Maybe there was still time to find out.

LA SEÑORA BLANCA

THE BLEAT of a train whistle greeted the couple's advance along the tracks, the jittering of the timber ties traveling up through the soles of their shoes, making their ankles wobble, their knees quake. In the distance, an owl mourned, crickets clacking in the tall weeds surrounding the tracks. No houses, no lights way out here. Just the Estrella del Norte headed south from Queretaro to Mexico City, right on time at 6:47 p.m.

Naldo lifted Lupe's hand to his mouth and kissed her fingers. "The train's coming, my love, are you ready?"

"Ready, Naldo."

"La Santa Muerte, she's keeping her promise."

"I can't wait to meet her, *mi amor.*"

They sounded like nervous young lovers, but they were old now, curled and fragile as two brittle brown leaves nudged along one last time by the breeze. Lupe tottered unsteadily, pendulous breasts flopping under her loose blouse, grey-streaked hair tumbling over the knobs of her spine. Naldo clasped her hand, guiding her over the tracks in the twilight. He was squat and sinewy, with bowed legs and a flamboyant, devilishly curling mustache that flared out on both sides of his square, pit-bull jaw. A knife scar pebbled the flesh at the side of his neck, and faded tattoos, souvenirs from numerous incarcerations, festooned his biceps and forearms.

"She's almost here, Naldo!"

The Estrella del Norte blasted around the curve up ahead and roared toward them at sixty miles per hour, lights blinding, disorienting, and the engineer must have spotted them, because bells suddenly clanged and the train commenced a terrible cats-in-heat keening. The engineer was giving the brakes all he had, but it wasn't enough. Naldo had explained to Lupe that, at the speed the train was traveling when it took the curve, the engineer would need at least a mile to stop.

Not that either Naldo or Lupe wanted to be spared. They'd planned their suicide years before, when Naldo had just gotten out of Mexico City's Prisión de Oriente and Lupe was being treated for a virulent cancer that nested in her uterus like a malefic fetus. They'd vowed they would survive into old age and then face death together.

"It's been a good life," Lupe said.

"The best, mi amor!"

"No regrets?"

"No regrets."

Adrenalin rocked Lupe's heart and she shuddered—not just with fear, but with pride and love and a terrible resolve. She looked at Naldo and mouthed *Te amo* and leaned over to kiss him—

—as the tracks buckled and roller-coastered into the starless black sky and the bruja-screech of the whistle rent the world as red rain spattered the front of the train.

LUPE AWOKE with a howl on her lips, eyes darting wildly. Something was wrong. It wasn't the dream that had wakened her. Something else.

In the room next to hers, Luisa Sentavo, a buxom former librarian, huffed and moaned in her sleep. From across the hall came the contralto rumble of Olive Pattala's snores and Vicente Montoya's drugged mumbling. Most of the residents of Sierra House Nursing Home slept like logs. Flora Espinoza, the night nurse, dispensed sleep aids as if they were Tums, but Lupe squirreled hers away in her cheek. She wasn't one of those old people longing to fade away in her sleep. She wanted her death to be memorable.

From outside came a soft scuffling sound like panther claws on the linoleum floor or the rattle of chicken bones around the neck of a *curandera*. A broomstick-thin shadow bent to the door of Lupe's room, peered in and then withdrew, leaving behind a heady cascade of rich odors—cigar smoke and rum and something else, the rank, pungent tang of decay.

The banging of blood in Lupe's chest rose so violently that she was afraid Pettigrew would hear it all the way to the nurse's station, but in spite of her fear, she slipped out of bed and mouse-crept to the door.

Her first impression was of a roiling black thunderhead that filled the corridor and dimmed the sallow glow of the fluorescent ceiling lights. She heard a hollow tapping and saw in stark relief the outline of vertebrae snaking against an inky cloak, vivid as veins in a winter-blasted leaf.

Lupe bit the inside of her cheek and reeled backward, so stunned by the sight that she feared her heart might crack apart on her ribs like a cheap earthen vase.

Prowling the hall was La Santa Muerte—known to her devotees as La Señora Blanca—regal and terrible in a hooded black cloak, heavy rings on her skeletal fingers. The stew of odors Lupe had smelled before wreathed her mottled cranium like a widow's veil.

Holy Death, in all her glory, come to call.

Watching Death stalk the corridor, creeping door to door with cat-burglar stealth, Lupe felt poleaxed with horror and awe. At the same time, her natural curiosity flared perilously high and she was beset with a rash desire to confront Death and pose questions. She opened her mouth, but her voice failed. She realized she was drenched in sweat and shivering. After so many years of praying to her image, to encounter Death—La Señora Blanca herself—was overwhelming.

Vividly, she recalled the first time Naldo had brought her to La Santa Muerte's shrine in Tepita, the most dangerous, crime-ridden barrio in Mexico City. Naldo had just completed a four-year stretch for robbery and had come out of prison a man in love, transformed with adoration for Holy Death, the most beloved and venerated saint in Prisión de Oriente. Lupe had gazed up in awe at the six-foot statue draped in velvet robes and a bride's taffeta veil, wielding a scythe in one hand and a globe in the other. Death's skeletal mouth seemed to twist in a cruel grin, as though she relished the terror she inspired and took pleasure flaunting her power over all living things.

With utmost reverence, Naldo filled a shot glass from a pint of Patron, La Señora Blanca's poison of choice, and placed it on the altar. From his pocket, he withdrew a pack of Marlboros and a fat joint, meticulously rolled, which he added to the offerings. "La Flaca isn't like the other saints," he said, calling La Santa Muerte by one of her many nicknames—the Skinny One. "She doesn't judge the poor people, the criminals, the *putanas*. She understands us best. La Flaca also appreciates the finer things. If we come to her respectfully and bring her gifts, she always answers our prayers."

"Always, Naldo?"

"Always."

Lupe had brought gifts, too: a red rose and white candles bearing images of La Santa Muerte's frightful countenance. She laid them on the altar and said a prayer: *Keep Naldo safe. Let us grow old together. When the time comes, let us die together, too.*

It was the memory of that prayer, heartfelt and fervently uttered, that restored Lupe's voice and snapped her out of her fear trance.

"Señora, Señora," she called.

Death halted midstride and twisted around with a click-clacking of phalanges. An inch of limp ash dangled from the Cohiba gripped in her teeth. Lupe could sense her disbelief and outrage. No one challenged La Señora Blanca. No one had the temerity to question Death.

Yet Lupe was a tough old bird who had lived almost ninety years, many of them in poverty and peril, so she blurted out, "Remember my husband Naldo, who was killed by drug dealers? He was a little man with a big mustache and an even bigger heart. Ever since he got out of prison, he was your devoted servant. Yet he was murdered eighteen years ago. Why did he die in such a terrible way?"

The silence that followed reverberated like a hail of bullets from an *arma automatica*. Lupe clutched the doorframe, legs liquid with fear. What had she done?

Death said nothing, but regarded Lupe as if she were a half-crushed insect she was about to put out of its misery.

Lupe wanted to scuttle back to her bed, but the thought of Naldo's bullet-ridden body, stretched out on a slab at the Mexico City morgue, gave her courage.

"Please, Holy Death, what happened? Why didn't you protect

him?"

La Flaca's gleaming cranium rotated to fix on the shriveled little woman who addressed her so boldly. Her limbs and torso were utterly still, but the tiny bones in her extremities crunched. The jeweled rings on her finger bones ticked together in agitation.

"Get lost," rasped La Flaca, her sepulcher voice somber and cold as the black of her pitiless eye sockets. Lupe heard the words as a thin hissing that burrowed its way into her flesh, the sound itself dry as broom straws sweeping a cement floor or a rattlesnake gliding through parched grass. "Be grateful I didn't come here for you tonight."

Smoke from the fat Cohiba snaked out of her eye sockets as Flora Espinoza passed by, studying a chart on a clipboard and drawing Death's attention. Espinoza was a plump, fortyish woman with neatly bunned hair, marshmallowy arms, and dull eyes that sometimes, unexpectedly, grew twinkly as though with secret, subterranean mirth. She had a lovely singing voice, rich with consoling, and often serenaded residents of Sierra House who were ill or distressed.

Death turned to stalk after Espinoza.

"*Please*, Santa Muerte, wait!" Lupe cried.

She fumbled in the bodice of her nightgown and plucked out a tattered prayer card that portrayed Death as a magnificent, bejeweled queen, her bones draped in a royal blue robe studded with gems. The card was torn and faded from handling and the bottom half bore rusty stains.

"This was in Naldo's pocket when he died—look, you can see his blood! Tell me why he had to die when he had just found you in prison a few years earlier? Naldo was devoted to you and brought you expensive gifts. He'd given up the criminal life, he was no trouble to anyone. And what about *me*, left to grow old alone and rot in this place, which is nothing but a prison for old people! We were going to grow old together. When the time came, we were going to ride the Estrella del Norte."

Death seemed to find this last remark uproarious. From her throat trilled a pinging xylophone sound that might have been a laugh. "Kissing the train—you call that a plan? That's a death for fools! *Idiotas* like you and your husband imagine the train's like a one-night stand—wham, bam, and it's over!" She lunged at Lupe and gave a guillotine snap of her jaws. "They don't see the ones I turn away—like chopped-down trees, all stumps. Mashed flat as a tortilla from the waist down or scalped alive when their hair tangles in the undercarriage. A fast and pain-free death, my knobby ass!"

She made a shooing gesture and strode up the hall to the room of Sylvia LaGuerta, an ancient, emphysema-stricken crone who, in her day, had dealt a mean hand of blackjack at the casino in Monterrey. Death peered into the room and, while her fleshless visage was incapable of real expression, Lupe heard her finger bones begin to agitate and her teeth grind together. The tip of her Cohiba flared and smoke began to puff from its ash. Death was displeased, and her fury altered the quality of the air, making it clammy and corpse-cold.

La Flaca stood at the foot of Sylvia LaGuerta's bed as though she were a vigil-keeping mother waiting for LaGuerta's eyes to open or her hand to twitch. But even Lupe, spying from the doorway, could tell that Sylvia, the *real* Sylvia, was long gone and that what remained was of no more consequence than a junked car on the towing lot.

Meanwhile, Death fretted beside the bed in mute pique, clicking her fingerbones together as though keeping time to an infernal song.

Lupe inched her way to Death's side and whispered, "About my question, Holy Death…"

La Flaca snapped her mandible and said, "Persistent pest, aren't you? I'll come again tomorrow night. Then we shall see."

"LUPE, SOMETHING dreadful's happened."

Lupe was watching a morning talk show featuring people who'd had sex change operations discussing their lovemaking techniques when Nurse Espinoza charged into her room, looking distressed and frazzled. She cut off the TV, pulled a chair up next to Lupe's, and sat down with a woebegone sigh. She looked close to tears, and Lupe wanted to comfort her, but it was difficult—Espinoza scorned La Santa Muerte, insisting that she wasn't a saint at all, but the fabrication of the ignorant and misguided, undoubtedly leading the lot of them to damnation.

Lupe tried to be forgiving, though, having heard that Espinoza's own mother, with whom she was very close, had died less than a year ago.

"Oh, Lupe," said Espinoza, dabbing at her eyes with a tissue. "Sylvia passed away last night."

"I know," said Lupe sadly.

A small frown line appeared in Espinoza's brow. "What do you mean?"

Lupe knew that Espinoza would think she was one of those old people lost in a fog of dementia if she talked of seeing La Señora Blanca go into Sylvia's room and tower over her bed, so she said quickly, "It was in a dream. I saw a great white sailing ship, like a magnificent swan, sailing across the ocean. Jesus was at the helm, the Virgin Mary by His right hand, and Sylvia kneeling at His side."

Lupe had to fight not to giggle at the banality of the image, a version of which she had once seen painted on a china plate in a Mexico City souvenir shop, but Espinoza's eyes flooded with tears and she nodded, *yes, yes*, as though she'd seen such a ship herself and talked with Skipper Jesus. Lupe looked away and rolled her eyes.

"It's for the best, you know," said Espinoza. "Sylvia suffered dreadfully with emphysema. She was fortunate to have an easy death." She plumped the pillows behind Lupe's back and squeezed her hand. "Would that we all could go so peacefully."

To hell with peace, thought Lupe. *I want to know why La Flaca let Naldo die.*

Munching fried potatoes at the evening meal, Lupe shot furtive glances around the room, wondering who La Flaca was going to take next. Would it be eighty-nine-year-old Guzman Torres, who lost a leg in the Great War and liked to brag that he'd lived through three marriages and two airplane crashes? Or eighty-year-old Bertie Angelina, who carried on long, rambling conversations with her dead brother and sometimes screamed out "Call 066!" for no apparent reason? Or maybe Vincente Montoya or Olive Patalla or even prissy little Luisa Sentavo with her nose stuck in a book all day and then moaning and groaning all night. Or maybe, Lupe thought, *she* was the one Death was coming for.

Later, she lay awake, alert and listening. Around two a.m., she heard Espinoza singing softly in another room, the sound so melodious and comforting that she almost drifted off to sleep, but jerked awake when the telltale odor of cigar smoke reached her nostrils.

Creeping into the corridor, she saw Espinoza leave Bertie Angelina's room, sighing and typing out a text message on her phone. Espinoza ambled toward the rec room, where Lupe knew the portly nurse often passed the wee hours playing Internet poker or watching heartwarming rescue stories on the Animal Planet. She didn't see what Lupe saw—the black-robed skeleton puffing on a cigar just outside Bertie's door, her skull head metronoming side to side as she moved with lithe, insectile grace into Bertie's room.

When Lupe tiptoed in behind La Flaca and saw what was on the bed, her heart wilted like a drought-stricken camellia.

Her old friend lay with mouth agape and sightless eyes bugged out, as though she'd watched La Santa Muerte come for her and died purely from fright. Her arms were outside the covers, hands clenched into claws. Even in death, she appeared to be trying to fight her way free of some terrible assault.

Lupe gave a little gasp, and La Flaca's head jerked up. She opened her jaw in a feral grin and snapped her teeth so viciously she almost bit her cigar in half.

"You again!"

"Holy Death," said Lupe, bowing low to show her deep respect and reverence, "if you would only talk to me a minute about how my husband died—"

Fast as a swung machete, Death lunged across the room, seized Lupe by the back of her nightgown, and hoisted her high. Lupe's bare feet paddled the air, the breath left her lungs in a whoosh. The prayer card she kept tucked in her bra shook loose and fell to the floor.

"What do you care why your old man died?" hissed La Flaca. "He's worm food now, there's no bringing him back. I'm a one-way door, don't you get it?"

"But what about all that Naldo did to show you his affection and respect?" Lupe exclaimed, her fear squelched by indignation. "What about the statue of you he carved with his own hands?"

"Ah, yes, the statue, I do remember that," La Flaca said, baring the toothy semblance of a smile. "Before he brought it to the shrine, he packed the nostrils full of snow. It was a thoughtful gesture."

"He did much more than plug your nose with cocaine. He also built you a shrine."

Death's mouth split wide with lethal mirth—she might have been hooting with laughter or braying with rage. "Don't talk to me about shrines! The only shrines I give a shit about are the bodies I leave behind. Every time you see a rotting corpse, a cadaver laid out on a pallet, that's another shrine to me. Remember that, Guadalupe Mendoza-Delgado."

Lupe gasped. "You know my name?"

"What do you think, that this whole dying business isn't organized? I know everybody's name, I know the names of your papa's bastard children and your *puta* of a grandmama's johns." She shook Lupe so hard that her head bobbled and her eyes bulged. "Besides, ungrateful *pendeja*, your name was on my ledger a long time ago—you're luckier than you know just to be sucking air."

"Then why wasn't I the one who died?" demanded Lupe. "Why Naldo?"

La Flaca ground her teeth. The cold silence of gravestones in the Panteon de Dolores radiated from the black depths of her ancient eye sockets. "You are a bitch, a *cabrona*," she said, "and your man made a foolish bargain." She impaled Lupe with a meat grinder stare. "Now get back to bed, and if you wake up, consider yourself lucky."

LUPE FLED back to her room and burrowed under the covers. Soon after, she heard footsteps and held her breath, but it was only Espinoza, come in to check on her. And though Lupe pretended to be asleep, the nurse must have sensed her distress, for she began to sing a soulful lullaby, part mother's love and part lament, that made Lupe think of times gone by and filled her with bittersweet longing.

She fell into a fretful sleep and dreamed about that terrible day when Naldo stormed into their little house, bloodied and shaking with rage.

Lupe was trembling, too. But before she could tell him her own dreadful news, he began to curse and shout, "*Mierde*, but a frightful thing has happened!" For a flustered instant, she thought he was talking about her test results, but then he went on, "The government sent soldiers with bulldozers this morning and tore down La Santa Muerte's shrine. The people who'd come to worship tried to stop them, but they beat us back. Everything's gone! The beautiful robes and the holy statues, the paintings and icons have all been carted off to the dump! They say we are a cult of criminals and devil worshipers."

Lupe, overwhelmed by this surfeit of sorrow, began to weep, and Naldo, not understanding that she was crying for herself, began to reassure her.

"Never mind, mi amor. I'll build a new shrine, you'll see. I'll make it bigger and more beautiful than ever."

He talked and talked, working himself up, until finally Lupe interrupted to tell him about her visit to the clinic and the cancer the doctor had found nesting in her womb. After that, he was silent for a long time, and then he cried.

All through that summer, Naldo worked alongside others in the barrio to build the new shrine. A few so-called upstanding folks chipped in, but mostly it was the outcasts, Gloriana the prostitute who stood in the alleyway all night selling her used-up flesh, the gangs and the drug addicts, the alcoholics, cab drivers and *policía*, fringe people whose lives were fraught with danger and risk, people who needed protection.

Lupe had lived that summer in mortal fear, but Death—whose fearsome image leered down from every wall in their house, whose face even stared out at her from across her husband's tattooed chest when he was mounting her, never came.

"LOOK WHAT I found in Bertie's room," Nurse Espinoza said. She held up Lupe's slippers, one in each hand, as if they were week-old kittens. Her eyes were smiling but her mouth was crimped tight as a fist. "These are your slippers, aren't they?"

It was early morning and Bertie's body had just been wheeled out on a gurney by two white-clad attendants. Along the hall, the residents of Sierra House crept warily out of their rooms to watch the sorrowful passage. Olive Pattala pinched Bertie's toes to make sure she was really dead, and Guzman Torres lifted up a corner of the sheet with one palsied hand and gave Bertie a smile and a little three-fingered wave. The same silent question played on all of their faces, a mix of dread and expectation—when does my turn come? Will I be next?

Having had little sleep the night before, Lupe had been dozing when Espinoza came in. Now she sat up, rubbed her eyes and squinted at the slippers as though she'd never seen them before. "They must be Bertie's."

Espinoza looked peeved, a teacher disappointed by a bright pupil's inadequate response. "But Lupe, these slippers are size six. Bertie's feet were big as barges. Your feet are like a doll's."

Lupe said, "I thought I heard Bertie cry out and went to see if she needed help. I must have left my slippers."

"And what did you see when you went into Bertie's room? Whatever it was, you can tell me."

"There was nothing to see. Only poor Bertie, looking like she'd been scared out of her wits when she died."

Espinoza's eyebrows lifted like elevators.

"How frightening it must have been for you to walk in and find her dead. Not only did you jump right out of your bedroom slippers, but you left behind this ugly thing as well."

From her pocket Espinoza whisked out Lupe's prayer card, which she flourished like a poker champ producing a winning Ace. She held the card up between two fingers, as though it were dipped in filth.

"La Santa Muerte wouldn't be pleased to hear you call her ugly," Lupe said.

"Death is no saint, and you're risking your immortal soul to worship such wickedness. I'm going to burn this, Lupe. It's an evil thing that can only bring you harm."

"But that was Naldo's!" Lupe cried.

For an instant, she glimpsed that tiny spark that sometimes flared up like an unvoiced scream in Espinoza's eyes, but then it vanished. Espinoza sighed forlornly and looked at Lupe with tenderness and sadness. "Haven't we had enough death around here, Lupe? For God's sake, let's pray there isn't any more."

TOO EXHAUSTED to keep her vigil that night, Lupe sank into a stuporous sleep and dreamed a young and virile Naldo suddenly thrust himself atop her.

She smiled and opened herself to him, but his urgency proved overpowering. Brutally, he held her down, smothering her face with hot, asphyxiating kisses. She began to kick and claw, trying to make him understand that she was suffocating.

You're crushing me, mi amor. Stop, please! I can't breathe!

But the reckless assault grew more merciless. A blow jerked her face to the side, her nostrils were pinched shut—she flailed out—*Naldo, no, don't do this!*—as his strength punched the air from her lungs. Lightning webbed behind her eyes, and a chainsaw chewed at the back of her brain.

Then it ended.

There was only silence and glacial cold, and Lupe thought she had died.

The pillow smashed into her face grew feather light and dropped to the floor. Gasping, her head spinning, she made out Espinoza's face, ashen and stupefied, trying desperately to free herself from the skeletal fingers that gripped her biceps so tightly they opened bloody punctures in the flesh.

"Cabrona!" Death rasped, rocking Espinoza side to side the way someone would shake a milk carton. "You go around snuffing people out like bugs and I let it go, because what's one more dead body here and there when I've got billions waiting. But then you make the same mistake as all the other psychos. When you decide who lives, who dies, you feel immortal. You imagine as long as you're in control of other people's dying, your number's never coming up!"

Espionoza's tongue planked and her eyeballs bled. Lupe could see her puffed-out cheeks working frantically to dislodge the object in her mouth, a wadded prayer card that suddenly began to blacken and curl at the edges. There came a branding iron sizzle of flesh as the nurse's face blazed a furious scarlet.

"Your *mamacita* called it right the day you murdered her," La Flaca said. "You are indeed a stupid puta and up to no fucking good!"

With a snort of disdain, she dropped Espinoza, whose body slithered to the floor in a burnt and boneless heap. Death lit a fresh cigar and tipped the ash into Espinoza's open mouth. She turned to Lupe, who was crouched in terror by the bed. "Still want to worship at my altar, cabrona?"

Lupe got to her feet on creaking knees. This time her question came out a whisper that was barely audible. "You said Naldo made a poor bargain. Tell me what you meant."

Death leaned so close that Lupe could look directly into her gaping, empty sockets—their fierce indifference to all human plight a stark reminder of her power. "Remember when cancer infested your belly and the doctors said you would soon die? What happened?"

"The cancer went away," said Lupe. "The doctors said it was a miracle, but I knew it was you, Santa Muerte, who cured me."

"You see?" said Death. "That's why you are a cabrona, I gave you back your life and still you bitch. It wasn't your paltry prayers that saved you, it was your husband's. He pestered me night and day to spare you. But don't be a stupid *zorra* about these types of transactions. Your life still came with a price attached."

Lupe absorbed this like a blow. "Naldo paid for my life with his?"

"Nothing's fucking free. The world is commerce, nothing else."

"But I was the one afraid of death," said Lupe, "not Naldo. That's why he promised me we'd die together."

"Tough luck, old woman. You got left behind." She gathered her cape around her. As it swirled and eddied about her ancient bones, Lupe saw time's passage stitched into the fabric, the rise and falls of city-states and nations, the scourge of plagues and mass exterminations, a vast and undulating tapestry of deaths past and deaths to come woven into the folds of La Flaca's robe.

Entranced by the terror and beauty of Death's garment, she reached out to touch the hem.

"Please, Santa Muerte. Don't leave me. Before you go…one dance."

The black pits in La Flaca's skull glowed, and she grew preternaturally still. "What a night! One puta tries to do my job, the other cabrona's so crazy she wants me to hang around for a *bachata*."

But then, after a moment, she took Lupe into her cold embrace and began to glide around the room, slowly at first, with a kind of stately measure befitting a last waltz, then picking up speed until they whirled and capered out into the hall, raising a draught of frosty air, like wind off of the highest peaks of the Sierra Madres. The icy breeze roused Vincente Montoya, who yelled out for his long dead wife to go downstairs and turn up the thermostat. It blew the roses on Olive Pattala's dresser so fiercely that she would awaken the next morning, astonished to find her bed covered in scarlet petals, and it chilled the bare butts of Guzman Torres and Luisa Sentavo, who were happily fucking away as they did every night, oblivious to Death passing by close enough to observe their octogenarian ardor and add one of their names to her To Do list.

Their wild bachata carried Lupe outside Sierra House and over the lawn, through dense woodlands and wild, weedy fields, down to the train tracks where Death spun to a stop and placed her spidery fingers against Lupe's heart, the grin on her face like that of a rigored corpse. *Tick tock, tick tock.*

Panting and gasping, Lupe stared into La Flaca's skull eyes. To her surprise, she saw not emptiness but all eternity, where universes were conceived and thrived and perished, only to be replaced by others in an endless cycle of creation and collapse.

From those twin voids, she heard her own voice and Naldo's echo and intertwine.

It's been a good life, hasn't it?

The best, mi amor.

A vibration began at her tailbone and lurched up her spine. She heard the blast of the whistle and the scream of the brakes and in the midst of the bedlam that built in her head, she managed a smile of relief and gratitude.

Even eighteen years later, the Estrella del Norte was still right on time.

MAKING THE WOMAN

D.J. AND me, we decided to make us a woman.

One all our own. To look at. Explore.

Not that we haven't seen real ones. We're both ten years old and we've seen a *lot*, let me tell you. Our mothers and sisters and aunts, bathing, dressing, fussing in front of the mirror— hypnotized before all that shiny, glittery *girly* stuff, the eye gook, the mascara, the brushes. We've seen them naked, too— squatting on the toilet, stretched out fish-pale and gleaming in the tub, scooping their boobs up into their bras like double dips of vanilla ice cream.

I even saw Mom fucking one time—while Dad was at work. I'd got sent home from school for giving some kid a black eye. When I walked in, she had a man on the couch with her. I'll never forget how her legs looked, straight up in the air like drumsticks, the feet twitching a little, and the guy's fat, pink butt in between.

And D.J. and I spied on my older sister Charlene and her boyfriend, dry-humping on the living room floor, making sucky-smacky noises, every now and then getting a glimpse of Charlene's tits while we huddled under the stairs, making gagging faces at each other, but fascinated, too, like at a really gross horror movie that makes you feel sick, but then you go back to see it two or three more times. I remember the excitement made my blood feel like carbonated soda, my belly tight as a fist.

Women. They seem so strange, so Other. Aliens pretending to be people, but not quite pulling it off. Always nervous, always warning us. Be careful, say our mothers and aunts and sisters, don't eat too fast, don't talk to strangers, don't run, don't yell, don't get dirty. *Don't*—it's like the only way they know to start a sentence, and it sucks.

Yechh to all that. Not our world. Our world is running and fighting and cursing and not being anything like them, making fun of how they walk and talk and smell. And how they act around the men—the phony sweetness, flirty sexiness—sometimes it creeps me out. It makes me want to hurt them, bite their fannies, pinch their titties, blow boogers out my nose and gross them out.

Painted and curvy and what they call femi-nine, always *doing* shit to themselves—shave the pussy, curl the lashes, wax the legs and eyebrows, always with the *I'm sorry's* when there's nothing to be sorry about, except that they ain't men—makes me want to puke, and slam their smiling faces with my fist.

If something bothers you, fucking *do* something to somebody else, says me and D.J.

So we decided to make us a woman.

Lucas, the twelve-year-old kid with a six-year-old's brain who goes to the special school across the street, saw D.J. and me headed up the block and wanted to come, too. Fuck that, I say. For one thing, Lucas don't think too good 'cause his mama drank so much 'fore he got born, she killed most all of his brain cells. He's also a nerd—soft and dimply and apple-round, *womanish*. He's even got small jiggly tits you can see under his clothes. His butt's like a plug of raw cookie dough with legs added on. Lucas the Doughboy, we call him.

Eat it, Lucas. Fuck you. Go play with your dolls.

Go bite the tits off your dolls, little boy.

D.J.'S DAD used to have a poster of a naked woman in his garage, her body carved up into sections and marked with words like Prime Cut, Shank, Rib Roast. He'd drink Jose Cuervo and brag about the bitches he'd fucked and how women were only good for one thing and not even that after their pussies started popping out kids.

D.J.'s dad is making license plates at the state farm now, doing two years on a domestic battery charge. When he gets out, D.J.'s mom better not be anywhere around here.

And my old man, he don't live here no more since Mom caught him in the basement taking pictures of Charlene and one of her friends dressed up in all that girly stuff—garter belts and push-up bras and panties slashed for the gash. Kinda makes me sick to my stomach, but I still wish I coulda seen Charlene and her friend with their boobs sticking out, wiggling around in hooker spikes, pretending they were grown-ups, doing all that disgusting stuff that grown-up women do.

WHERE D.J. and I live, only a few of the houses have people livin' in 'em. The rest are broken-down junk houses, roach motels, flophouses for street bums and bag ladies and cracked-out hookers walkin' stiff-legged like they got a pair of pliers up their cooze.

So the day we decided to make the woman, D.J. swiped some tampons from the Circle K and I took one of Charlene's hair pieces and Mom's rubber douche bag, and we headed up to where the buildings are most all of 'em empty.

Woulda been nice, I thought, we'da had a beach to go to, soft pale sand scooped up round and firm, make tits and ass, but this neighborhood ain't no Malibu and all we had to make our woman from was dirt.

Plenty of that, though, in the lot behind the empty Rexall Store at the corner of Fifth and Pearl. Nobody to see either, dumpsters block the view from up the street.

D.J. used a pocketknife to trace the woman's outline. Big hips, a skinny waist and neck. For boobs, we scooped up fistfuls of dirt and packed them firm, used bottle caps for the nipples. I found a clump of weeds and used it for pubic hair. D.J. unwrapped a tampon and stuck it up into the weeds like it was coming out of the woman's snatch. Then we drew a head and stuck on Charlene's blond wig. I found a crumpled condom, and we used that for the mouth. We both laughed, D.J. and me, till our sides hurt.

I put the douche bag on the woman's head. I wanted to plug a tampon up her ass, too, but she was just an outline in the dirt. She didn't have no backside or no inside or no feelings. She didn't really exist.

Suddenly I felt so mad I wanted to tear somethin' up.

I picked up a rock and threw it at the woman. "Bitch!" I hollered.

"Cunt!" yelled D.J. and did the same.

"Pussy!"

"Slut!"

"Whore!"

But it wasn't enough, and my anger still boiled. I jumped up and down on the woman's legs while D.J. stomped on her head. Hatred for our woman—for *all* women—spilled out of us like puke.

In the shadows near the dumpsters, I heard something move, and I picked up another rock.

"Whatchoo guys doing?" said Lucas, ambling into view, gawking at the woman's boobs like he was seeing a ten-car pileup on the freeway. "What's this? Pitcher of a fuck?"

I don't know which one of us threw the first rock. Maybe it was both at once, but a stone cracked Lucas in the temple and he oozed down like chocolate melting, and then D.J. bashed him with another as he groveled on the ground, flopped and foundered on top of our woman like he was tryin' to figure out how to fuck her.

"Him!" I shouted, grabbing D.J.'s knife. "Make him our woman!"

We pulled his pants off, yanked down his jockey shorts. He was crying and thrashing around, so D.J. sat on his face and pinned his arms. I yanked his little dick up with one hand and—I hesitated. For a second I couldn't breathe and I felt afraid right down to my bones. What the hell was I doing? But then I remembered all the things I'd seen and heard in my ten years— Dad whippin' Mom's ass and her takin' it, Charlene with a black eye, a split lip, courtesy of her boyfriend, and all the words, the words like punches, *cunt* and *pussy* and *gash*, and before I'd even thought of all the words I knew for woman, Lucas's dick ripped loose in my fist. I raised it over my head and war-whooped as blood poured from the hole, gushed like a bitch on her period.

Lucas howled and his eyes rolled back in his head.

D.J. leaped up and danced around the blood spigot where Lucas's dick used to be. "Lucas the Dickless Doughboy! Lucas is a woman now!"

"You cunt, you gash, you piece of shit," I screamed, throwing the wet tube of flesh to D.J., who caught it and tossed it high in the air, blood spattering Lucas's flip-flopping body.

"Bitch! Pussy! Cunt!" we screamed, our voices raw and savage with something beyond hate, something personal and terrifying.

Lucas is a girl now!

"A girl! A girl!" roared D.J.

"A girl! A girl! Like us!"

THINGS OF WHICH WE DO NOT SPEAK

"Hit me," said Elaine.

I thought I hadn't heard her right.

"Hit me!" she demanded. I stopped in midstroke.

She might as well have screamed that the sheets were on fire. My cock slithered out of her like a clubbed snake.

Rolling off her, I stared at the cracked plaster and wondered why ceilings weren't routinely decorated with some groin-enlivening mural—Delacroix's *Rape of the Sabines,* maybe, or some nice nineteenth-century Japanese porn—something to provide spent males, or prematurely limp ones, some focus for contemplation other than their own untimely detumescence.

"Why did you *say* that?"

"That was Little Elaine."

"Oh, Christ, not that inner child crap again."

I flopped onto my side, willing myself not to say anything else. I mean, I loved this woman. Even if I'd only known her for a few months, I loved her passion and her energy and the way she craved sex like some kind of cock junkie, but sometimes her incessant psychobabble, pop psychology, Survivors of Shitty Childhoods Anonymous, or whatever the shrinks on the bestseller list were hyping these days, really got old.

After all, nobody has a perfect childhood, right? But you grow up, you forget about the bike you didn't get for Christmas or the cat that got hit by a car. You get down to the business of being a grown-up, and you leave your childhood behind.

I stole a glance at Elaine. She appeared to be meditating on the area between her eyebrows.

"I *asked* you to hit me."

"That doesn't turn me on. I care about you. I want to kiss you and caress you."

"You don't get it, do you?"

"Evidently not. Care to enlighten me?"

"I don't want you to *hurt* me. Getting rough during sex doesn't have to mean anything sexist or sinister. It just adds to the rush, like going over the top of a rollercoaster. My therapist says it's really Little Elaine, my inner child, who wants to be slapped. Little Elaine grew up with lots of yelling and screaming and hitting. She's addicted to chaos."

"Do you have any idea how ridiculous you sound when you talk about yourself in the third person? I feel like I'm in a threesome, and one of us is underage."

"Fuck you, Matthew. You're just being a prick because you lost your hard-on."

She flung the sheets aside and leaped out of bed.

Suddenly I felt very alone.

"I wish you wouldn't go."

My pecker wished it, too. Elaine was a dancer and part-time fitness trainer. Her body radiated a fierce, androgynous energy. Riding Elaine, it was like making love to a lust-struck python. Now she stormed about the bedroom, snatching up items of her clothing that had been cast about in a frenzy of libido that, given the present circumstances, now seemed sad and ludicrous.

"Elaine, I'm sorry."

"Look, I won't ask you again to do anything you're not up for—" She realized what she'd said, and we both laughed. At least it broke the tension, but she didn't stop getting dressed. "I have to leave anyway. Cory's probably sweet-talked the sitter into letting him stay up to play video games all night."

"Hey, tell Cory I got that backgammon set he wanted."

"That was sweet of you, Matthew. I will."

AFTER ELAINE left, I lay on the damp, musk-scented sheets, feeling angry and confused, marveling at the peculiar masochism of people who seemed to relish the rehashing of their traumatic pasts. I had always avoided thinking of my own family. Yet now, perversely, the memories came, each with its own distinctive sting, like an angry acupuncturist jabbing in needles and setting them aflame.

My father had died in '98, and Mom lived with my sister RuthAnn in Illinois. I called occasionally, but the mere sound of their voices was like hearing the language of a foreign land where I once was held prisoner. I had no wish to ever revisit it.

If Elaine's family had been drunken and violent, mine had been the opposite: quiet, pious, restrained. Grace before meals, Mass on Sunday. No alcohol, no swearing, no voices raised in either rage or exultation. Boundaries were rigidly observed and privacies respected.

Dad taught high school chemistry and coached football.

RuthAnn, two years my senior, was a high school track star.

I was a "brain" who could master trig but blundered about in gym class like a lobotomized brontosaurus, a timid tourist in my skin to whom the language of the body seemed as alien as Sanskrit.

Football was Dad's great passion. A winning team meant conversation at the supper table, a losing one evoked grim silence. Sometimes I couldn't help but wonder how he felt, coaching other people's athletic, strapping sons, then staring across the table at his own pimply, uncoordinated progeny.

Freddy Burton was a year ahead of me, a sixteen-year-old junior, and even pudgier and less athletic than I was. For that reason, I suppose, I tried to be his buddy. I'd invite Freddy over for dinner and watch him scarf down two desserts and hope Dad noticed how truly disgusting Freddy was, how his gut lopped over his trousers and his chins jiggled. I figured if I couldn't make Dad proud of me, at least I'd make him less ashamed.

Like that time I dislocated my shoulder in a sledding accident, and Dad drove me to the hospital. He didn't comfort me, but only said he hoped I wasn't going to cry. I nearly bit my tongue in half not crying.

I was thinking of that ride to the hospital when I fell asleep, and the old nightmare surfaced in all its terrible clarity: My throat feels like I've gargled with Drano. The school nurse has diagnosed strep throat and sent me home. Now I stand at the foot of the stairs, looking up at my father, thinking maybe he's come home for lunch. He holds one hand out like a traffic cop and says, "Don't come up here."

But my room is upstairs and my bed and my books. I have a

sudden, urgent need to be there. To crawl into bed with a book and escape into a jungle of squiggly black bug tracks on a cream-colored page.

I start up the stairs.

"No!" commands Dad.

A fierce heat radiates from above. My eyelashes feel scorched, my forehead burns. At first I think it's fever. But suddenly I understand—our house must be on fire! And Mom and RuthAnn! Where are they?

Now I remember a story I read about a boy who saved his family from a burning building. How I longed to be that boy, to be a hero better than any football star. To see the pride and gratitude in Dad's eyes, to be someone who mattered.

I rush up the stairs, oblivious to danger, determined to rescue Mom and RuthAnn, to make Dad proud.

Dad blocks my path.

No!

He grips my shoulders, forces me to meet his eyes. They gleam like pale, ice-encrusted stones.

He says, "Some things we do not speak of."

This was the nightmare from my youth, with Dad saying those words I always thought I had imagined, until the night Elaine asked me to hit her.

After that, it seemed as if I heard Dad's voice every time I closed my eyes.

ON SATURDAY, Elaine couldn't get a babysitter for Cory, so I took the Lexington #6 train over to Eighth Street and walked up to Avenue A, stopping at the corner market to pick up steaks and a bottle of Chianti, some Orange Crush for Cory.

When I left the store in the early twilight, the neighborhood was already acrawl with people who looked as though, a few hours from now, they'd be filling up the local emergency room, psych ward, and drunk tank. A bearded old man pushing a shopping cart waddled past me, spewing gibberish with the panache of a Pentecostal speaking in tongues. A slant-eyed hooker—some exotic mix of Chinese, Hispanic, and black—leaned a leather-clad hip in a doorway.

Rap blatted from an open window. Across the street, a couple stood on the porch of a dilapidated walk-up, bickering in some dialect that sounded like corn popping. I could smell weed, hear obscenities shouted, taste the grit and swill of the city.

Dammit, how could Elaine raise her son in such a pit? Once the neighborhood had held hopes for gentrification, but tonight the little ragged clumps of street people, the pairs of sullen hookers, fouled it like the droppings of a thousand diarrhetic pigeons.

"Hey, mister!"

They were on me before I realized what was happening. A tribe of them, four half-naked boys, their complexions varying shades of brown and black and sickly alabaster. They sauntered over from a doorway, all sinews and skin, like scrawny wolves wearing tight jeans and sneers.

"You party, mister?"

The tattooed boy who spoke surveyed me with the black, predatory eyes of some wild, nocturnal raptor. His skin looked the color of dusk, all soot and smoke, and his neck was way too supple and long and unblemished to belong to a boy. His face bore a mocking smirk that I longed to rearrange with my fist.

"You talk, man?" said another. I glimpsed gold teeth, heard gum pop.

I elbowed my way past them, clutching my parcels.

"What you like, man? Blow job? Hand job? You like it in the ass?"

I reminded myself these were just kids trying to shock. Their high-pitched laughter sounded like Cory's the time I took him to a PG-13 movie and, to my embarrassment, every other word was a four-letter one.

"Fuck you then. You ain't from this neighborhood. What is it? You a cop?"

I shifted the shopping bags to one arm and shoved the boy who blocked my way. He lost his balance and stumbled off the curb. A stream of curses flew at me like darts. I reached Elaine's building and hurled myself through the door.

I didn't mention the encounter on the street, but when Elaine asked me to go back to the store for salad dressing, I pleaded fatigue. While she chopped up veggies in the kitchen, Cory and I played backgammon on the set I'd bought him. He was a bright boy, quick to learn. I watched him concentrate on his next move, brows furrowing, a small black mole on his left cheek accentuating the pallor of his skin.

The whiteness, the fragility of that skin made me think suddenly of the vermin I'd encountered on my way here. A sudden appalling image: Cory, a few years older, posturing and smirking, eyes bright with meth and menace, thumbs thrust into the pockets of his too-tight jeans, fingers angling down to form a V.

"Cory, does anyone ever bother you?"

He looked up, surprised. "You mean at school?"

"Or here in the neighborhood. You know, older kids."

"You mean drug pushers? Pervs? We took a course in that last year in school—'How to Be Street-Smart and Safe.'"

"But *do* you feel safe around here?"

I made my move. Too fast, a blunder so obvious Cory had to think I was deliberately throwing the game.

"C'mon Matthew. You can do better than that."

His move.

"Hey, look, I know this ain't—this isn't Fifth Avenue, and people get mugged here and all. But I can look out for me and Mom." He glanced behind him to make sure Elaine wasn't looking, then dug into his school bag and produced a set of nunchucks.

"Cory, you've got no business—"

But at once I saw in Cory's face the fear that I'd tell his mother. I knew that such a betrayal would mean a rupture in the friendship we were forming. So I nodded, respecting the trust he'd placed in me by protecting his secret.

Later, though, helping Elaine do the dishes, I voiced some general concern. "You really ought to move. It isn't safe to raise a child in this neighborhood."

"Cory's a tough kid. You should have heard what he said to the panhandler who cussed at me the other day. He's a tiger."

"He's only twelve years old, Elaine. He needs protection."

"From what?"

"Christ, Elaine, don't tell me you don't see the kind of hoodlums that hang out around this neighborhood? Just tonight on my way here, there was a gang who…"

But then the implications of what I was about to tell her struck me, and a queasy, seasick feeling roiled liquidly in my gut. What if there was some significance to the fact that the young thugs had chosen me to waylay? What if the street kids had sensed something in me that even I was unaware of?

Elaine was staring at me strangely. "What happened, Matthew? You look sick."

"There was a younger kid, that's all," I quickly lied. "They roughed him up a bit. I put a stop to it."

Later, after Cory was tucked in bed and we'd made love, we lay with only our fingertips touching, letting the sweat dry off our bodies. Elaine's bedroom was stuffy, airless. A ceiling fan turning dissolutely overhead stirred air that seemed the temperature and consistency of tepid porridge.

She stroked my hand. "Cory likes you. You're good with him."

"Cory makes it easy. He's bright and well-behaved. I don't know how I'd be if he were a brat."

She rolled onto her side, pressed against me. Her skin felt hot and slick. She smoothed the damp hair off my face, then let her fingers trail along the inside of my thigh. A dangerous heat radiated off her. She made small circles with her hips, her belly muscles flexing. She was wet when I pushed inside her.

"Matthew? Did you hear me?"

She'd murmured something in her "naughty" voice, her Little Elaine voice, but I hadn't been listening.

"Suppose I was a brat...?"

Her words knifed through the sex trance.

"...and I'd been bad?"

I tried to get into the spirit of this without losing my concentration, without letting my mind leave its dark, preverbal rapture. "I'd cancel the cable TV."

"I mean *really* bad."

"Put you up for adoption on Craig's List?"

"Matthew, please." She stopped moving, but her internal muscles were at work, pumping, milking. "Punish me."

"You haven't done anything wrong."

"*Pretend.*"

I wasn't good at fantasy. Whatever the appeal of make-believe, I'd tried to leave it behind in childhood.

"Elaine, I can't get into this."

"Of course you can."

(I *mustn't.*)

"I don't know what you want."

"You do."

(I *do.*)

She gazed up at me, hungry-eyed.

"Hit me," cooed Elaine, all honey and heat.

"Elaine, this scares me."

My erection was diminishing like a popsicle thrust toward a flame. I tried to reconnect with sensuality by pinching her nipples and swirling my tongue along the curve of her neck. All for naught.

She sucked my lower lip between her teeth and bit down hard. The pain was like an ice pick up the ass, unprecedented, scalding. I tasted blood.

"Christ!"

She lunged at me. I fended her off, pinning her arms above her head, but it felt like she had twice as many joints as an ordinary woman and three times the strength. She broke my grip on her wrists and flailed at me with long acrylic nails.

I knew this was Elaine's idea of a game, but suddenly I felt terrified, like I was battling for my life.

I did what she wanted.

A timid blow at best. Yet a smile of both relief and lust and yes, even childish triumph, spread across her features.

God help me, I wanted to hit her again.

Not just hit her, but pound her face until her nose shattered, until her eyes were fleshy slits echoing the larger wound between her legs, her cheekbones like crushed eggshells, and then I'd work her over down below, starting with her penis—

Penis?

Shame flayed me. I muttered "Damn you," got out of bed, and headed for the bathroom, where I knelt before the toilet, close to puking. The hand with which I'd struck Elaine still tingled.

She tapped on the door.

"Matthew? Matthew, listen. You didn't hurt me. Matthew, are you okay? What's wrong?"

But how could I answer her, when I truly wasn't sure? And how could I go to sleep, when I knew what I would dream?

I'VE LEFT school early, sent home with a sore throat. Dad's Olds is in the driveway, but he isn't in the kitchen or the den, so I start up the stairs to look for him.

This time Dad doesn't stop me. A cold dread ices my stomach, and I try desperately to wake myself up, but it's as if I'm trapped in the dream, drowning in it, and I have to go on.

On the threshold of my parents' room, I hesitate. I've never intruded here, not even when I was five years old and woke up screaming, convinced the silhouette of the neighbor's cat outside my window was a bloody-fingered corpse, freshly self-exhumed, scratching at me outside the glass.

I give a timid knock before entering, but the room is empty.

Isn't it?

From the bathroom that adjoins their room, I hear sounds. The door's half open, so I peek inside.

And almost blurt out "excuse me," because isn't that what you say when you catch someone on the commode, except the toilet seat Dad's sitting on is down, and Freddy Burton's head is bobbing up-down, down-up on his lap.

Dad looks at me, but doesn't disengage. In fact, I think he smiles. It's as if Freddy's head is growing out of my father's crotch, a gross and bloated cancer complete with jug ears, sprouting from his genitals.

"You bastard!" I shout. "You bastard, I'm going to tell!"

I shut the door and run.

Outside, a light snow's falling. I run until my lungs hitch. Then I walk until I'm able to run some more. It goes like that, until I'm numb in every part of me except my heart, the part that hurts the most and that I cannot soothe.

Fury keeps me going long past the time my lungs and muscles scream to quit. What brings me home at last, though, is something else, that most exhausting of emotions, shame. I feel that I will choke on shame, because, as the anger recedes, what's left stranded on the shore of my soul isn't disgust or rage or revulsion, but something much more terrifying: black envy of the boy my father's used. Envy and, God help me, desire.

Part of me would like to die, to be found frozen in the snow, my corpse a mute accusation far worse than any words.

Instead, of course, I opt for warmth over melodrama. I hide out at the mall until it closes, then slink home.

Mom and Dad and RuthAnn are finishing supper. Mom looks up and says, "Thank God! We were about to call the police," but I know that's just to scare me. Then Dad takes me into the den and unbuckles his belt. I know this ritual well, know what's expected. I lower my jeans and briefs, brace myself against Dad's desk.

"Say it," says my father.

I can't. My throat feels cauterized.

"Say it!"

The belt hisses down, strikes the desk chair.

"What do you want? Say it or I'll make it worse."

The words dribble out of me like tears.

"Hit me."

"So I can hear you!"

"Hit me!"

I have to say it each time, before each stroke, even when I'm crying too hard to get the words out in any coherent form.

After it's over, my father says, "There are things that decent people never speak of, Matthew. And if you ever threaten me again, I'll make it worse for you. Much worse."

And that is all he says about it. Ever.

I KNEW I shouldn't go back to Elaine's apartment, not with the weight of those memories. But on the phone, she purred and promised enticements so seductive my cock lifted like a charmed snake, while in the background, I could hear Cory urging me to come over so he could beat me again at backgammon.

A humid drizzle was falling, leaving the streets sodden, rain-slicked as I came up out of the subway.

Before I even saw them, I heard their voices. The sharp, mocking chatter of parrots, curse words in English that were interspersed with bright, harsh snaps of Spanish. Three of them were huddled under the rain-sagging awning of a fruit stand. Eyes glittery and feral, voices like little shards of glass, snipping at arteries.

"Where're your groceries tonight, man?"

Snickers, hoots.

The skinny one canted a hip. Batting of lashes, slicking of tongue.

"Hey, man, whatchoo want?"

I wanted to bounce their skulls off the sidewalk and watch them splat open like dropped melons. They were evil boys who singled decent people out for prey, who imagined others shared their vile desires.

By the time I reached Elaine's door, I burned with indignation. I would call the police, report the hooligans for prostitution, harassment.

Elaine greeted me wearing a little see-through teddy with cutouts in strategic places. "What's wrong?" she said.

"Those damned boys out on the street. They're dangerous. I'm going to call the cops."

"Matthew, calm down. Can't it wait?" She took my hand and kissed the knuckles, the inside of the wrist. Her palms felt hot, as though she'd warmed them over a stove.

"I sent Cory to the store," she said and led me toward the bedroom, where we made love with all the fervor of the first time, or maybe Elaine made love and I just fucked, I couldn't tell. I only knew I didn't want to look at her, that every time I closed my eyes I saw the sneering faces of the street hustlers.

She thrust her hips to meet my cock.

"Hit me, baby. I've been so bad."

She bucked beneath me. Our bellies slapped together, sang of sex. She moaned, "I can't...come...if you don't..."

"Then don't fucking come."

"Damn you. Do it!"

"No."

I can't. I won't. I want to.

Elaine stopped moving. We were suddenly no longer joined. The urgent, hormonal energy that a moment earlier had galvanized my body simply vanished, and with it went my hard-on.

"Jesus, Matthew, not *again.*"

"So understanding, aren't you?"

"Okay, you've got a problem."

"Yes, I do."

She got out of bed, grabbed her robe. I came around the bed to intercept her.

"Elaine, I don't want to..."

hit you

"Maybe you'd better leave."

But I did.

I did what she had wanted all along.

Suddenly she became small and light, almost weightless. My

blow was open-handed but she flew backward, struck the wall, did not slide down, but blinked, astonished, *hurt*, and after that first time, it was easy, fun, like so many evil things, and the next blow spun her in another direction, against another wall.

"Matthew, no. Stop!"

This time she didn't rise so fast. Her mouth was bleeding. I grabbed her by the hair, flung her across the bed.

Straddled her.

Her eyes took on a bright, uncomprehending terror. The next blow made her scream. My fist rose up, as powerful and potent as I wished my cock to be, but I didn't get to hit her. Something smashed my ear, my neck, then slammed my ribs from the other direction.

"Let her go!"

I tore my hand lose from Elaine's frantic grip, whirled and caught Cory's wrist. The nunchucks clattered to the floor. I threw him down and pinned him. In the dim light, I could see anguish on his young boy's face, the skin so pale, like marble, eyes black and fierce with rage. A lovely face, the pink mouth opening like the sweetest of promises.

Then the room exploded as Elaine grabbed the bedside lamp and swung the metal base against my head.

Neon pain, Times Square on New Year's Eve inside my skull. Elaine and Cory fleeing. I heard the lock turn inside the bathroom door, got up and stumbled toward it.

"Matthew, go away! If you try to get in, I'll yell for help. I'll scream 'Fire'! Everyone in the building will come running."

"But I...it shouldn't end like this. Elaine? Cory? Cory, *talk* to me."

"Go to hell, motherfucker!"

Elaine shushed him. "Don't make him mad. He's crazy." Then, to me, "Just go. You've terrorized me and my son enough."

I leaned my head against the door. It felt like I was standing outside that other bathroom door again, the door behind which Freddy Burton knelt between my father's feet, head bouncing up and down, and I wished it had been me. *Me.* I knew I wasn't supposed to cry, but I couldn't remember why not.

Before I left Elaine's apartment, I found Cory's nunchucks on the floor and took them with me. He was too young to have such a dangerous possession anyway.

Then I went looking.

I didn't have to go far. Two of them were lounging up against the wall of Elaine's building. Passing a bagged bottle back and forth, stoned and sultry-eyed as heat-struck snakes.

I motioned to the one with the curvy white throat and the blank, executioner eyes.

"Still want to party?"

The worst part was he didn't look surprised.

I let him lead me to a room in a squalid walkup used by hustlers and heroin addicts. There were just the three of us tonight, though, me and the boy and Cory's nunchucks.

He wasn't shocked by what I said I wanted him to do. Perhaps he'd played this role before. Perhaps other men had asked such things of him, men who cherished the seductiveness of pain, the cleansing power of suffering.

After I gave him his instructions, he stood behind me, in the shadows, while I braced myself against the wall. But I could sense the bunching of his muscles, the gauging of the force he'd use on that first downward blow. My dick stiffened in remembrance of that place I once thought I'd escaped forever, my childhood.

And the words came like a long-forgotten prayer: "Hit me."

SPREE

Chapter One

I HAD only eleven days left as a guest of the glorious State of Colorado in Canon City Penitentiary when I got a postcard from Delores asking me to call her at Gary's Tavern at ten Friday morning. Now I'd been expecting mail, but I'd hoped it would be from my girlfriend Julia, or maybe Liz or Donna or MaryLynn—some of the women I've been pen-palling with these past months.

The last person I expected to hear from was Delores, who I loved dearly, but who I rarely heard from. In the two years and five months I'd been in the joint, Delores and I had probably talked on the phone less than a half-dozen times. This was partly because Delores had fucked with Western Bell so often they weren't about to let her have phone service and partly because at Canon City, like most other prisons, inmates are allowed to make collect calls to the outside world, but the outside world can't call in.

Phone calls weren't Delores's style anyway, but neither was writing—maybe once a year she'd send a long, complicated letter, thick as a small-town phone book, that took me days to muddle my way through. No punctuation and sentences running on for pages at a time, all prettied up with exclamation points and question marks and those little double-dot things that look like a snake bite thrown out when you least expected it—more for decoration than anything else—plus the occasional stain I figured to be Jim Beam or Jack Daniels. From her letters I could never tell if Delores was drunk or high or just being her old crazy self when she wrote them and, when you got right down to it, it was all about the same.

Some days Delores was crazier than others.

So I was a little bit nervous when I called collect to Gary's Tavern on Friday morning. Gary himself answered the phone. He and Delores were tight, so he accepted the charge and handed the phone over to her.

Soon's I heard her voice, I knew right away she wasn't alone in her skull, that her madness had hatched out new demons that were chasin' around in her brain like a convention of Shriners on those little go-carts. Now Delores had been a few short of a six-pack as far back as I could recall, and usually it didn't get on my nerves, but I was feelin' so good, bein' so close to free, and then she gets me remembering that sometimes the worst prison of all is inside your own head.

"Saw J.D. at the Dark Horse t'other night. He was shooting pool. Tryin' to anyway. That arm you broke for him still stiffens up in cold weather."

"Fuckin' fine," I said. "Somethin' for him to remember me by."

"Why you hate J.D. so?"

"He's a scum-sucking lowlife, for starters."

"He bought me a coupla shooters, said tell you hello."

"Tell him I'll see him in hell. Is this why you asked me to call? Catch me up on the guy sent me to this fuckin' hole in the first place?"

"Well he *asked* about you and how you was doing. Got right pale when I told him they was lettin' you out early to free up some beds for others more deserving than you." She paused. "Hang on a sec, hon. It's Annie. Hey, Annie, honey, love the new hair color!"

Annie. Another of Delores's drinking buddies no doubt.

"Annie says give you a big kiss."

"I don't even know who the hell Annie is."

"Lonny says hi to you too, hon. Anyway I think J.D.'s still scared of you. When you get out, you ain't gonna come after him or nothin'?"

"J.D.'s not worth skinning my knuckles. I was gonna come after all the assholes you've been hooked up with, he'd be at the end of the line."

"He'll be relieved you said that."

SPREE AND OTHER STORIES

"Long as J.D. stays outta my way and away from you, he'll live to die of cirrhosis of the liver." (Which—who the hell knew—at the rate he chugged it down, might be as much as a few months or more.)

"You're mad, ain't you?"

"I'm not mad."

"You're mad, I can tell."

"I'm not mad."

I was mad that she didn't ask about *me*, that she'd got herself wrought up over this no-good cook in a greasy spoon who's got a porn collection would fill up the Library of Congress.

"You're mad, just like Luke said you'd be."

Shit, not Luke again. "I thought Luke was gone."

"It was a trick. He just made me think he'd gone. He really just changed places with Martin. He's a trickster that one."

Did I mention that Luke and Martin are two of the voices that periodically rented space in Delores's skull? There were others, too, but I don't remember the names. You didn't know Delores and God forbid, you struck up a conversation with her on the bus or in line for food stamps, you might get the impression she ran a halfway house for nutcases who were forever escaping, returning, perpetrating blackmail and thievery and indecent exposure. Until, if you were dumb enough or bored enough to listen for a while, you'd figure out Delores *was* the nuthouse all by herself—her brain had more activity going than Bellevue on a full moon Saturday night.

"So what else did Luke say about me?"

"That it's a mistake them lettin' you out. You ain't ready for freedom."

"Bull*shit* I ain't."

"Luke says you still ain't learned your lesson. God's gave you chances over and over—but the minute you're out, it's back to the booze and the bitches."

"Nice language, Delores. You used to slap me upside the head when I talked like that."

"Luke said it. Not me."

"Yeah. Right. Look, let me know if Luke says what the winning lottery combination's gonna be. Otherwise tell him to shut the fuck up."

A guy across the hall opened a centerfold. A pair of tits that took up the whole middle page lolled out at me. I stared like a starving guy looking at pictures of pastry. Jesus, over two fucking years. It's inhuman to go without pussy two weeks, let alone years.

What I said next was a question posed by my dick, not my brain. "You seen Julia lately?"

"Why you ask?"

"'Cause she's stopped taking my calls all of a sudden. You seen her or not?"

"Hold on, hon, I need a cigarette. Gary, you got a light?"

I waited a few seconds, heard the flick of the lighter followed by the long, sultry inhaling of breath.

"Well?"

"Actually I saw her just yesterday. She was in town and stopped by with Andy. Brought me some literature 'bout her religion."

"Yeah, I know. She sends that shit to me, too. Guess she must think my soul needs savin'."

"I told her you'd be getting out early."

"Yeah, I've called her a shitload of times to tell her the good news, but she never answers her goddamned phone. Or maybe she wants to keep the line open in case Jesus phones."

"You know how much these prison calls cost, hon. She's watching her money."

"Yeah, well, makes a man feel pretty low, his own girlfriend won't take his calls."

"You been away two-and-a-half years, hon. That's forever when you're missing someone." I heard her sigh and it was long and slow and unbearable, like wind rattling through bare winter trees. "God knows, I ought to know how long it is."

"Yeah, well, I'm sorry, Delores. I know I let you down. I was gonna whip J.D.'s ass, I shoulda caught him in a dark alley where he wouldn'ta known who'd hit him. I fucked up big time, didn't I?"

"You did it 'cause you love me."

"Yeah. I guess that was it."

Love's a funny word. Coming out of Delores's mouth it made me squirm like an old spinster lady when she heard the word "fuck." Made me want to turn and look behind me, make sure nobody heard.

I guess Delores was waiting for me to say something else, and when I didn't—when I couldn't seem to get my lips around the L word—she kept talking.

"Andy's getting big. He said to tell you he went sledding the other day."

"Did you tell him Uncle Lonny was spittin' distance from walkin' outta this hole? That right after I come visit you, I'm headin' straight to see him and his mama and ball her brains out?"

A long flat pause, as though all the air had been sucked out of the phone. I'd forgot Delores didn't like to hear me talk that way about Julia. Or anyone else. After a few seconds, I could hear her whispering to herself in that weird, mumbly language she'd use to consult with Luke and her other disembodied buddies. "Look here, this ain't easy to say, Lonny, but—I think it'd be best if you stayed away from Julia."

"You crazy. Just as soon as I take her legs down from over my shoulders, I'm gonna marry that girl."

"You leave her alone."

"No way in hell."

"No, I mean it. You know how it is, Lonny. Things change."

"And how would you know? You psychic now? Did she say she don't love me no more?"

"It ain't that. Listen to me. Listen hard. I want you to do something for me. It may sound crazy, but—"

"What is it, Delores? Who you want me to shoot?"

"That ain't funny."

"Okay, okay."

"If there's guards monitoring this call," said Delores, real loud, "Lonny was kidding. It was a joke. He ain't shootin' nobody."

"For God's sake, ain't nobody listening to this conversation. *I'm* not even really listening to this conversation. Now what is it? What you want me to do?"

"I want you to stay there where you're at a few more months."

"In prison? What? Are you fuckin' out of your mind? If it weren't for the grace of God and the tightwad voters not wantin' to pay for more prison space, they wouldn't be lettin' me and your minor fuckups out early to make room for the real psychos."

Another whisper-filled pause, then Dolores said, "I'm scared, Lonny. When I was eatin' my cereal this morning, that man in the commercial for term life insurance came on again. Luke says it's a sign."

In Delores's world, everything is a sign. The way a little bit of pot falls out of the paper when she's rolling a joint is a fucking *sign*.

"He talks to me, Lonny. Right to *me*. And he come on again right after Julia left. He was tellin' me what I need to do."

"He's not talking to you, Delores. He's on TV. He comes on again, get up and change the goddamn channel."

"You get outta prison now, I think somebody may die."

"Bullshit. Don't care if God comes down and carves it on a goddamn tablet, I ain't stayin' in jail."

"I can tell by how you talk about J.D., you ain't learned what you need to in that prison. You ain't learned to love. You ain't learned to forgive."

"Hate to tell you, Delores, forgiveness ain't what they teach in here. The curriculum runs more to larceny, burglary, and assault, with sodomy thrown in as an elective for your pervert population."

"That attitude got you where you are to begin with. Luke says it's gonna get you drunk when you get out again."

I was biting the inside of my lip to keep from saying something I'd hate myself for two minutes later. "Delores, baby," I said just as nice as I could considerin' a big chunk of my cheek was between my back teeth, "you're the one hittin' the bottle. Get a grip. I'm a free man in a week and a day and I ain't about to let nothing, nothing, bring me down now. So you tell ol' Luke to leave me out of his prognostications or I'll come over and whip his imaginary ass with my imaginary fists."

"Please, Lonny, I ain't askin' much. Mouth off to a guard or get in a scuffle. Some little somethin'. Make 'em tack a couple more months on your time."

"What do you think I am, Mr. Popularity around here? I got a record as long as Secretariat's dick. I fuck up, a few years is what they'd tack on."

"Will you at least think about it?"

"Like hell. I know what's goin' on, you're fuckin' J.D. again, ain't you. You're worried I get out I'll bust him up again. Goddammit, I don't believe you. I can't believe you'd go back to that son of a bitch when he's the one got me put here in the first place!"

"I'm not *seein'* J.D. no more," said Delores. "I'm not seein' nobody. That's the God's truth. I love you, Lonny. That's why I called today. 'Cause I know I've screwed you up bad, but I didn't mean to. I never ever meant to hurt you, Lonny. I—"

"Jesus, Delores, are you crying?"

"I can't help it, Lonny."

"Please, Delores."

"I just feel so guilty, so worthless, so—"

"You're drunk aren't you? Jesus Christ, it's not even ten thirty in the morning and you're fucking drunk."

"I'm not, Lonny. I ain't had a drink since I can't remember."

"You're lying."

"I ain't had a drink since—"

"Since when? Since you woke up this morning. Hey, I've had it with you, you drunk bitch."

"That's what you think I am? That's what you call me?"

She started to sob. Deep, lung-crunching sobs that smacked into my ears like brass knuckles.

Fuck.

"Delores, I'm sorry. Really. I didn't mean it. I'm sorry. I— Delores, don't hang up. Don't. Please don't hang up. Mom? Please don't, Mom. Mom?"

She hung up.

I walked back to my cell and bent over the sink and splashed water into my face, so nobody would know I was crying. Damn Delores. I couldn't stand to hear the fear and desperation in her voice. I'd let her down. Not just in one or two things, but in everything. My whole life had been one huge fuckup. And not even all those years when I stayed drunk or high almost every day had reduced my IQ to the point where I actually believed real men spent their lives fighting and partying and passing out in alleyways and waking up in jail. And Luke or no Luke, she was probably right—it don't take no genius to figure out guys like me don't generally die of old age and if they die in bed, it's cause they got caught one time too many fuckin' some guy's old lady or they slapped the wrong woman around one too many times.

But knowin' that never had stopped me from bein' an asshole and nothin' Delores or none of her "advisors" could say was gonna make me do somethin' to stay behind bars.

Delores—damn the woman—now that she'd called, I couldn't stop dwelling on her and on Julia, too, and all the ways I'd let both of them down. Bein' locked up in prison when I shoulda been out there looking out for the both of them.

But then I got to dwelling on what Delores had said, and I got worrieder and worrieder. Why would Delores want me to stay in this shithole for even one extra day? What was it she didn't want me to know? That she was fucking J.D. again? What about Julia? If something had changed between Julia and me, if she really didn't want to see me, then why didn't she tell me herself?

One thing I knew, if I got out and found Julia with another guy, I'd feed him his balls on a shish kebob stick. And Christ, but I hate it when I start having thoughts like that. It's thoughts like that got me put here in the first place.

Chapter Two

THE LAST time I saw Delores I'd just had another blowout with Julia. From being one of the wildest, horniest women I ever balled, Julia had gone and joined up with them Seven Days at Venice folks who can't fuck without a permission slip from God and can't enjoy it even if they have one. She wanted to be on her knees for Jesus and I wanted her there for a blow job. So when I couldn't jump her bones without running the risk of a domestic violence charge, I went over to the Dark Horse for a beer and from there to the Down Under Lounge and on and on, barhopping my way toward a trailer park on the north side of Boulder.

Toward Delores.

Because the more I thought about Julia, you understand, the madder I got at how she was treating me. I knew Delores would understand. I knew she'd never turn me away.

I come into the kitchen, grabbed one of the two items I found in the fridge, both of which were beers, took a piss in the john and studied myself in the mirror. Nose peeling from being outside operating the forklift. Hair sticking out at weird angles, bloodshot blue eyes. Still when I flexed for the mirror and saw my biceps bulge up, I couldn't understand why Julia hadn't liked what she saw. And, hell, that was only *above* the waist.

Upstairs the stereo was booming away—nothing new about that. Delores liked her music loud. She always said when things got too quiet the voices in her head committeed up and started to gab.

The bedroom door was partway shut, but I nudged it open and walked in.

First thing I saw was Delores's face in the mirror over the bed. Eyes shut, hair flying, beads of sweat on her brow. Underneath her, grunting and bucking, was J.D. Barnes, a short-order cook at Jake's Spoon over on Twenty-Eighth Street who'd been in and out of her life like a bad case of shingles for the last five or six years. Only good thing I could say about J.D. was that he'd leave his porn tapes stashed all over Delores's trailer. He had lousy taste in porn—fat mamas and women squirting breast milk out of their tits—but it'd do in a pinch when there was nothin' on HBO.

"Dammit, you fuck me like I tell you to do!" he was yelling. He raised his hand up and brought it down hard on her hip. I saw her wince. He smacked her again. Pain furrowed her face and she wasn't pretty no more. She looked old and beat up and used.

"Come on, harder, harder," J.D. was hollering, in the same tone of voice he'd probably tell a busboy to wipe off a table. "Grind your fat ass, you lazy bitch!"

I reached over and slapped the light switch, and the bedroom lit up like noon. Then I shut off the stereo.

"What the fuck—" yelled J.D.

Delores jumped up, J.D.'s dick pulling out of her with a sound like a cork leaving a bottle, and grabbed for her nightshirt. J.D. leaped out of bed, all sweaty and red-faced. "What the hell are you doin' here?"

"I could ask you the same thing."

"You punk kid. What's it look like I'm doin'?"

"A pretty half-assed job of fucking my mother that's what it looks like you're doing. Now get dressed and get out of here, before I throw your ass out."

"You arrogant, shit-faced, son of a—"

He punched me in the jaw, but I was so drunk the blow felt like a love tap. I bounced off the wall, grabbed his shoulders, and head-butted him to the floor.

"Lonny, stop it!"

"I thought you threw this washed-up piece of shit outta here the last time he hit you," I said. "What'sa matter, you that hard up for somebody to screw?"

I saw the look on her face and turned around in time to see J.D. picking himself up off the floor, coming at me with an empty beer bottle. I grabbed his wrist, twisted it behind him, and slammed his face into the wall. Heard the crack-pop as his wrist broke, but I wasn't done yet, and I kept putting pressure onto his arm until I heard that snap, too, and he slithered to the floor like a filet of sole.

"What've you done?" screamed Delores.

"Saved you from another scumbag. What was it he gave you to fuck him—a fifth of Jack Daniels, a half ounce of coke?"

"Nothin', Lonny. You know I'm clean. You know I haven't had a drink in three months." She knelt down by J.D., took his head in her hands. Patted his face, which was white and slick as a wet bar of Ivory soap. I saw tears in her eyes. I felt sick.

"He was hittin' you, goddammit! I saw it with my own eyes."

"We was *playin',"* she yelled. "He weren't hurtin' me. I wanted him to."

"You're fucking lyin'."

"What are you doin' here anyway? What right have you got to barge in?"

"Shit, all I wanted was to fucking *talk* to you! All I wanted was to fucking *talk!*"

"You *go!*" yelled Delores. She picked up the beer bottle J.D. had come at me with and threw it at my head. I was too drunk and too stupid to duck and it hit me in the forehead and opened a cut.

"You happy now!" I shouted. "You fucking happy now you goddamn crazy bitch!"

The look on her face made me wish the bottle had gone into my mouth and cut out my tongue. She looked like I'd tore out her heart.

"Delores, I'm sorry. I—"

"You get out of here," she said. "I got to get help for J.D."

I left Delores's place and drove straight to the Dark Horse. Ordered a double, then went into the john to clean up my face. I didn't want to wash the blood off. I wanted to go back to Julia's place later on and let her see me cut up like I was, 'cept I'd tell her it was J.D. done it, not my mom, but people were givin' me funny looks. Guess outside a pro-rasslin arena guy with dried blood in his eyebrows does raise a touch of suspicion.

Minute I walked out of the john all eyes turned to me. For a second I wondered had I forgot to fold my dick back in my pants. Then I saw it weren't my pecker had their attention but the cops who were aiming their guns at me.

Cops. Can you believe that? My own mother I was protecting from that asshole and she called the fuckin' cops.

So, see, it wasn't my fault I went to prison. It was Delores's fault for calling the cops and Julia's for thinkin' she was too good to fuck me no more.

That was why, soon after I got to prison, I got me a hobby suggested by a guy who'd been in the slammer five times. Seems there's a breed of women—lonely, shy, chubby, desperate—who the hell knows—but 'stead of getting a boyfriend and sooner or later seein' him behind bars, they just skip the first part and go straight to the second. They like cons. Like to write to 'em anyway. Think they can change them, I guess. Reform them with love and boxes of cookies. So I put my name on a list of inmates who'd like to get letters and pretty soon I had me a regular little harem of letter writers. Lonely and desperate. Who the hell cared? I figured maybe they were the one kind I could trust.

Chapter Three

I WAS pouring Jack Daniels over Julia's big, pillowy breasts and licking it out of her cleavage when suddenly blood squirted out of her nipples. It splattered my face and the ceiling and walls. The image scared me awake. I lay there gasping, my mouth tasting like somebody'd pissed in it, hoping like hell I was either at Julia's place or Delores's. But I didn't smell Delores's poison, which she'd pour over herself to overpower Jim Beam, and I didn't smell that oh-so-sweet honeysuckle aroma of pussy and weed that, before she took up with God, was Julia's home-blended perfume.

I took a deep breath and opened my eyes.

Fuckface Franky, one of that strange breed of wingnuts who actually think working inside a prison is significantly different from being locked up in one, was shaking my shoulder. Real gentle, like he scared of hurtin' me. That alone shoulda told me somethin' was plenty wrong.

"You gotta come with me, Lonny."

I didn't ask. You learn not to. Just rolled out of my bunk and went with him.

We traveled through the endless labyrinth of corridors, each one sealed off from the others by steel doors that clanked shut behind us, then down some stairs and—fast—through the piss 'n' puke smells of the infirmary to Warden Joe's office, a journey only a little farther than Denver to Houston. By the time we got where we was goin' my head had cleared some and I'd figured it out. Delores's phone call the day before had been a dream come up from my subconscious that somehow I'd acted on. I'd fucked up somehow, done something to get myself in more trouble. I weren't walkin' out of here next week. I was fucked.

"Come on in," said Warden Joe. His chubby little face was knotted up with concern, and he was fiddling with a staple gun, turning it over and over, like he was trying to figure out what it was. With his beady little eyes, lady-like hands, and chirpy, high voice he was definite wet-dream material for those who'd been in so long they'd lost hope for real pussy.

He nodded to Fuckface, who stepped outside, but left the door cracked in case—I suppose—I decided to make an escape attempt holding the staple gun to Warden Joe's neck. "Have a seat, Mr. Flynn," he said.

That "mister" sounded like trouble. In court or in prison, I've found that formal usually means fucked. I steeled myself like you do when you see a kick comin' and you're too drunk or too dizzy to duck. "What'd I do, Warden?"

I waited while he cleared his throat and looked out the window at vistas of chain link and barbed wire and a guard had his gun slung at the angle of a cock just got the aroma of cunt.

"It's about your mother."

"Delores? Don't tell me, she got drunk and showed up at the judge's house in the middle of the night, yellin' and screamin' I'm innocent?"

He didn't smile.

"Did she forget I'm gettin' out next week and try crashing her car through the front gate?"

"I'm sorry, but—"

I was on my feet. "Jesus Christ, was is it? What's happened?"

"She was found—"

I started shaking my head, saying "No, no, no!" so I couldn't hear what he was telling me, but still the words connected—*naked in Boulder Creek*—like a boot to the head—*combination alcohol and pills*—but I couldn't pass out or scream—*jogger walking her dog found the body.*"

"Jesus, somebody murdered her?"

"There were no signs of foul play. Boulder police say it was suicide."

"Delores wouldn't never have killed herself. Some son of a bitch, some lowlife she met in a bar, went and killed her."

"What it is, she got drunk and threw herself in the creek, but the water wasn't deep enough for her to drown, so she lay there and froze to death."

"Jesus God."

"The cops found an empty bottle on the creek bank. She left a note inside."

"Bullshit. I don't believe it."

"She wrote—" and here he read from a piece of paper where he must've scribbled some notes when he talked to the Boulder police, "—she couldn't keep on with life the way it was going. That she'd screwed up one time too often." He looked up. "She said she wanted to slit her wrists, but somebody named Luke told her the ice water would hurt less." He looked up. "This Luke guy anybody you know? It's against the law aiding a suicide."

"Naw, I don't know any Luke."

"According to the police, your mother had a history of mental problems—trips in and out of detox, arrests for drug possession, disturbing the peace. Her death wasn't exactly a surprise."

I shook my head. "But how could she've killed herself *now*? When she knew I'd be gettin' out so soon? When it was so close to us seeing each other again?"

"It's a tough break," said Warden Joe. "You want to, you can talk to the cops when you get back to Boulder."

"I ain't gonna talk to no fuckin' pig cops."

Warden Joe's nostrils flared like he'd just gotten goosed. He looked like he was getting ready to say something, then changed his mind.

"Funeral's at the end of the week. Your sister Amber's takin' care of the arrangements. If you'd like to speak with a chaplain or a therapist, I could..."

"Fuck it. I'm done here."

I didn't need to listen to no more. In the space of thirty seconds, my whole life had changed. Delores was dead.

Delores.

Dead.

I went back to my cell and lay down and stared at the ceiling.

Shit, that wasn't supposed to happen. That couldn't happen. I was supposed to die first. Not Delores. Not the pretty young blonde who dressed like a hippie chick straight from the Haight even in the late seventies, who took me fishing for the first time in that same creek she died in, who held me and hugged me and sat by my hospital bed that time I rode my bike out in front of a car when I was ten and her touch felt so good, made it almost worth getting my leg broke in two places.

Who was I kidding with all my tough talk? I loved Delores. I was terrified I'd inherited her crazy streak, but I loved her to death. She was the first woman I'd ever loved or seen naked or been held by and every other woman after that, even Julia, was just a model, an imitation, a pale reproduction of what Delores had been.

I'd been a lousy son. For all the ways I'd let her down, with my whole heart I begged her forgiveness.

Oh God, Oh God, oh GodohGodohGod...

Something started to hum at the base of my spine, an energy surge like I'd just got plugged into a giant electrical generator. I gripped the armrests of my chair cause it felt like if I let go I might float up to the ceiling.

Oh fuck, not here! Not now!

The sensation of white light rising up from my tailbone hadn't happened to me in such a long time, I thought it was gone for good. That maybe God had forgot about me or, more likely, given up. At least, I'd hoped that He had.

Cause nothin' on this earth scared me as much as that leaving-my-body, not-being-Lonny sensation. It's the foreplay for craziness, the wet kiss of insanity that leads down those dark corridors where Delores spent most of her life. It's the sneak-up-on-you-in-the-dark boogeymen that keeps my sister Amber a prisoner in her own house, 'fraid to walk out the door cause the sky's gonna crash down on her head.

It's the ticket to a journey outside my own self, a feeling that usually came when I let myself soften, when I let myself feel something and allowed my heart to come out of hiding.

It was incredibly pleasurable and, at the same time, it was pain beyond pain, because it changed how I looked at the world—instead of me being the center of the universe it made the whole universe seem like the center of me.

Usually I fought it with alcohol, but in a pinch, pure hundred-proof rage could do the job, too.

I bent my head over and ran a tape through my head—a tape of all the fuck-ups and scumbags and con men who'd fucked with Delores over the years, of what they'd done to her and to me and to Amber. Nights staying awake while downstairs the dishes flew and the voices of Mom and her boyfriend battered the ceiling like hail. Floyd Payne running around drunk with a .38 in each hand, Claymore Epps with Amber's brassiere wrapped around his dick when I walked into the bathroom that time, Dabney Bowles coming at me with his bowling-ball-sized fists. As I concentrated, the sparks of white light that spiraled up from my tailbone dimmed down, and I was burned through with the clean, fierce fire of hatred.

I knew two things.

I needed to find the men who were responsible for Delores's death. Maybe they didn't get her drunk and push her in the creek that night, but the way I saw it, she was already dead when she jumped in. Freezing to death just made it official.

Second thing was, I needed a drink.

Needed one bad.

Figured I'd have to get me the second before I started in on the first.

Chapter Four

A BARE-BREASTED woman slunk toward me, wearing a silver G-string and carrying a tray full of drinks.

I'd been calling Julia from the pay phone at the Conoco station up the street ever since I took the bus back to Boulder and moved into Delores's trailer, but I was still just getting a recording.

The half-naked waitress paused long enough to hand me a beer and a shooter. I slid a dollar bill under her G-string and tried to make eye contact, but she put her nose in the air like a buck was an insult.

"Fucking whores," I said as she walked away, loud enough so's she could hear.

I was sitting at the bar of the Bustop in North Boulder. One of my favorite hangouts before I got sent up. Just up the road from the Trailways bus terminal and a greasy spoon called the North Boulder Cafe. Before I met Julia, I dated a dancer here, name of Cynthia. She had cantaloupe tits and she could move her hips like a boa constrictor. Her pussy left my dick tingling for days. I couldn't get hold of Julia, I figured Cynthia might be willing to welcome me home.

Cynthia wasn't here tonight unfortunately. What *was* here was a bunch of frat boys from up on the Hill—C.U.'s finest, seeing who could piss away more of their old man's money into the G-strings of the guttersluts on stage. One guy was stuffing the dancers' G-strings with ten-dollar bills.

Assholes. I slugged down the shooter and beer that the waitress had brought me. Then ordered another.

When I got up to go to the john, I had to pass a whole table of those assholes. One of 'em, about my height, but with twenty pounds of gut in addition, looked at me all smirky and smartass. I knew what he was thinking: how much better he was than me, how much richer, how much better educated. That he'd never been in the slammer and he'd fucked higher class pussy than me.

He didn't say it out loud. I heard it in my head. But that was enough. I hauled him up out of his seat and threw him across the table he and his buddies were sitting at. Beers spilled in every direction. College punks scattered like cockroaches.

"What are you *lookin'* at?" I yelled at him and threw a right to his gut that turned his face a sick shade of green.

One of his buds tried to tackle me from behind, but I was too fast and I decked him. It felt good. Not as good as it would've felt to ream Julia or Cynthia, but close.

The guy on the table was wheezing, blowing blood out of his nose. Somebody grabbed my arm and twisted it so far up my back I could've patted myself on the shoulder.

"Come on, asshole, you gotta get out of here."

A bouncer, I figured. Fine, I'd take him on, too. I let him hustle me outside into the parking lot. The minute his grip on me loosened, I spun around, aiming to kick his legs out from under him. Get him on the ground and take it from there.

Instead I ran into the guy's fist.

Smashed backward into a car. Tasted blood on my teeth.

"You dickhead, what the fuck are you doing? Or are you so shitfaced you don't even know me?"

I blinked. The neon sign over the Bustop threw a sickly light over the parking lot, turning everything the color of piss, but I recognized my old buddy Tommy Gleason. Musta been mid-forties by then, but I had to give the guy credit—he looked hard as brick and the deep lines in his face made him look more like the Marlboro man than a geezer.

"Thought you were in prison."

"I was so good they let me out early."

"Looks like you miss the joint already. You can't wait to go back."

"Yeah, well, some college punk started it."

"Maybe, but some college punk won't be the one going back to the can."

All of a sudden, about half a dozen black-and-whites came racing up North Broadway. More headlights flashing in that parking lot than I'd seen on the stage.

"Fuck, can you believe it? They called the cops."

Tom grabbed my arm. "My truck's over there. Come on, let's get the hell out of here."

I followed him. We jumped into his Chevy and eased past the police cars and out of the lot. I ducked down in the seat.

"What about my truck?" I said, meaning, of course, Delores's truck, but I figured what was hers was mine now.

"We'll come back for it."

"Where we going?"

"To where you shoulda been in the first place."

"Shit. Fuck. Piss. What kinda friend are you anyway?"

"A good enough one that I don't give a shit how mad you get. I'm gonna say what you need to hear and take you where you need to be."

I guess about now's where I ought to say that Tom Gleason was my best friend in the world. Almost fifteen years older than me, he'd had a short marriage to Delores's sister Andrea when I was a kid. A man of the world who'd served in the Army and traveled all over Europe and Southeast Asia. A strange guy, too. He drank, but he never got drunk and he never got mean. From time to time, he'd take off into the woods and camp by himself for a week or two. He said that silence was the language of God and those days alone were his time to listen.

Then later, when I was older, we did dry wall and carpentry for the same construction outfit, and worked together for almost six months on that big industrial park project in Westminster. We'd also been cellmates for a few days in Boulder County Jail.

Me for drunk and disorderly. Him for trying to buy pot off a vice cop. We'd drank together, screwed hookers together, gone on a road trip down to New Mexico on our bikes. Believe it or not, we even prayed together on a couple of occasions.

Not that Tommy was perfect. He'd gone to chiropractor school for exactly one week, but he had cards printed up and he liked to tell women that's what he did for a living, see if he could get them to let him "work on their backs" or someplace farther south. I know that scam got his ass kicked a few times.

If I had a soft spot in my heart for Tommy, though, it was because of Delores. He never come round to the house that he didn't bring her a carton of Luckies or a bottle of hand lotion, some little somethin', and when she went into the hospital for an overdose—he visited her every day. Read to her from the Bible and the Big Book, sneaked her those Oreo cookies she craved.

"You ought to be more like Tommy," she'd tell me. "He does what he wants to do, but he uses his head and he don't drink too much and he remembers it's God in charge, not Tommy Gleason."

Delores, I thought. *Delores is dead.*

The police cars weren't following us, but Tommy was still driving about ten miles under the speed limit. I turned around, getting ready to say something smartass, when suddenly my eyes flooded over and my hands started to shake.

"She's dead, Tommy." I bent over and started to sob. "Delores is dead, Tommy. What am I gonna do?"

He put his hand on the back of my neck and rubbed me there, way I imagine a father might've done if I'd had one of those, and I bawled like a baby.

We hadn't gone very far south on Broadway when Tommy pulled in front of a long, low-slung building with the words Alcohol Rehabilitation Center on the front.

"You oughta check yourself in here. Tell your parole officer your mom just died and you're a mess, and they'll prob'ly send you straight to rehab."

"Oh no, man. No way. I ain't going in here."

"Fine," he said. "Then I'll just turn around and drive you back to the Bustop, so you can keep tryin' to get your ass busted."

"Shit, why are you doin' this to me?"

"'Cause one, I'm your friend, and two, your mom used to say, anything happen to her, she wanted me to keep an eye on you."

"What? Like I'm twelve years old?"

"Hell, I knew you when you was twelve years old and you were way more mature."

"I got my fill of these fucking meetings in prison."

"Yeah, I can tell you're all cured."

So we got out of the car and went into the A.R.C., which has been a kind of second home to me over the years, I've detoxed there so many times. It was an open AA meeting Tom had brought me to, meaning it was okay for non-drunks like himself to be there. We sat on the back row, next to a couple of panhandlers from Pearl Street who stank like three-day-old garbage.

"Now just keep your ears open and your mouth shut," Tommy said.

"Don't worry, I got nothin' to say."

The topic, it turned out, was gratitude. I didn't think I had a fuckin' lot to be grateful about. Delores dead, only a few hundred bucks in my pocket from pawning her TV set and stereo, Julia still not taking my calls.

The guy who'd been talking got through. I changed my mind about not wanting to talk. Raised my hand. "I got somethin' to say."

Tom reached down and clamped a mean grip on my knee, but I didn't understand why he didn't want me to talk. I was too drunk to remember that it's one thing to show up at an AA meeting tanked to the gills, but the AAers don't want you to share 'less you're sober. Maybe scared the alcohol fumes from your breath will get somebody high.

"This is what alcohol's done to me."

"Who are you?" somebody asked.

"Oh yeah. My name. I'm Lonny and I'm an alcoholic and I'm shitfaced."

An uneasy silence spread over the room. A few people murmured, "Hi, Lonny."

"I just got out of prison," I heard myself say. "And you prob'ly think I'll be back in prison soon, but that ain't the case. I'm not drunk 'cause I'm an alcoholic, I'm drunk because my mother just killed herself. I let her down. But I'm gonna make it up to her. I got a purpose. A plan. I got me a reason to live, and that's somethin' I never had before. Fact is, I'm feelin' so good that if we were all at a bar, I'd buy this whole room a round."

That was when I got forcibly evicted for the second time in an hour—when Tommy jerked me up and hauled my ass to the door.

"You dumb fuck. You can't even sit through an AA meeting without running your mouth."

He was pissed. All of a sudden I felt scared. I'd always looked up to Tommy. He was my best friend in the world.

"You mad?"

He shook his head. "I ain't mad, Lonny, but when you're drunk, you flat out disgust me. Remember I knew you when you were a boy. I know what you coulda been and what you could still be. Fucks with my head when I see you haven't learned shit, that you're still hellbent on pissing your life away."

We headed out toward Tom's car. I heard him say something about coffee and eggs over at Coco's.

A few minutes later, as I watched Tommy fork some of the greasiest eggs I've seen outside the joint, I said, "I know who killed Delores."

"So do I. She's been killing herself for the last twenty years. The other night she just finished the job. Now drink your coffee. It'll help clear your head."

"But I do know. I wasn't just bullshitting back there in the meeting. I do have a plan. I can't tell you what, but I figure I'll need a few days at least. Then I'll head on up to Julia's. Find out why she's not takin' my calls."

"Look, you can't expect things to be how you left them with her," said Tommy. "Don't forget your life's been on hold for two years. Hers hasn't."

"You mean you think she's met somebody else?"

"She's human is all I'm saying."

"But everything was dandy until just a couple of weeks ago. I mean, I used to call Julia all the time. Got letters from her every week. And then Delores calls and says she saw Julia the day before and *that's* when everything changes, and I ain't heard from her since."

"People change," Tommy said.

"Not Julia. And not so goddamn all of a sudden."

Tommy held out his coffee cup to the waitress and she refilled it. He emptied in two creamers and five packets of sugar and stirred it real slow. "You said she goes to church now."

"So what? I don't care how much religion she's got, the quickest way to that woman's heart is still through her pussy. She's a sex witch—like Delores."

Tommy put down his fork. "Looks like she put some kinda spell on you."

"Hey, Julia don't want me no more, I can get along fine." I pulled a letter out of my back pocket, one wrote by the Kmart cashier. "Look here, I got half a dozen women I been writing to in the joint. Sendin' me stamps, puttin' money on my books. All of 'em lonely and horny and countin' the days till I get out."

"So you're sayin' you expected Julia to wait for you, but meantime you're carrying on postal romances with these other women?"

I realized how it must look to Tommy. "Hey, it don't mean nothin'," I said. "It was just somethin' to pass the time besides jerking off."

I stared down at my waffle, realized I'd puke if I tried to get any down. "Look, take me back to my truck, okay? I gotta make an early start tomorrow morning. I gotta go to Glenwood to see Amber."

"You ain't supposed to leave Boulder County."

"Aw, fuck that. I gotta at least see my sister."

"Who else you goin' to see?"

"It don't matter. C'mon, man, you packed enough grease in your arteries. Let's go."

Tommy shook his head. "Why don't you take a few days to calm down? Get used to your freedom and let some of the shock wear off. Come on up in the mountains with me. Like old times."

"Another sweat lodge, Tommy?"

"Might not do you no harm."

"Can't. Gotta take care of some things. And don't try talkin' me out of it."

"I got some time between construction jobs. How 'bout I go with you?"

"Thanks, man, but I gotta do this alone."

"Your mom made me promise I'd look after your ass if anything happened to her. That's a promise I intend to keep. If you're taking off, I'm going with you."

"You are one stubborn bastard, you know that?"

Tommy paid the check and we walked outside. The night air stung with the promise of snow. "You never did tell me what happened that day at the sweat lodge," Tommy said. "It's only been fifteen years. Maybe it's time."

I smiled. "That was a long time ago, Tommy. I'm not sure I remember myself."

Chapter Five

TOMMY DROPPED me off at Delores's place. I waited for him to leave, thinkin' I'd take off as soon as he did. Daggone, but if he didn't come in, make himself at home, and then fall asleep on Delores's old couch that the neighbor's rottweiler had pissed on last summer. Pretended to sleep anyway. I had an idea I wasn't gonna shake Tommy Gleason as easy as I might've expected.

So I went back in the bedroom, smoked the joint I'd found earlier when I was looking for Delores's drug stash, and took a shot at falling asleep, but I couldn't get used to the noises—dogs barking, cars goin' by, a stereo playing somewhere. Not prison sounds, but the noises of normal life.

And besides, in spite of what I told Tommy, I did remember

the sweat lodge. Remembered too well a day that started off being one of the best in my life and ended up one of the worst. So I lay there tossing and turning, just stoned enough for my mind to start drifting into places it should've stayed out of, and thought about that weird trip up into the mountains with Tommy when I was eleven years old.

Delores was living with a coke addict named Dabney Bowles at the time. Dabney was a mean drunk, and I know Tommy worried about me and her both. He used to try to talk her into coming to live with him and Aunt Andrea, but she always said no and made excuses for the way Dabney treated her. Truth was, she'd trade a black eye and a busted lip for a few lines any day.

So one Saturday, when Tommy asked could he take me with him up into the mountains, Delores didn't even ask what for. I figured she wanted to fuck and get high, and she was glad to get rid of me.

We drove Tommy's pickup 119 past Barker Reservoir, through the scruffy little mountain town of Nederland into the mountains. It was early October. In the high country, the leaves were already turned. As we got higher, there were patches of snow on the ground and the aspen leaves glittered like polished brass spoons.

"Where we going?"

"You'll see," Tommy said.

We left Tommy's car and got out and tramped through the woods for a couple of miles. I knew Tommy went up in the mountains sometimes, but I didn't know for what and I had a lot of wild thoughts, most of 'em involving drug smuggling and drugged-out guttersluts just lookin' to give it away.

The trail we were on intersected another. There were boot prints in the snow. We left the path and bushwhacked up the slope for a couple of miles.

Tommy stopped and made some kind of birdcall. Someone answered back. I wondered what kind of a game we were playing and why Tommy had brought me along. The thought even came to me that maybe Delores was tired of having a kid around. My sister Amber had already been placed in a foster home by social services. Maybe Delores had asked Tommy to take me into the mountains and lose me up there.

Just when I was wondering if this whole expedition was some kind of trap, we came to a clearing with the biggest tent I'd ever seen. There was an opening in the top with a pale column of smoke rising from it. Next to the tent was a pile of backpacks and boots and, beside that, an even bigger pile of clothing.

"We get undressed now," said Tommy and started to take off his clothes. I thought he was crazy. It must've been ten degrees on that mountain and the snow was a foot deep. Still I did what he told me and stripped down a fast as I could. Inside the tent, the heat was so intense I couldn't hardly breathe. Smoke and incense stung tears to my eyes, but I could tell there was a circle of men around a small fire. I took a seat. A minute later, Tommy joined me.

What now, I wondered.

But the answer was nothing. We sat. And sat. Then we sat some more.

A pipe got passed around. I thought it was gonna be reefer, which I already knew about from smoking with Mom, but no, it was just plain old tobacco.

I caught Tommy's eye, but he just put a finger to his mouth and motioned me to stay quiet.

We sat.

My body started rebelling. There were itches and twitches and tickles and cramps. I wanted to pee. It was hell not to squirm.

We sat.

My mind went through all kinds of the usual thoughts—sex and school and the Broncos and sex and whether my dick was as big as it ought to be and whether Dabney had started beating Mom up by now and what I should do about it.

I thought about Mom and the creeps she was with, about Amber stuck in some foster home over in Louisville, about how lousy life was. I thought, *fuck you, God, this isn't right. Why does it have to be like this?*

Why am I locked up all alone inside this sack of skin with no way out till I'm dead and maybe not even then?

Why do I have to feel so separate? So scared? So alone?

Then my mind just kind of quieted down and, in the quiet that followed, I started to drift. Wordless, thoughtless, emotionless— like the inside of my skull was as big as the whole universe and I was just floating inside it.

And words came to me that seemed to answer what I'd wondered about earlier. They weren't my words, so I figured they musta been God's: *I'm not separate. I'm you. And you're not alone I'm with you. I've always been with you.*

Scared the shit out of me. Delores heard voices, too, and Delores was nuts. My biggest fear was that I'd end up like her, talking to the air, people giving me funny looks and crossing the street when they saw me.

Shit, was this how it had started for her?

My heart started to race.

A buzzing began at the base of my spine. Soft at first, and then louder, like a hive full of bees were suddenly swarming out of my asshole. I thought maybe I'd been sitting so long that the cheeks of my ass had fallen asleep. I shifted my weight back and forth to get the blood going and looked around to see did anyone else hear the sound.

The buzzing started to rise. It plucked my vertebrae like a guitarist twanging strings. Getting louder and stronger the higher it climbed up my spine. The pipe, I thought. It wasn't just tobacco. There was drugs in the pipe, peyote or hash. I was going on some incredible drug trip.

The noise reached the base of my neck. Stinging distance away from my brain. My hair felt like it was catching on fire. I glanced at Tommy. His eyes were shut and he looked to be in deep meditation.

The bees entered my brain with an explosion of white, and a sound like bacon frying up inside my skull. Everything changed. I wasn't me anymore. I was outside me, watching. At the same time, I was seeing everything from the viewpoint of everyone else. Like the minds of every man in that tent had been melted down into one huge, swirling stew and everything that we saw, felt, or thought was all mixed together in the same giant pot. Rippling outward and outward in a circle that included everybody in the world, living or dead. It felt like I'd been taken backstage at the biggest play in the world where I got to see all the actors out of costume and not mouthing their lines. Like nothing mattered, either, because it was all just a game. There was a me, the real me, underneath Lonny Flynn, but Lonny himself wasn't real. Lonny was just something made up and the sooner I shed him the sooner I'd know who I really was.

I told myself to sit still, not to flip out and embarrass myself, but more bees were rushing up my spine, filling my head with fire and noise. The top of my head opened up and what felt like a column of white fire erupted out of my skull. My bones started to melt. My jaw clenched and the fire burned up out of my gums and into my teeth. Flames surged through my dick and it started to get hard.

And with all this came a feeling so rich and so wonderful, it was almost more than I was able to stand. I loved every man in that tent. Every person in the world. I even loved Lonny—didn't matter if he was a scared, lonely fuckup who couldn't admit any of that to himself. I loved him and God loved him and somehow it was all one and the same. The white fire was melting Lonny down into ashes and soot and, when it was done, all that was going to be left was silence and the pure love of God.

I thought this is it, this is what I've always been scared of. That I'd turn out to be crazy like Mom. She hears voices, I hear bees and feel fires. Two loonies together. We deserve each other.

It was too much. I got up and bolted toward the tent door, stumbling over somebody's knee, almost falling, then catching myself and staggering outside into the snow.

I kept running and, as I ran, my body started coming apart.

Pieces fell off. I looked back and there was my hand and my arm. There was my leg. I didn't understand how I could keep running when most of my body was strewn out on the snow, but I did. I kept on running till something clamped down hard on my shoulder, and I screamed.

Tommy whirled me around. "Where're you going?"

I looked down at myself. I was naked, but at least the intense cold had got rid of my hard-on. My bare feet were covered in snow. My ankles were red as raw meat.

I stared into Tommy's worried eyes. In a heartbeat, I knew everything there was to know about him—things he knew about himself and things even he didn't know, everything he'd ever done and why he'd done it. He'd done bad stuff, but it didn't matter. He was full of love for me and for everyone—the white fire had burned through him, too—behind the scruffy two-day old beard and the anxious blue eyes, I swear I saw God.

"What happened?" he asked.

"I—I couldn't breathe. I had to get out."

He stared at me. "You sure that's all it was?

I nodded.

"Because sometimes in a sweat lodge a man's life force starts to rise, the God force in the base of his spine climbs up to join with the God force in the top of his head. In the East they call it Kundalini, the divine serpent. It's a holy thing, a mystery."

"Hey, I just got too fuckin' hot," I said, brushing him off. I turned and walked back toward the tent. When I got there, I picked up my clothes and started to dress.

Tommy caught me by the arm. "Come back inside."

I jerked free. "I'm done."

"Lonny, if something happened in there—"

"Nothin' happened," I yelled. "I *told* you that, didn't I? And fuck you and the whole fucking bunch of you."

So I sat in the truck and waited while Tommy went back into the sweat lodge. I thought about what I'd felt. Tried to puzzle it out. But I couldn't tell Tommy what had happened in that tent. I was scared he'd think I was crazy or on drugs or maybe even a faggot, if I described the love I'd felt for him and the other men.

I couldn't tell him how scared I had been.

It was like I'd edged up to a cliff, come a thumbnail away from jumping, and then moved back. I was safe. I was on solid ground. But whatever I'd backed away from, whatever it was that announced itself by the noise of the bees, it still called to me. Whispered and tempted and offered itself. Like a beautiful woman too scary to fuck. Like a sunset too gorgeous to look at.

WHEN I got home, it was late. Delores and Dabney were stretched out on the couch watching TV. Delores's blouse was unbuttoned. I tried not to look at her chest, but I did—she had great tits. Dabney saw me and shot me a look of pure snake venom, but I didn't hate him the way that I usually did. I felt sad for him and wished I could give him a taste of whatever it was I had felt in that tent, because I knew that would change him forever.

You're God, don't you know that? I imagined saying to him and then almost laughed out loud, thinking of the reaction I'd get.

Back in my room, I prayed for a while. When I was through, I'd decided to talk to Tommy about the experience after all. He was one person I knew wouldn't laugh. Besides, he already knew about it. He had a name for it. Koonta-something. Sounded like an African name. I decided I'd call him first thing in the morning and say I was sorry for how I'd acted and tell him just what had gone on.

It didn't work out that way, though.

I woke up in the night to what sounded like an explosion.

It was Delores slamming the door as she came into my room. I reached over and flicked on the light. There she was in her black baby-doll nighty and those silly white slippers with the powder puffs on top, down on her knees, fumbling with the lock on the door.

I said, "Mom, what's going on?" and then I heard Dabney's boot hit the frame of the door and the whole house creaked and swayed on its foundation. The second kick knocked the door off its hinges and he roared in like a freight train derailing. He grabbed Delores by the hair and hauled her out of my room. I heard him smack her, once, twice, three times.

"Fucking whore!"

I pulled on my pants and ran out into the hall.

He had her backed up against the wall in the living room. Lip bleeding, eye swelling, starting to turn black.

I thought, *Okay, just be cool. He's got it out of his system now. He'll lay off. He'll go home.*

But he didn't. He cracked her across the face two more times. I heard her jaw pop. She screamed, "Stop it, please stop. I'm sorry. I told you I'm sorry," and he hit her again. Her head banged against the wall and her eyes started to glaze.

I tackled Dabney from behind, wrapping my left arm around his neck while I punched him in the eye with my right fist. He bellowed and shook me off. Backhanded me across the room and turned back to Delores, who was trying to crawl out of his way.

"Fuckin' whore and your fuckin' brat!" I heard the impact of his boot meeting her ribs. She shrieked and curled up in a ball, clutching her stomach. He moved in on her. Aiming another kick.

I ran to my room and got the hunting knife I'd stolen off some old passed-out tramp and I ran back and found Dabney on top of Delores, smacking her in the face so her head rocked back and forth. She wasn't making a sound. I held the knife handle in both hands and brought it down.

I don't know how he saw me. How he knew. Years later, I

wondered if he could've seen my reflection in Delores's eyes, but her eyes were closed, so maybe it was just animal cunning or plain dumb luck.

But he knew. And turned away from Delores in time to intercept the knife. I still got him, though. Got him good. The blade sliced through the fatty part of his palm. Blood spouted out like I'd opened a spigot. Blood on my face, my neck, blood I could taste in my mouth, salty and hot.

He made a weird, furious sound deep in his throat. Not a human sound or even an animal, but mechanical, like gears grinding together in a machine getting ready to break. To explode and spew out shards of metal and spikes of steel.

I drew back the knife to stab him again and suddenly it was flying out of my hand, soaring up toward the ceiling and then clattering down to the floor while I went in the other direction, weightless in spite of the fact that the bones in my arms and legs had turned into lead. Now the blood I was tasting was mine. He threw a punch at my face—fist crashing in like a huge hammerhead—and I dodged and moved right into the same punch that was coming from the left side, too. Things shook loose in my skull. Brains oozing out of my ears, teeth rattling around like so many Chiclets.

Delores screamed something, but I couldn't make out her words. An enormous roulette wheel was spinning in my head. Every time it would almost stop, he'd hit me again and the wheel would take off at a furious rate, the ball bouncing from number to number, me wondering where it would stop, *if* it would stop.

I heard Delores wail, "Jesus, you're killing him."

She screamed it three times. Each time she did I believed her a little bit more.

"Jesus, you're killing him!"

Then the roulette wheel stopped with an ear-splitting crash, and I knew Delores was right.

I had to be dead.

But I could still hear it, the sound of bees buzzing.

So faintly, receding.

Back to their God-hive.

Leaving me empty.

Then everything black.

Chapter Six

I SWEAR if Tommy Gleason wasn't harder to shake than a summer cold. Like trying to scrape chewing gum off your shoe. I kept trying to get rid of him so I could get on with the business at hand, but he wouldn't get gone.

Finally I decided, if he was so eager to miss work at his job site and buddy up with me on the road, then shit, I'd let him come with me. Long as he didn't try to interfere with my drinking no more, this might be okay—for a hundred miles or so anyways.

We had us another breakfast—this one I managed to get down with the help of a bloody mary—and headed west toward Golden, then took Route 6 up into the mountains. A little ways south of Idaho Springs, where Route 6 intersects with I-70, we came to Clem's, a biker bar that had always been one of my favorites. A half-dozen pickups were parked out front and, even in this weather, a couple of Harleys. I pulled in beside them.

"Gotta get me a drink."

"That's the last thing you need."

"I know, I know. One drink is too many and a hundred isn't enough. Don't worry. I'm not gonna get shit-faced. We'll be in and out faster'n you can fuck a truck-stop whore."

Tommy reached over, plucked out the car keys, and dropped them into the pocket of his parka. "I'll hang onto these. Just in case you was thinkin' of ditching me."

"You hurt me, man. I thought we had *trust*."

"Only thing an alcoholic can be trusted to do is have another drink. I'm keepin' the keys."

I shrugged, trying not to show how right he'd read me, and we went inside.

Now Tommy Gleason was maybe better than most men I knew, but lucky for me, he weren't no saint. Soon's we got in there and he saw I wasn't fixing to leave right away, he started to check out the women. A couple of 'em I could tell blew him off, but this one gal, a biker chick with big square turquoise earrings about the size of belt buckles, started flirting. She musta liked Tommy's ass, way she stared when he walked to the men's room, and I admit I felt jealous—here I'm just out of the joint and horny as hell and an old guy like Tommy's got this chick wet. When he come back from the can, I couldn't hear what he was saying, but I did see him reach into his wallet and hand her what had to be one of his phony chiropractor cards.

I was standing over by the pay phone, waiting to call Julia when the guy using it finished explaining to his boss how he was laid up with the flu, and I noticed a couple of guys at the pool table whose insignias matched the one on the chick's black leather jacket.

The guy on the phone was whining about how bad he had diarrhea and chills. I gave up on trying to call Julia and struck up a conversation with the pool players.

After a while, I looked over at Tommy and laughed. "Shit, would you look at that. He's giving her the old chiropractor routine."

The taller of the two guys, whose left cheek and forehead looked like he'd rolled his bike on loose gravel and had his face sewn back together by a plastic surgeon on speed, zinged the five ball into a corner pocket.

"You mean your friend over there?"

"Not my friend. We did time together, that's all. He used to brag how he'd carried these phony chiropractor cards and tell women he'd work on their back if they came back with him to his office. Said it was amazing how getting fucked on a hardwood floor does wonders for a gal's back."

Five-Ball called the eight in the right corner pocket and scratched. His friend, a balding guy with prison pallor and a set of homemade tattoos that indicated he, too, was a newcomer to the free world snickered and lined up his shot.

"Hey, I wouldn't worry. Most he'll do is take her outside, cop a feel in the parking lot, maybe get her to suck his dick. He's a con artist, that's all."

"Yeah? Maybe I need to have a word with this asshole."

The guy stalked past me and marched over to the bar. Ignored Tommy but had some words with the gal, who musta mouthed off because all of a sudden Five-Ball landed a right to her chin, sent her flying back into the pool table so hard her legs went up in the air and balls flew every which way.

Made me think of that movie where the gal gets fucked on a pool table because the chick was out cold, arms and legs spread. She looked better like that, and it was all I could do to tear my eyes off her.

Meantime, the guy was trading punches with Tommy while the bartender, a squinty-eyed little dude looked like he missed his Prozac one too many days, tried to break up the fight by hauling out one of your basic bartending implements, a baseball bat, and banging it down on the bar.

"Quick! Gimme the car keys," I hollered to Tommy, but seeing as how Five-Ball's knee was on his throat, he was otherwise occupied. As Tommy's friend, though, I figured the least I could do was realign the guy's jaw before I took off, so I punched him, made like I was reaching down to help Tommy up off the floor and grabbed the keys out of his jacket.

Then I hauled ass.

"Hey, you little shit. You came in with him. Where you think you're going?"

A guy only a little bit smaller than a Frigidaire blocked the door. I dodged a right, belted him in the windpipe, and watched him career into the cash register.

Behind me I heard what was getting to be way too familiar— the sound of somebody calling the cops. Tommy and Five-Ball were still going at it, and to judge from the peculiar angle of Five-Ball's nose, he mighta been losing the fight, but his looks had at least been improved.

For the first time since I'd been driving it, Delores's truck started up on the first try, which I took to be an omen for luck.

Now don't think I didn't feel like a snake, leavin' my best friend to fend for himself at a bar where most of the occupants were fellow alumni of the fine Colorado penal system, but Tommy shouldn'a been so pushy about coming along. I knew he'd done what he felt like he had to, 'cause he'd promised Delores to look after my ass, but I had my own shit to take care of.

Guy name of Floyd Payne was the first turd on the list.

Near Estes Park, I stopped at a liquor store, bought me a fifth of Jack Daniels, and looked up old Floyd in the phone book. A woman—cranky-sounding and old—answered the phone. Said she was Floyd's wife and he was up to Gem Lake ice fishing.

"Now why would he wanna do that?" I said, sincerely impressed with the stupidity of anybody'd wanna plunk their ass down on a slab of ice in the middle of winter.

"'Cause he thinks he's a polar bear," said the woman—Floyd's wife, I supposed.

"We're old buddies. You think he'd mind company?"

"Not if you bring him a six-pack."

"Will do," I said. I asked for directions to Gem Lake and she give 'em to me, just as nice as could be, even waiting while I got a pen and paper so I could write it all down.

This time of year the only gem that Gem Lake resembled was a huge, cloudy opal with the sun on it so bright, hurt your eyes to look at it. Stands of spruce and fir, dusted with snow, crowded down to the edge of the ice while, up above, the sky stood as empty and still as the day after Creation.

The quiet was huge. Loudest I'd heard it since that day years ago at the sweat lodge with Tommy. I thought Floyd Payne must be crazy to come here alone, to a place where the sky had no roof to it and the ice had no end and a man could get swallowed up by the silence.

I took a pull from the bottle of Jack, then stuck it back in the glovebox for safekeeping. I left the truck and hiked along the edge of the lake. The frostbit grass crunched under my boots. The air was so cold that it hurt to breathe deep, and every time I exhaled, my chest made a sound like a teakettle. Finally, way yonder toward the opposite shore, I spotted a vehicle out on the ice. A hundred or so yards away was a heavyset guy hunkered down on a bucket, a jig pole in his hand. His light-colored vest and tan pants blended into the silvers and greys of the ice and the sky so closely he looked like something that should be haunting a graveyard.

I started toward him, but it was all I could do to make myself walk out onto the lake. Sounds dumb, I guess, 'cause there was a Chevy Blazer sitting out there, but I couldn't help imagining I heard the shifting and popping and cracking of ice slabs getting ready to break.

When I was within twenty feet of the guy, I hollered, "How ya doing? Catching anything 'sides pneumonia?"

The man turned to face me. He had a wool cap pulled down over his head and damned if I couldn't tell if it was Floyd Payne or not. I'd been about nine the last time I'd seen him and, if this was Floyd, he had about thirty pounds more gut and considerable less muscle. Delores had always liked her men to be about the same suit size as Godzilla, and Floyd Payne fit the bill. He'd played defensive back for the Denver Broncos for a year in the '70s before he went to prison for dealing methamphetamines. Judging from the bulk of him, I figured it was a toss-up which would go through the ice first—this fat dude or the Blazer.

As I approached, he said, "You call this cold? Hell, wait till the sun goes down, this'll feel like Hawaii."

Minute I heard that twangy, slow-as-syrup south Texas drawl, I knew I'd found Floyd. Not the forklift-sized gun nut who once showed his dislike of loud music by shooting out the stereo when Delores had the Grateful Dead turned up to about the volume of front row at a rock concert, but a paunchy middle-aged married guy more interested in snagging pike than pussy.

"Catch much?" I said.

He squinted into the pitifully faint sun that was trying to sneak around the corner of a cloud.

"Got a few yellow perch this morning, but they were mostly throwbacks. This lake's got its share of humpbacks, though. Later in the day's when they come out." He indicated a good-sized white bucket over by his gear box. "Have a seat if you feel like it. Extra jig poles over there."

Friendly guy, this older, fatter Floyd Payne, but then as I recalled he'd always been right down decent to his fishing and hunting buddies. It was me and Delores got treated like shit.

I picked up the bucket and inspected the gear box, which contained a selection of lines and lures, a cigarette lighter, pack of Winstons, and a keyring with about twenty keys. He had a couple of bait buckets, too, and three more jig poles, each with a different lure on the end. There was also a motherfucker of a power augur that he'd used to cut out a hole in two feet of ice.

I upended the bucket and took a seat a few feet from Floyd. "I hear the pike are biting this year."

"Hell yeah. The Serengeti's got its lions, the mountain lake's got your pike."

If there'd been any doubt in my mind that I had the right man, it was gone now. Floyd always had been a fishing nut. I'd like to've had a dollar for every time I'd heard him use that line about pike and lions, and I still didn't get exactly what he was talking about.

I lay my pole down, reached into my backpack, and took out a six-pack.

"Have a drink?"

He smiled and accepted, then offered me a swig from his thermos. Fire all the way to my toes. I figured he must like a little coffee with his Jim Beam.

"You're Floyd Payne," I said.

He took a long time to answer. "We know each other?"

"Sure we do."

You could almost hear the creak of mental wheels in desperate need of a lube job. "I know. You were on the crew of that renovation job in Dillon last year."

I shook my head.

"Bartender at LeRoy's."

"Nope. I'm Lonny Flynn. Delores's boy."

"Shit. So you're Lonny? All growed up." His mouth twisted into a smile. His eyes got hard and glinty as the lure on the end of one of his lines. Looked me up and down like he was trying to decide how tough a fish I'd be to land if it came to that. He switched the pole to the other hand so we could shake.

"How'd you find me?"

"I called your house and spoke to your wife."

"Surprised she could leave her soap operas long enough to answer the phone."

"She give me directions and everything."

"Weren't that nice of her."

I lowered my jig pole into the water and took a swallow of half-froze beer.

"You ever ice fish before, Lonny?"

"Naw, I think ice fishing's for fools. Freezin' your ass off, trampin' around on ice could break anytime, end up bein' a popsicle for some fish."

He moved the canteen up to his fat, whiskered mouth and took a long pull. Made a "haaa" sound of contentment.

"Ice here won't break. It's two-foot thick. You see the size of the augur I had to use to drill through it."

"So even if you don't go for a swim, you still just pissin' your time away."

He laughed loud enough to scare the pike twenty feet down. "Coming from you, that's funny as hell. I still got friends back in Boulder. I know you been doing time. What do you call that, an enriching experience? Hell, from what I hear, you've pissed your whole life away."

The sun lost its fight with the clouds that were trying to smother it. Wind felt like it came from a glacier burned the tips of my ears. All of a sudden I felt scared, unsure what to do next. It was like sitting down next to a girl you've dreamed all your life about fucking and here she is with her legs open and all you know how to do is hem and haw because for all that fantasizing you never really thought it'd come true. Never thought the day would come you'd sit there lookin' up her twat and wonder would you be able to get it hard.

But damn it was cold! That musta been why my hands was shakin', why my tongue felt like it was three sizes too big for my mouth.

"You didn't come all this way to share a six-pack and shoot the shit. What d'you want?"

"Wanted to let you know 'bout Delores."

"Delores—how is she?"

"In an urn on Amber's mantel, for all I know. She killed herself a little over a week ago."

"Fuck. That's a damned shame. I really mean that. She had a lot of problems, your mom did."

"No shit. One of 'em named Floyd Payne."

"Hey, I know I got rough with her a few times, but there were two sides to it, you know. You didn't know the full story. Your mom was hell to live with. She musta been hell for you, too. Remember the time she just walked out the door to go to the liquor store and never came back? Next time I heard from her she was in Colorado Springs with a guy she'd been buying dope from."

"You ran her off is what happened."

"And you'd just got out of juvie and hell, I didn't know how to handle a young kid who wasn't even my own. 'Specially not one with a mouth like yours."

"So you busted my arm."

"And I'd do it again if you raised a hand to me like you did that day."

"You forget something, Floyd, I'm not no kid anymore."

I took a glove off, walked over, and stuck my fingers down through the hole in the ice. The water was so cold it nearly burned through the flesh. I yanked my hand back.

I looked down and down into the hole, thinking about the fish swimming around in that skin-searing cold, about the ache in my fingers where they'd got wet. About the water in Boulder Creek, which must've felt this cold to Delores when her whole body was suddenly under it.

When I turned back, there was Floyd Payne as I remembered him best, with a .38 in his hand. The gun was exactly the color of the slate sky and as glittery grey as the ice.

"So when were you plannin' to kill me, Lonny?"

"What the fuck you talkin' about?"

"You think I'm stupid. You was always a bad kid. Crazy. Crazier than your mom and she was whacko for sure. You didn't come out here for no social call."

I held my palms up.

"Hey, I'm gone, man, okay? I don't wanna mess with you. You kicked my ass too many times already." I took a step toward him. "Jesus, man, you lookin' at me like I'm some kind of maniac."

"You just stay right there."

"Hell, you can't shoot me. What're you gonna tell the cops? I come out here and threatened to steal your damn jig poles. Hey, please, man put the gun away."

"I know you, Lonny. If you took the trouble to track my ass down out here, there can't be but one reason."

"Lay the gun down and we'll shake hands and I'll be on my way. That's the God's truth, you hear me."

I took a risk and stepped toward him again. I knew then he wasn't gonna shoot me—no way—'cause he knew I was right— I'd given him no reason, no goddamn reason at all.

He stepped back again—one time too many—his heel came down on the edge of the power augur, which might not've mattered if we'd been on dry land, but on the ice, the augur slid out from under him and his back leg slid, too. The gun flew up in the air and came down a few feet away. For a middle-aged fat guy Floyd Payne could move fucking fast. He was up and charging me when my knee drove his lower jaw up into his sinuses. He fell back spewing blood and tried to crawl toward the gun, but I snatched up one of the jig poles and wound the monofilament line around his fat neck.

His eyes bugged out and he kicked over the bait box, lures and lines sliding all over. And, I swear, for the minute or two that we struggled, he did just about the finest fish imitation I've ever seen. Then he collapsed onto the ice, skidding on his butt like a fat woman gettin' fucked on satin sheets before he came to a stop and lay still. To the average person he would've looked dead, but I know dead when I see it, and he weren't.

I stood over him. Down there on the ice he looked so much smaller than the gun-toting asshole I remembered who once explained to me, after he'd beaten Delores, "Only way you keep a woman is through fear, Lonny. You got to keep 'em in fear."

His eyelids started to flutter. I bent down beside him, checked his pulse. "You're okay, Floyd. You'll live. And you know what else, I never told Delores about that time you beat the shit out of me 'cause I wouldn't let you play with my dick. I knew she wouldn't believe me anyhow, her thinking you loved her and all. I figured that was just between you and me."

His lips moved, all purple and blubbery, but no sound came out.

I walked over and picked up the gun off the ice, a nice little semi-automatic. Then I picked up one of the bait buckets and emptied it out. Brought it back over, dunked it down in the hole, then splashed the heart-stopping cold water over Floyd.

He screamed.

"You stay there and take it, you son of a bitch. Delores drowned herself in a fucking creek. You think this is cold? At least you can breathe. At least you ain't up to your neck in it."

I doused Floyd with water three or four more times, till the ice was starting to form on his eyelids and whiskers and his face looked like that fellow who tried to climb Everest and come back without any nose.

But I knew I wouldn't kill Floyd. I couldn't kill nobody. I wasn't that kind of man.

Floyd was starting to sit up, shake the daze off his brain. Which was a damn good idea, because if he didn't get warm, hypothermia was gonna set in real soon.

I walked over to where the bait box had got knocked over, scattering things every which way, and picked up the keys to Floyd's truck.

"Go get in your truck, turn the heat on high, and go home," I said, sounding stern and kind of ridiculous, like that guy who came round the prison one time, give a talk on how to put on a rubber.

I tossed him the keys, but he didn't get his hand up in time. The keys went over his shoulder, hit the ice, and skidded straight toward the hole. We'da been playing miniature golf, it've been a helluva shot. The keys plunked into the water. I threw myself at the hole and stuck my arm in all the way to the shoulder, but I knew it was too late—the keys were probably already in the mouth of some pike with evil eyes and a big grin on his face.

I turned back to Floyd. Shit, now what did I do?

"Dwop m' off at my house." The words came out smooshed and soggy as waterlogged potato chips. "Or'nto down. S'place can det 'arm."

Shit. I pondered it. Prayed on it.

Ponderin' told me one thing and prayer told another.

I said, *God, I take him with me, when I leave him off he'll sure as shit call the cops, which he's gonna do anyway, but now I won't have no time to get away. Plus he thaws out in my truck, he may start to get ornery, and I can't drive down a mountain and fight off Floyd, too, so I'd have to kill him anyway, wouldn't I?*

He looked at me. He knew what I was thinking. He started to blubber and babble and beg.

"I'm sorry, Floyd. Hey, man, really I am."

I turned and ran. He tried to follow but his clothes were already froze to the ice. He squirmed out of his ice-crystaled jacket. When I got into my car he was trying to rip his pants free of the ice.

Fuck, I thought. *This is fucked.*

I drove fast as I could down the mountain. About a half mile down the road, *it* started up. Felt like fish was nibbling just above the crack in my ass. I reached back to gouge the sensation away with my nails and the damn bees started up. Whole hivefuls erupted inside of my backbone and buzzed up the marrow toward my brain, and each bee felt like a chunk of molten rock as big as a dime, shearing off bits of vertebrae which plunked down into my bowels and made me feel like I was going to shit fire.

The craziness came over me. The same craziness that maybe killed Delores. I couldn't stay inside my skin. It wasn't even my skin. I was Floyd Payne. I was everyone everyplace everywhere. God help me, I was God and if that ain't the definition of crazy, I don't know what is.

The ice, the ice that I sprawled on, even that was on fire. My skin burned and a strip of wrist between my glove and my shirt that was in contact with the ice had frozen to it. Hypothermia was slowing everything down. I wasn't cold, I was beyond cold, meaning I was starting not to feel the cold anymore, to feel almost warm. Almost drowsy.

Oh, fuck, oh, fuck! A wall of trees loomed up, black and scary as jail bars. I swerved the car, careened from one lane to the next, and spun to a stop with a jolt that whiplashed my head so hard my eyeballs almost spun out my ears.

Then I sat there, half of me in my truck on the side of a snow-glazed road, the other half froze to the ice of Gem Lake, while the synapses in my brain turned to icicles and an invisible hatchet went to work on my fingers and toes.

I was dying of bee stings and Floyd Payne was dying of cold and I knew the only way to save myself was to get him off that ice.

I backed the truck up and started to turn it around. Suddenly I remembered—how could I have forgotten, like forgettin' there's a fifteen-year-old virgin with tits like honeydew melons and an ass pink and sweet as cotton candy in your bed, but I had—until now. I reached over and popped open the glove compartment. There it was, the pint of Jack Daniels.

Oh holy night! Sweet Jesus! Medicine and sacrament, liquid stronger and sweeter than anything ever poured out of a hot slut's pussy, and I swear I almost got an erection, so intense and so nasty the pleasure was.

I musta guzzled a third of the bottle before I pulled it away from my mouth, and by then my stomach was settling and the bees were shrinking and falling away just as sure as real bees you'd just zapped with Black Flag.

Floyd Payne no longer existed, either dead or alive. I was alone in the dark cell of my skull where, as long as I couldn't see out into anyone else's, I felt safe.

I was sane again.

At least for a little while.

AN HOUR later, at a bar in Grand Lake, I tried Julia's number again. Somebody picked up, and Andy's little kid voice asked "Who'zit?"

"Hey, it's Uncle Lonny. You 'member me? Lemme speak to your mom."

"Yeh," said Andy vaguely. A long pause, but he hadn't put the phone down 'cause I could hear his nasal breathing, like maybe he was gettin' over a cold.

"If your mom ain't home, lemme speak to your babysitter," I said, but I was already annoyed. What kind of babysitter lets a six-year-old kid answer the goddamned phone anyway?

"Wait here," Andy said. I heard him patter away, feet that must've been slippered thump-thumping on tile.

I waited, growing madder and madder, and then Andy came back to the phone. "She's out."

"Your mom or your babysitter?"

Silence while he tried to puzzle out the answer without asking Julia for help.

"Look, forget it," I said. "I'll call another time. Okay?"

"Okay."

"Love ya, buddy."

"Love you, too."

I hung up.

So she wasn't taking my calls now. What had the goddamn Seven Days at Venice people done to her anyway? Julia, who used to give head with the urgency of someone whose only source of air was through my dick. Who used to get on her knees with her ass in the air, head down on the pillow, and spread her butt cheeks wide open so I could inspect her while I greased up my cock and slid it into her rosy pink asshole.

Fuck Julia, there was plenty more pussy where she came from.

I thought of the packets of letters in my knapsack. Letters from Donna and Liz and MaryLynn. Hot, sexy bitches who had *I Cum for Cons* tattooed on their asses, who wanted my dick in all of their holes.

I sat down at the bar, ordered another Jim Beam.

Who was I kidding?

Weren't nobody I felt about the way I did Julia. Nobody 'cept Delores and now she was gone.

Chapter Seven

I CHECKED into a motel near Granby and tried to sleep, but soon as I lay down, guilt got ahold of me like one of them leg-hold traps, so I had no choice but to start gnawing my ankle off and go to work finishing up the bottle of Jack. Floyd Payne deserved what he got, I reminded myself. 'Sides I learned a long time ago, there's nothin' wrong with revenge if it's well-deserved and long overdue. 'Specially if it's over a woman.

Uncle Zack taught me that when I was fifteen. Now of all Delores's boyfriends when I was growing up, the one who came closest to being an all-round decent guy was Zack, so naturally—since he didn't beat her or break up the furniture or drink the rent money—she kicked him out after just a few months so's she could marry a douchebag named Claymore Epps. But Claymore hadn't come down the pike at this point, so things weren't as awful as usual.

Zack was shaped like a cinderblock, thinning grey hair spiking out in every direction, eyes like little insects buried in his skull. When he walked into a bar, you could see people get uneasy and look toward the exit. But when the bartender hurried over to see what he'd have, and Uncle Zack ordered a soda or (worst of all) a big glass of milk, you could feel everybody relax. Some even smiled.

They shouldn't have. Uncle Zack was one mean motherfucker. And if his peculiar taste in beverages embarrassed me as a kid, I was proud of his emerald green custom Harley, his naked lady tattoos, and the leather vest he wore almost always, decorated with grinning devils and teeth-baring angels and the words *Sober Souls* in black and red letters on the back. The Souls didn't do drink, do drugs, or lend out their old ladies. And Heaven help the S.O.B. who violated those rules.

One Saturday night when I was fifteen, Zack told Delores he had some business in Fort Collins and he wanted to take me along. I thought maybe we were going to a whorehouse, that maybe Zack thought it was time I lost my cherry, but I'd already done that—with an older woman of sixteen who was my babysitter when I was twelve.

Along the way we were joined by two more Sober Souls, C.J.

and Hank, both decked out in leather, both straddling big mean-looking Harleys.

We got on I-25 headed north and roared up toward Fort Collins. I rode with Zack. Along the way, he told me what we were going to do.

"We got a member, Gil Paugh, who went on a drunk last night. Beat up his old lady bad. We're gonna have a talk with him."

"About the drinking or the beating?"

"Both."

"I thought women liked rough stuff," I said, remembering the advice Floyd Payne had given me.

He roared almost louder than the Harley, "That's bullshit! Only an asshole and a coward says shit like that. You understand?"

I didn't. Not really. I knew Mom didn't like being slapped around by her men, but I also knew that, whether it was me they was beating or her, she wasn't in no hurry to leave. I also knew getting beat up gave her an excuse to call up her girlfriends and cry and get drunk. Maybe that part she liked. I thought Delores was stupid and weak, and I didn't know who I hated more—her boyfriends for beating her, her for taking it, or me for being too young to stop it.

Uncle Zack shouted into the wind, "We're gonna pull this S.O.B.'s badges. He won't take kindly to it. That's why I brought backup."

We left the highway at the first Fort Collins exit, zigzagged through streets at the south end of town before parking in a dirt driveway back of a run-down little house. Gravel yard stubbled with weeds. Reeking of food stamps and despair.

Zack walked to the back door and banged on it. Me, C.J., and Hank behind him. A big-busted woman with dyed blonde hair and a tank top without any bra under it stared out at us, eyes deader than somethin' you'd see on the wall of a hunting lodge. It was a look I knew too well: *Do what you want to. I don't give a shit.*

Her face was banged up. A front tooth was gone and an eye blacked. One side of her mouth looked puffy. She smelled of tequila and shame and of the two, the tequila was stronger.

"He ain't here," she told Zack.

"Then we'll come in and wait for him."

"Can't do that."

"We're doin' it, Babs," said Zack. "We're asking nice cause

we're good people, but we are comin' inside."

That look again: *Fuck you, do what you choose.* She stepped back from the door, losing her balance and reeling a little 'cause she was so drunk. We trooped in. The house was about two sizes too small for the whiskey and pussy smells that it held.

"Where's he at, Babs?" asked Zack.

She shrugged and poured herself another drink. Lit a cigarette. We started searching the house. Didn't take long—we just followed the sounds of the TV to the bedroom. He met us in the doorway. A big, mean-eyed fucker. Tattoos all over his bare, fleshy chest. Black handlebar mustache like the bad guy in a John Wayne movie.

"What're you guys doin' here?"

"We come to pull your badges," said Zack.

"What for? 'Cause I had a few drinks?"

"That," said Uncle Zack, "and Babs."

"Fuck Babs. She tell you what she did? We'd gone to Fanny's Pub for supper, and she was flirtin' up a storm with every man there. Then we go home and she wouldn't have sex with me. I'm her husband. I got my rights. 'T'weren't for that cockteasin' bitch, I wouldn'a had to drink in the first place."

"Listen, you asshole," said Zack, "you don't drink and you don't call your old lady a bitch."

"Bitch is too good for her. Fuckin' cunt."

C.J. started to move in, but Zack was closer and his fist got there first. Knuckles to cheekbone and a sound like a giant egg cracking. The guy didn't go down, didn't even sway. He punched back and Zack took it, and then C.J. and Hank and Zack was all pilin' into the room. Furniture flying, and somebody put a foot through the TV screen. Punching the guy till he went down flailin', then taking turns kicking the shit out of him.

Watchin' it all, I felt the anger rise up inside me like a hard-on, only tougher and huger than any boner I've ever had. I saw my chance and drove my boot into Gil Paugh's fat belly. It felt like stomping concrete, so I did it again. And again.

Gil Paugh was grunting and moaning and, incredibly, getting up off the floor. Which under these circumstances was not a smart thing to do. C.J. waited till his head was up high enough, then brought his knee up underneath the guy's chin. Sent him crashing into the wall and probably some other time zone. He oozed down to the floor and stayed there.

C.J. found Gil Paugh's Sober Souls jacket and ripped off the patches and insignia. I wanted Gil Paugh to wake up and start fightin' again. I wanted to get hit and then hit back double hard. It was like bein' so hungry for so long that you forget what hungry feels like, till somebody gives you some food and then not all the food in the world would be enough. Not all the punches and kicks in the world would be enough to get all the anger from inside me.

C.J. tossed the remnants of the biker jacket onto the floor.

"Where's Babs?" asked Zack.

"I think she went downstairs when the fight started," C.J. said.

"Go find her," said Zack to nobody in particular. "Tell her this asshole hits her again, we'll come back and hurt him this time." He looked around the destroyed bedroom. "We better clean some of this up 'fore we go. Lonny, go downstairs make sure Babs is okay. Tell her we did what we had to."

I nodded and tromped on downstairs. There was a big room with a pool table and big screen TV. Babs was sprawled out on the couch. One arm dangled over the edge of the couch and loosely held a bottle of tequila.

I noticed there was still some alcohol left, so I slipped the bottle out of her hand and took a drink. Good stuff, I thought. Too bad she went and passed out before she could finish it.

"Mrs. Paugh?"

I shook her arm.

I remembered the time a couple of years before when I found Delores passed out on the kitchen floor. She'd thrown up, so I cleaned her up, which meant I had to take off her shirt and while I was wiping her off with a wet paper towel, her nipples got hard and I touched her—just a little bit—but she woke up. I'll never forget the look she gave me.

But Gil Paugh's wife didn't say nothin', so I emptied the bottle in a half dozen big gulps. It went north to my head and south to my dick, and damn, if it didn't feel like an angel was giving me head.

"Hey, Mrs. Paugh. You okay?"

I shook her again. Not hard, but hard enough that her tits bounced side to side inside her T-shirt.

"Mrs. Paugh? Mrs. Paugh, you awake?"

Her T-shirt had ridden up over her belly so I could see a couple of inches of smooth, fatty flesh. I laid my hand down over her tit. She didn't move. I slid my other hand up under her T-shirt and rubbed her nipple in a circular motion. Her skin felt warm and damp.

Shit, don't do this, I thought.

"Mrs. Paugh? Babs?"

I pushed the T-shirt up so I could see her tits. White, meaty breasts pale as cookie dough under the tan of her bikini line. I put my mouth on the nipple, swirled my tongue around. I swear her tit tasted like tequila.

Then—I swear I didn't plan to do it, I didn't even realize I *was* doing it—but I opened her jeans and rolled them down and her panties down over her hips and off of one leg so I could open her up. She had a tattoo of a pink pussycat just above the pubic hairline and soft, fleshy thighs. I spit on my fingers and moistened her. My cock was throbbing so hard it felt like I might shoot my wad before I even touched her. I took it out and eased it inside her. All the while thinking, *what if she wakes up? What if somebody comes down here and sees? I'll get charged with rape*, but I couldn't stop by this time. My cock was like iron. There's something—don't know how to explain it exactly, but—something about fucking a woman who don't know you're fucking her. Not dead—I'm not one of those sickos that likes fuckin' 'em dead—but a woman dead drunk or unconscious and you know that when she wakes up her pussy might be a little sore or a little wet, but she'll never know for sure if somebody's fucked her. She'll never know who it was and it's like you've got this sick, terrible secret but every time you think about it, through your whole life, you get hard. You get hard just remembering.

I rammed myself inside her maybe half a dozen times and then I came so hard it felt like my brains was bursting out the end of my dick, and I pulled her jeans up again and pulled down her top and my secret was safe. I hadn't got caught, and I wouldn't have to pay for what I'd done.

At least I hoped not.

Chapter Eight

I HADN'T seen my sister Amber in almost five years. She and Delores didn't speak to each other. That was on account of the fact Amber ran away from the foster home she was living at when she was seventeen and came home to live with me and Delores and Delores's brand new husband Claymore.

Now Claymore was what I guess you could call a gore-may, which I guess could be funny since he had managed several of the most roach-ridden greasy spoons I've ever risked food poisoning in. But Claymore, he risked food poisoning all the time. He had these food allergies. If his fish wasn't fried just the right way or the beans were too stringy or the roast not up to par, he'd express his irritation by smashing the contents of the whole dinner table onto the floor. Sometimes he'd make his point even stronger, by pushing Delores down and trying to mop up the mess with her hair or making her gobble the ruined dinner right off the floor. If I tried to interfere, he'd beat me black and blue, but if Amber started to cry or begged him to stop, he'd back off a little bit.

Delores, of course, made excuses for Claymore's tendency to play with his food. It was his allergies, she explained. Due to some kind of defect—inbreeding maybe—Claymore's system was hypersensitive to all kinds of seasonings normal people don't even think twice about. Curry would make him gasp and break out in hives. And Heaven help anything didn't fit into the category of regular food got into his system. Delores said he'd almost died once from a bee sting.

"Claymore has to be cautious about what he eats," she said. "He puts the wrong thing in his mouth, he could *die*."

Too bad Claymore weren't allergic to his stepdaughter's pussy or we'da all been spared some bad times.

One night I come home and found Amber sitting on the sidewalk crying and her stuff strewn all over the front yard. Seems Delores had caught her making it in the bathtub with Claymore. Somebody had to go and it weren't gonna be Claymore.

That marriage lasted less than a year 'fore Claymore took off while Delores was at a treatment center in Grand Junction. Didn't take him long to hook up with Amber again and within a couple of years, they got married.

Didn't have a pot to piss in, either one of 'em, until Amber got lucky and was rear-ended by a rich lawyer drunk on his ass who settled with her for a bundle. First thing Amber did was go into therapy and then start divorce proceedings against Claymore, who'd turned out to be as big a shithole as a husband as he was as a stepfather.

Turned out, though, Claymore was harder to shake than one of his famous allergy attacks. Amber wrote me that, even after the divorce became final a few months ago, he still came around, hitting her up for money, threatening to try to get custody of the two kids on the grounds that she's crazy.

That weren't the truth, though. My sister weren't crazy. She was just a homebody type who liked to stay in her beautiful house and enjoy it. At least that's how she explained the fact that—'cept for that one time the kitchen curtains caught fire— she hadn't left the damned house in over three years.

Amber's house was one of them cookie-cutter deals—one of four different layouts and designs repeated over and over in a paint-by-the-numbers kind of subdivision that looked like the only folks who'd really like living there were Barbie and Ken. I swear when you went in there you needed to unwind a rope from the back bumper just to make sure you could find your way out. The streets all had similar names and ended in cul-de-sacs, and the kids and the dogs looked as cookie-cutter alike as the houses. After half an hour of driving around looking for Maple Tree Drive I was ready to smash my truck through some suburban yuppie's new picture window.

When I finally found Amber's street, I pulled over and shoved all the empty beer cans up under the seat and ate a roll of breath mints before I went to the door.

I knew she'd be home. I'd've been shocked if she wasn't. Says she can't leave the house without having an anxiety attack and feeling like she's going to pass out. Agoraphobia. I read up on it one time. She won't admit to having anything wrong with her. Makes all kinds of excuses—she's got allergies, it's too cold or too hot or too rainy. When she was married, her excuse was that Claymore liked her to stay home. Now she's divorced from the son of a bitch, doesn't seem like things have changed any.

Amber musta been watchin' me out the window 'cause before I could even knock, she opened the door. I tried not to show any reaction, but it was hard. Let me put it this way, my sister had changed. She hadn't just got fat, she'd gone straight to hell. That lean foxy face I remembered was so larded up I hardly recognized her. Her blonde hair was dyed red, her nails painted to match.

She threw her arms around me, held on to me for all she was worth. "Lonny, I can't believe it! God, but I've missed you. Come on in. Make yourself comfortable. Can I get you anything?"

"A beer would be good."

She brought me one and we sat in the living room together while the two kids, four-year-old Margret and five-year-old Bud, played some kind of board game. It seemed like an awful nice day for kids to be playing inside. I hoped this agora stuff wasn't hereditary.

"So how was the funeral?"

She turned away and fussed with her hair, which was sprayed so stiff and flat you coulda served tea off the top of her head. "I'm not real sure, Lonny. I didn't go."

"Fuck, Amber, our own mother, and you didn't go to the funeral."

She shot me a look. "Watch your mouth, Lonny. The kids."

"Sorry."

"I bought a nice casket. Mom's friend Edna—you remember, Edna volunteered at the homeless shelter—she picked it out, white with pink trim."

"I still think you ought to have gone. That or waited till I got out."

"Better you weren't there. Edna said it got kind of rowdy. Bunch of barflies showed up—her old drinkin' buddies come to pay their respects. A couple of 'em got in a fight, and the police had to come. That's Mom for you—only person in the world whose funeral turns into a bar brawl."

I laughed. "Well, she'da liked that. If you're gonna say good-bye to the dead, you might as well wake 'em, too." I set down my beer. "Another one of those would be nice."

"I was hopin' you'd quit."

"Can't," I said. "Things get strange when I quit. I stay drunk so that I can feel normal."

"Normal," said Amber. "Like you'd know what that was. Like

either one of us would."

"So can I have another beer or do I need to go buy a six-pack and come back?"

She brought me the beer. The kids playing their game on the floor snuck glances at me, wondering, I suppose, who this stranger was that had showed up out of the blue claiming to be their uncle.

"When was the last time you talked to Delores?"

"Mom, Lonny. Call her Mom."

"When did you talk to her?"

"Not for—God, Lonny, you know how it was. You know Mom and I hadn't spoken in years."

"She was willing to forgive you for what you did to her, you know. She told me."

"Forgive me? What about me forgiving her? She's the one threw me out on the street when she found out about me and Claymore."

"Well, what'd you expect her to do? He was her husband."

"I was her daughter."

"Well, shit, Amber, you musta liked it. You up and married the fucker after he and Delores split up."

"Oh you. You always took up for her. It's like you was blind where Mom was concerned."

"You stole her husband, you expect her not to get pissed?"

"Lonny, please. Margret, Bud, do Mommy a favor and take the game up to your room. This minute. I'm serious."

They did like she asked. Sulky, though, like they knew good and well they were missing important family stuff that they'd probably spend years of their lives talking to therapists about.

"Whatever Claymore and I did, I've paid for it, understand. A thousand times over."

"He still come around?"

"When he needs something. Money, mostly."

"Mostly."

"Or sex. Usually I say no, but once in a while—oh, hell, Lonny, I get so lonely."

"Yeah, it's hard to have a decent sex life when the only men you meet are the ones come to deliver pizza or Chinese."

She ducked her head down like she was going to take a sip of her tea and when she straightened her mascara had run and covered her face with what looked like prison bars.

"Oh hell, Amber, don't cry."

"You think it's easy? Makin' arrangements for the kids, gettin' people to come pick 'em up, take 'em here, take 'em there? What am I gonna tell them when they get older? They already ask why we never go anyplace. Everybody thinks it's my fault, but I—I can't go outside. I just can't."

I drained my beer, went into the kitchen and got another from a fridge overflowing with food. There was a phone, so I decided to call Julia. She didn't answer, but while I was letting it ring, I noticed Amber's telephone bill, which she'd left next to the phone. The usual shit, but then something I hadn't expected— there were two numbers listed that Amber'd had blocked, followed by the charge for that service. I jotted those two numbers down and went back in the living room.

"Claymore still managing restaurants?"

"Not exactly."

"What do you mean? He's managing one or he isn't?"

"He got fired from his last management job. He's still in the restaurant business, though."

"Where at?"

"It doesn't matter."

"I might want to look him up."

"I know what you want to do—cause trouble."

"Where's he work, Amber?"

"Leave it alone, Lonny. You just got out of prison. Why you wanna go back?"

"Hey, at least I'm a free man. You're still locked up."

"Dammit, Lonny, why're you so mean?"

"Fuck, I guess I was born that way."

"No, you weren't. You were the sweetest boy in the world, Lonny. You were—"

I was mad all of a sudden. Mad at Amber. Mad at her fatness, mad at her fucked-up head that kept her trapped in her own house, most of all mad because she didn't seem mad enough herself.

I stood up. "I gotta go. It gets dark, I'll never find my way out of this fucking neighborhood."

She started to cry again. Fat tears running down fat cheeks rolling down what passed for a neck but was really a series of chins. Amber used to be beautiful. Dammit, what had she done to herself? I wanted to hit her. I didn't.

Instead I got in my truck and found a pay phone where I called the two numbers Amber had blocked. One didn't answer. The other belonged to a place name of Dolly's Cantina.

I got directions from the spic I was talkin' to and headed that way.

Damned if Claymore didn't drive the same piece-of-shit Camry he'd had when he was married to Amber. I parked next to the Camry and waited and watched.

They were closing up shop. Two greaseballs and one asshole. The greaseballs were waiters. The asshole was Claymore. Amber had said he'd lost his last job, but she hadn't added he'd sunk all the way to scrubbing the kitchen floor.

I watched the greaseballs leave from where I was parked in the alley out back of Dolly's. Then I opened the back door, which weren't locked, and I walked in and greeted old Claymore, who was down in Julia's favorite position, on his hands and knees— only difference, he was pushing a scrub brush, not sucking my cock.

His glare was all belligerence and attitude as he got to his feet. "You here about the busboy job, it's been filled."

"Oh damn, I am so disappointed. Why that was my one goal in life to become a busboy at a fine establishment like this." I grabbed a mop from where it was leaned up against the sink and brought the end up under his chin so hard it musta rattled his eyeballs.

"Hey, asshole, I ain't no busboy. It's Lonny, your ex-stepson and ex-brother-in-law. Thought I'd stop by and have a bite with you."

I opened one of the big refrigerators and swept the contents of the top shelf out onto the floor. Strips of raw bacon and eggs that smashed on the floor, mixing in with the detergent suds to make a nasty ooze. I kicked him in the stomach so he doubled over and then brought my knee up under his chin. He went down on his back. I kicked him over onto his stomach so his face was in the suds, bacon, and eggs mix, and I kicked him in the butt and he skidded a few inches.

I stuck Floyd's .38 in his eye and said, "Lick it up. Remember that, Claymore? Remember how you used to do Delores when she didn't get dinner cooked right? So lick it up, you son of a bitch. Lick this fucking floor clean or it'll be your fucking brains on the floor 'stead of the eggs."

He started to lap. I straddled his back and kept the gun to the back of his head, riding him, giving his ear a little tap with the gun to keep his attention.

He started to snivel and weep.

"Lick it!" I screamed.

I made him lick the floor from one end to the next, raw egg ooze mixed up with cleaning suds, and by the time he'd got done with that, the game was losing its kick. I felt tired and wore out and every time I'd look down it'd look like Claymore was crawling over an ice-covered lake, licking up ice chips, 'stead of washing the floor with his tongue.

"Get up," I said. "Clean yourself up and get on outta here. You promise you won't hassle Amber no more."

He looked up, face twisted into a terrible mask, bits of food and soapsuds foaming over his lips so that he looked like a mad dog in a feeding frenzy.

"I promise."

"You fuck with her and I'll come back. You know I will."

"I—" Suddenly his face went the color of tripe. He bent over clutching his stomach. "Oh shit, oh shit."

I figured he was gonna throw up and I stepped back 'cause last thing I needed was get my boots shined with projectile puke.

He started to claw at his pants pocket. A really gross gesture, like he was trying to jerk off.

"I need—I need—help—"

He reached his other hand out to me.

The way Floyd Payne had done. That same gesture, desperate and pitiful. And that terrible fear that seemed to foul the air the way bad perfume does, I could feel the stink settle into my clothes and my hair and my soul.

If I let myself, I could almost feel sorry for him.

The tingling didn't come at the base of my spine, but just the faintest sensation between my eyebrows. Like electric lips had just kissed me there. A reminder from something that wasn't altogether dead in me yet.

"Shit, get up already," I said. I grabbed his hand and helped haul him onto his feet. He stood there for a second, making this weird underwater sound from way down in his throat. Then he pitched forward and landed face first in a big pile of egg froth and cleaning suds, and he went into convulsions like that time he got bee stung only this time it was like his body was being jerked around on puppet strings, and the last time his back arched, I swear I thought that his spine would snap, but his heart musta stopped first, 'cause he made this terrible gurgling sound and rolled over with his face in the suds and then he lay still.

I walked over and put my hand on his head and damn if he weren't dead already.

Then I fished in his pants pocket and saw what he'd been trying to get to was an inhalant—the kind I remembered him using to help him breathe that time he had a reaction to Delores's meatloaf.

I picked up the box of cleaner he'd been using and saw it contained something called trisodium phosphate. Now I don't know what that is or if it's fatal to everybody or just those with bad allergies, but it'd sure done a job on old Claymore.

Cleaning suds. Shit. Or hell, maybe it weren't that at all. Maybe the bacon was bad.

I thought about Amber. She was gonna be pissed. Not pissed enough to call the cops on me, I hoped, but pissed.

My hands shook. I started to scream. "This is your fault for being an asshole! You made me do this! You made me!"

I kicked Claymore's corpse in the ribs. In the teeth. In the head. Kicked and kicked and kicked until the cleaning suds near his body were bright red and the toe of my boot and the floor was all streaked with red.

Claymore, you fucker, this is your fault!

It was starting to snow when I left Dolly's place, and the only liquor store I came to was closed, so I smashed one of the windows and grabbed a bottle and ran. Jim Beam didn't give a shit if Claymore was dead.

After a while, I didn't either.

Chapter Nine

I LEFT Glenwood that night and headed back toward Boulder. Toward Nederland, too, and Julia.

It started to snow when I got to Vail Pass and got worse as I kept going east. By the time I went through the Eisenhower Tunnel, the night was made up of a zillion white dots—enough to make your brain ache—and all of it in insane, twisting motions. Twirling, swirling, spiraling. Like each snowflake was alive and angry and tryin' to break into the car, snow dancing and spinning, making me dizzy, sick to my guts. Big angry flakes of snow— white hornets—and when I turned on the high beams it got worse—glittering pinwheeling snow hurtling into the windshield like Fourth of July candles going off.

I cut off the brights and slowed down some, cause dependin' on how I focused my eyes, there was either an outside world beyond the curtains of snow or there was nothing in all of Creation but just me and the black hole of the night sucking in a galaxy of snowflakes.

I grabbed a beer from the six-pack on the seat next to me, popped the top with my teeth, wishing it was Julia's nipple instead, and took a deep angry swig.

If Delores was alive, I would've phoned her up, told her what I had done, but I couldn't so I figured I'd try—one more time— callin' Julia. Damn but I missed that girl!

I wished I had one of them car phones. Wished I could dial Julia's number from here in the dark, hear her sugar voice purr over the phone, tell me she loves me, she wants me, come on home, Lonny baby, it's all right, I'll suck your dick till it falls off. And the snow would've stopped swirling and the dark would have dimmed to somethin' manageable, somethin' I could see past.

Somewhere just north of Idaho Springs, I pulled into a Conoco and stood freezing my ass off, fumbling for change so I could dial Julia's long-distance number. Like always, her machine picked up and I told her get her ass to the phone, it was me, it was Lonny, but she didn't pick up. Here it's ten thirty Saturday night and Julia's not home, and then I thought, wait a minute, what about Andy, Andy's got to be there with a babysitter. Unless Julia *is* home. Unless she can't come to the phone 'cause she's got her legs up in the air. I slammed the phone into the cradle so hard it bounced off. I left it dangling and went back to the truck and drove north faster than any sane person would go.

Damn women, I thought, why ain't they ever there when you need 'em? Why can't you trust 'em? Why is their goddamn skin the only bridge between hell-on-earth and just earth? Why is sex the only way that God lets people taste Heaven and then, just like any other rotten, fucked-up dad, he takes it away? And then, ever after that, dangles it, dangles it, the prospect of peace, the solace of Beaver Heaven, like a promise that never comes true.

A kaleidoscope of snowflakes launched themselves at the truck. Made me half-drunk to look at 'em. Made the road out there seem like a memory, a dream.

Then *he* come out of the dark on the left side of the car. I saw him and hit the brakes, but I already knew and he did, too, I could hear the knowledge of death spreading over his mind like dark water, a small death that preceded the real one by a tenth of a second.

I *knew* him. Felt him. Smelled his blood and his fear and his life.

Then I hit him.

He was big with a huge spread of antlers and the impact knocked the car sideways. I braked hard and the car went screaming into a skid that took me over into the left lane and then back to the right. It came to a stop and I jumped out and ran back to where the force of the impact had thrown him.

His huge eyes were open and blood was leaking out of his nostrils. Part of his tongue dangled out of his mouth and a front leg was bent underneath him. The snow fell on his open eyes and melted. I reached over and closed them. Then I started to sob.

I'd never hunted. I thought hunters were lower than dirt and I always prayed the guy who thought he was taking aim at a buck would actually blow the balls off his buddy. I'd never willfully hurt any animal. But here I'd killed a deer, a creature of God, and I knelt in the snow by his body and sobbed. I could kill men, but I couldn't kill a deer, even accidentally, and live with myself, and I knew why: because a deer was a creature of God with no ego and no evil in its heart, and men, it seemed to me, always teetered on the line between love of self and salvation.

I tried dragging the carcass off into the woods, but he was too heavy and I only succeeded in moving him a few feet. I wanted to bury him, but the ground was froze solid and I had nothing to dig with.

Finally I just knelt by his body and said a few prayers. For his soul, which I knew was safe because I'd felt it depart, and for my own, which I weren't nearly so sure about.

Then I got back in the car and drove on, and I tell you, it was the strangest drive I ever took in my life, because all the while, the deer's soul stayed with me.

I knew it was him, that he was traveling with me a little while because what I'd done was an accident and I mourned him. His soul got lighter and lighter as I drove north. I knew he was moving on, and with every mile I knew more intensely that he had forgiven me.

I had killed him and he had forgiven me.

My eyes were so full of tears I couldn't drive, so I pulled over to the side of the road, put my head down on the wheel and cried. Forgiven. Just the notion of it, just the word made me shake. At first I thought it was forgiveness I wanted—from Delores and Julia, from Floyd and from Claymore, all the people I'd hurt, all the folks I had disappointed, the probation officers who believed I could turn it around, the judges who let me off easy, the sponsors I'd had in AA who spent night after night reading the Big Book with me. Then I realized it wasn't so much their forgiveness I wanted, but to be able to forgive those that had wronged me. To let go and leave it in God's hands and set free their souls.

Forgiveness.

What a balm it would be to my heart.

But I couldn't.

I wouldn't.

To forgive would mean letting go of my hatred and rage, and those I clutched with more passion than ever I'd held on to a woman.

I drove on through the night and presently I felt the soul of the deer detach itself from my body and move on. It grew very distant and its touch very faint and when it was gone, I was emptier.

I'D MEANT to drive straight into Boulder, but I was needing a drink, so I stopped in Golden at a biker bar called The Rebel Yell.

First thing I did after orderin' a beer, I went to the pay phone and called Julia. The fucking recording came on again, and I slammed the phone down. Dammit, I knew she was there! Where would she be this time of night, at a prayer meeting for God's sake?

I went back to the bar, ordered a shooter, and reached into my pants pocket to pull out a crumpled sheet of purple paper. Liz always wrote on purple paper with little penguins in a row at the top. She was the one sold cars for some outfit in Thornton and liked country music and car racing and smoked Marlboro Lights. My kind of gal.

I hope to meet you sometime in the near future, she wrote in handwriting so spikey and sharp, looked like she was drawing a picket fence. *I hope you won't be disappointed with me. I know how hard it must be where you are and I can only say how much I admire you for having the courage to make up for your mistakes.*

Even when two people don't meet right off, I think a lot of affection can develop just the same and...

"Love letter?"

I turned around. The woman who'd slid onto the bar stool next to mine was at least ten or fifteen years older than me. She'd lived hard, you could tell. Deep lines mapped her face and her voice had a brittle edge to it so the words sounded like dry twigs popping, but her tits were centerfold-sized and her dark-rooted hair curled wavy and blonde around her face.

"Don't tell me you're sitting here getting shit-faced moonin' over some love letter from a gal who ain't here when you could be talkin' to one who is."

I folded the letter up, guilty as if I had stole it. "It's from my mother," I blurted, before I realized how sappy that sounded. "She's been real sick."

"I'm sorry to hear that, baby." She motioned the bartender. "Another round here. This boy's got a sick mama."

I reached for my wallet. She put a hand on my wrist, letting her fingers whisper close enough to my crotch that if I'd done it to her, she'd prob'ly of slapped me.

"Naw, baby, this is on me. Name's Barbara. You can buy the next round."

So we sat there knocking back shooters. I found myself telling her about Julia, about how she'd let me down by not writing or taking my calls after I went to prison, and she made me feel good by saying what a dumb bitch Julia must be to give up somethin' as hot-looking as I was. I knew it was just a game, she was just another gutterslut lookin' to get laid, but still I lapped up her flattery the way Julia used to do cum.

She was too drunk to drive—or said she was anyhow—so I drove her back to her place, an efficiency next door to a Liquor Mart, which she said, only part joking, I think, was the reason she'd moved there.

First thing she did was turn the TV on. We sat on the bed and pretended to watch some old late-night movie. I unbuttoned her blouse and fumbled around at the back of her bra, feeling angry when I couldn't get it open right off, but then she unsnapped it herself at the front. She had big, soft, comforting tits that reminded me of tires just a little low on air.

"You're a nice boy," she said. "You're real cute."

"Cute is for Bambi."

"Well, cute-*looking*, I mean. I know you been around the block, hon."

"Cell block," I said, trying to make a joke.

Her eyes narrowed a bit. They were blue and close-set and outlined thickly in black, so they looked more like doll eyes than real ones. "You mean you been in prison?"

"Yeah, but hey, that was a long time ago, and besides, I didn't do it."

"That's what my ex-husband used to say."

"Well, I'm not your ex-husband, so relax."

She lay back, her tight skirt riding up to show off plump, pretty thighs. "Cut the light off, would you, hon?"

"Naw, I want to see you. Pretty girl like you, don't tell me you're shy."

I got on top of her, kissing her tits, kissing my way down her belly which had pale, silvery stretchmarks, not ugly at all but kind of like the icicles you put on a Christmas tree. I pushed her skirt down over her hips.

Down to the edge of her underpants.

Stopped.

"Somethin' wrong, hon?"

I just stared.

"Hon? What is it, you don't like my pink pussycat?"

"You said your name's Barbara. Anybody ever call you anything else?"

"Honey, I been called *lots* of things."

"I mean, something besides a nickname. Your *real* name."

"Well, Babs. My husband—he called me Babs. But that was a long time ago."

"So you were Gil Paugh's wife?"

"Yeah, in another lifetime. Small fucking world."

I rolled off her. "No fucking joke."

Her hand slithered down and she started to open my fly. I grabbed her wrist.

"What's wrong, hon? You don't want that?"

"Look, I've changed my mind. This don't feel right. I gotta go."

"What? You a friend of Gil's or something? Look, hon, we were divorced over ten years ago and I ain't seen the son of a bitch since."

I sat up. "Yeah, whatever, I still gotta go."

"I know what it is. You're not feeling guilty about Gil. It's that gal with the purple stationery you're thinking about." She reached between my legs. "Hate to tell you sugar your dick's not thinking about her."

"It's not that."

A picture flashed through my head—Delores passed out on the floor in her own vomit, and me taking her blouse off and washing her off, and she wouldn't wake up and I was too little to pick her up off the floor, and I knew I should cover her up again, cover her up, and—then I was seeing Babs that day at Gil Paugh's house and what heaven it had been when I slid my dick into her, when I knew I was doing this and she'd never know—and now I saw Delores and now Babs, now Delores...

"Hon, are you crying?"

"Look, I gotta tell you something."

And I told her, I told her everything, and she didn't remember me, she said, had no memory at all of a teenaged boy come into the house with the men, but she remembered that day and what had led up to it, how Gil had wanted sex and she'd said no 'cause she wasn't on birth control, she'd forgot to pick up her scrip for more pills, but Gil said he was gonna fuck her anyhow and she fought him and he beat her up, but they didn't have sex, and—

Her blue doll eyes changed. They got small and rattlesnake mean, and my hard-on shriveled away like she'd held a match to it. I couldn't believe I was scared of a woman. I wanted her gone then. That minute.

"You bastard. You fucking bastard."

"Hey, I'm sorry," I said. "I only told you 'cause I feel bad about it now. It was wrong and I'm sorry, but that's why I can't fuck you. This was a big mistake. I gotta go."

I started to stand up. She grabbed me by the shoulders and threw me back on the bed and put her weight on me, and I knew I should hit her, throw her off me, do something, but I was too scared to move.

"Do you know what you did to me? Do you fucking know what you did?"

She started shaking me. The back of my head cracked against the headboard of the bed.

"I never understood how I coulda got pregnant. I thought Gil musta done it weeks back, the last time we'd had sex, but it always felt strange, the *baby* felt strange, like somethin' evil growing inside of me. Now I know why."

She shook me harder, and still I felt paralyzed, like her voice had wrapped itself around me like chains. "You fucking bastard, you raped me, you ruined my life, that child ended up with social services. She brought me nothin' but misery!"

She hit me and I hit her back. She flew off the bed and I jumped up and got on top of her and hit her again and again. I mean, I had no choice really. I had to defend myself, didn't I?

I found a half-full pint of Scotch set down next to the bed, and I drank it and got dressed. When I left she still hadn't moved, but I don't think she was dead.

I'm sure she weren't dead.

But if she was dead, it wasn't my fault. I didn't mean to. I had to defend myself, didn't I?

Chapter Ten

TWO DAYS after I ran into Babs, the sun was out bright and the snow had almost all melted, and I had drove back to Boulder. I stood across the street from the homeless shelter and looked through a book about the totem animals of Native Americans that I'd bought a few hours earlier on the Pearl Street Mall. Every few seconds I'd glance up at the door of the homeless shelter, scan the windows and the little alleyway between the shelter and the used clothing store next door to it and then go back to my reading.

The deer symbolizes...

...means...

A middle-aged Hispanic woman with a face as shiny and blank as an aluminum frying pan and a slutty sway to her fat-larded hips came up the block, paused like she was lookin' to see was anyone lookin' at her, let her shoulders sag and shuffled into the shelter.

...means...

A city bus pulled up and let off a raggedy-looking geezer looked like he'd been on a diet of Antabuse and Thorazine a couple of weeks.

I crossed the street and called over to the guy. "Hey man, I'm lookin' for somebody to help me haul wood. You interested?"

He acted like he didn't hear, so I repeated the offer. "How much you payin'?" he said.

"Six bucks an hour."

"How many hours work?"

"Four or five—plus lunch."

He stewed on this. I wondered if I should be offerin' a severance package and benefits, the indigent bein' the uppity lot that they are these days, but finally he must've consulted his day planner and since no golf or tennis was planned at the country club, decided he might as well help haul the wood.

He slid in the truck next to me. With him came a God-awful odor of beef stew and B.O. and nicotine.

"What's your name?" I asked, just to be sure.

"Dabney." Just the name juiced up my spine like a cattle prod'd been put to my ass. "Where we goin'?" he asked.

"I live a ways outta town," I said. "Don't worry. You're on the clock."

We drove. Neither one of us said much. I'd slipped the tape of that night I got beat up into my brain and was playin' it over and over, working myself into a rage-trance, pretending the wheel was his turkey neck.

At the outskirts of town, he started to fidget. I wondered if he was nervous 'bout where I was takin' him.

"Not much farther," I said, but that wasn't what he meant.

We were passing a seedy strip mall with your usual greasy spoon at one end, laundromat at the other, and discount liquor store in between. He rolled down the window and stuck his head out the way a dog does.

"How about we stop here for a sec? Get a little nip to start off the day?"

"You do that on your own time after I pay you."

"I'll work better with a little somethin' to settle my stomach," he said slyly. I imagined I could hear the saliva swishin' around in his mouth at the thought of a drink, but then again, maybe it was my own.

"Got a bottle in the glove compartment," I said.

He was thirsty. I had to practically wrestle the bottle away from him 'fore he emptied it. Then I wiped the neck on my coat and took a swallow myself. It burnt a hole in my belly that traveled all the way down to my dick and I started to get an erection. Because here I was by myself with ol' Dabney Bowles. I wasn't eleven years old anymore and he wasn't a two-hundred-pound bruiser. For once, things were going my way.

With the liquor in him, he got chatty. "Bet you think all my money goes for liquor," he said. "Bet you think I'm an old alcoholic bum lives on the street, eats at soup kitchens."

"No," I said, "I think you're Donald Trump and Halloween's late this year."

"I could get me a wife, I wouldn't be in this fix," he went on. "Money wouldn't go for booze then, it'd go to pay the bills. I could put a little somethin' away. Bein' all alone, not havin' nobody leads to bad habits."

"Don't you mean you need a wife so's you'd have somebody to beat the shit out of? Maybe a kid or two besides. Sendin' a few people to the hospital, I bet that'd brighten your day."

"Naw, I just wanna home. A wife who'll keep me off of the

booze."

I saw a clearing where the snow didn't look so deep I'd have to worry about getting stuck. I pulled over.

"Get out," I said. "We're gonna walk."

"Soon's I get back on my feet, I'm gonna get me a place of my own. Then I can start seein' women. A woman, she don't like it if a man don't have a place of his own."

"So you like to fuck women?"

"Don't you? Hey, you ain't queer or nothin'? Naw, you don't look queer. I can tell. There's a coupla queers at the shelter. I don't stay there if I see they got a bed. Can't be too careful with your asshole when them perverts is around."

We walked a few paces into the woods. "You know who I am?"

"You didn't say and I don't rightly care."

"I'm Lonny Flynn."

"So?"

"You sent me to the hospital when I was eleven years old. You beat the shit out of my mother."

"I think you got me mixed up with somebody else. I don't know your mother and I don't know you."

"Delores Flynn. When you knew her, she lived in Boulder off Twenty-Eighth Street. Chink restaurant on one side. Lube job joint on the other. The two of you shot up together."

He studied the ground. "How much further we gotta walk? These shoes they give me at the shelter don't fit me worth shit."

I grabbed him by his shoddy jacket and slammed him up against a tree so hard that snow shook loose from its branches and fell onto his head. "You fucker, when I get done with you, you'll be lucky if you *can* walk."

I punched him in the face. He fell back onto the ground, blood from his split lip staining the snow. I walked over and kicked him in the kidney. He moaned and rolled over, clutching himself.

"You feel better? That make you feel better?" he wheezed.

"Fuck yeah, it makes me feel better."

I kicked him again. "Makes me feel so much better I might do this all day."

Except that it didn't feel anywhere near as good as I expected it to. I kept waiting for God to send down the bees, but God was elsewhere today. I didn't feel myself sliding inside the old douchebag's skin, didn't feel my mind flowing into the crepe-paper nooks of his addled-pated brain. Didn't feel much of anything at all.

I pulled out the .38.

"You gonna kill me?"

"I sure as sin should."

He licked the blood off his lips. "Well, go on then. I don't give a shit."

"Yeah, right. You're as scared of dying as anyone else."

"You think so, huh?" He hauled himself up off the ground, spat some blood. "Look, asshole, I don't recall beatin' you up, but seein's how you turned out, I'm sure you had it comin'. That Delores bitch, now *her* I'm rememberin' now. It's comin' back to me. She was that loony who heard voices, lived on another planet half the damn time. Yeah, Delores. How could I forget a fucked-up bitch like Delores?"

"Shut up!" I backhanded him so hard his jaw popped.

He staggered backward and bumped into a tree and just leaned up against it, shooting me a loony, lopsided grin with a dribble of blood leaking from it.

"Hit me all you want. Can't hurt me. The booze melted my nerves a long time ago. I could be lyin' on a feather pillow with you kissin' my dick—it wouldn't feel a goddamned bit better."

My hand was hurtin' where I'd punched him earlier. It was cold as a witch's cunt and a sharp wind was kickin' my balls.

"You are one pathetic old wreck. You ain't fit to piss on."

"You wanna piss on me, go right ahead. Take a dump on me, too. You'll be dumpin' on yourself you sick fucker."

"I ain't nothin' like you."

"You *are* me, you dumb asshole. You kill me, you die, too."

"Shut up."

I couldn't believe I was runnin' out of steam. All the nights I'd fantasized about this moment, about catchin' up to Dabney Bowles someday and kickin' his ass from here to hell, givin' him every inch the beating he gave me and more. Makin' him *feel* what I felt and *know* what I knew.

Only now I was just cold and tired and Jim Beam was cooin' to me from the glovebox in the voice of a sweet, horny slut. I needed a drink. I needed the safety of that dark, closed-in cell no wider than the distance between my ears.

"Fuck you," I said. "You ain't worth killin'. You ain't worth dirtying my hands."

"You take me back now, you're even stupider than you was as a kid. You think I'm gonna tell folks I fell down. You think I won't have the cops on your tail? Shit, you're as dumb and dotty as your mom was."

"I said shut the fuck up."

I grabbed him by the collar and shoved him ahead of me. He walked a few paces. Turned around.

"Yeah, it's all comin' back to me now. Your dippy old whore of a mother. She wasn't cookin' on all the front burners, but she sure as shit knew how to suck cock."

"Shut up and walk!"

"I 'member one time when she was drunk as a sailor, I brought home four of my buddies from work and lined 'em all up with their pants open and their dicks hangin' out. She didn't even have to be told what to do, she got down on her knees and let every one of 'em face-fuck her. An' you know what, she loved it. She lapped up their cum off the floor like a cat lappin' up cream.

"You know what she tol' me one time?"

"I don't give a shit."

"You was on the football team, weren't you? When you was in high school?"

"Yeah."

"That equipment you needed didn't come cheap. New uniform, helmet, knee pads. Your mom ever tell you how she paid for it?

"Naw, I reckon she wouldn't've. Your coach, I don't recollect the man's name, but I do recall seein' him—in your Mom's bed, he was boinkin' her brains out and she was hollering fuck me harder, fuck me deeper, and then he commenced to slappin' her on her behind. You shoulda heard her squeal then and he just kept spankin' her harder and harder till her butt cheeks got all red and she was cryin' but I didn't interrupt 'cause I liked watchin' too much. I didn't even bring it up to her—I knowed she was a whore when I met her—"

"I swear to God, if you don't shut up—"

"—but she tol' me one time why she fucked him. It was to pay for your uniform and then after that she fucked him a few more times, to keep you on the team 'cause you was such a piss-poor wuss of a player. You didn't like gettin' hit. You didn't like when the bigger boys fell on you. You'd come home cryin' to mommy and she'd take you in her arms, her all boozed-up and out of her mind, tits bouncin' around on her chest like peach-colored balloons, I wonder could she even tell the difference between you and one of her boyfriends—"

"You motherfucker, I'll—"

His voice had changed—it was a scary, sing-songy lisp— nothin' human about it. He was butt-ugly before but now his face shriveled and his cheekbones caved in where the teeth were gone. His face bones moved under the skin like the branches of tiny Japanese trees all bent into tortured positions.

His mouth pruned up and bloody spittle flew out of it.

"Shut up, Dabney, shut up while you still—"

"Oh I'm shakin'. Shakin' in my shoes. You tell me I'm pitiful. That you'll give me another chance out of the goodness of your goddamned heart. Look at yourself, a mama's boy who's spent his whole life tryin' to get back in the same hole he come out of."

I pulled the .38 out of my jacket and took two steps forward and put it to his forehead and fired three times, till, from the mouth up, there weren't nothin' left of his head.

I went back to the truck and drove into town and headed for Gary's Tavern. God didn't say nothin', God only watched, and I felt so rageful at Dabney Bowles I wished he was alive so I could kill him again. 'Cause he'd tricked me. The old bastard wanted me to kill him. That had been his revenge. Puttin' his blood on my head along with the others.

I drove and drove and the world looked six shades of black.

Then I got to the bar and had six shots of tequila and damn, if all the color didn't come back.

Chapter Eleven

AFTER DABNEY fucked me over like he did, I spent the afternoon and part of the night drinkin'. Met some guys from Fairplay, did a couple of lines. Played some pool and tried Tommy's chiropractor scam on a girl with a black eye who'd come to the bar to hide out from her husband. She didn't buy the chiropractor routine and when her old man showed up lookin' for her, she trotted off with him nice as you please.

Women, I thought. *Whether they're cryin' for help or cryin' for more, it all comes out sounding the same.*

I left Gary's toward dusk, buzzed but not blind, and headed for Nederland. Canyon Road, from Boulder to Nederland, was slick as a frozen waterslide. Tree branches, brittle-looking as bone, clawed up at a fat, streetlamp-yellow moon. I passed the turnoff for Magnolia Road, where Delores and I lived for a few months when I was seven or eight. I used to play in these dark woods, to pretend I was an Indian escaped from the white jail, on my way back to my tribe. Tired and hungry and lost, but determined to make it to a safe place. Determined to find my way home. The way I felt now.

Snow was fallin' by the time I reached Nederland. Highway 119 was eerie, untraveled, the night all black ice and cold silence. Finally the truck was skidding so bad that I parked on the edge of the highway and hiked on up the road. Julia's cabin was a good quarter mile back from the highway, but it coulda been ten miles and I'da still got there. That's how eager I was, how hungry for just the sight and the smell and the taste of her.

When I saw her house with its frosting of icicles and smoke curling out of the chimney, I broke into a run and banged on the front door. Inside, I could hear the TV on and Andy babbling along with the show the way kids will do, repeating everything the characters said after them. I tried the door, but it was locked, which pissed me off. Way I see it, a locked door is a door askin' to be kicked in. I heard footsteps and a "Who is it?" but before I could answer, Julia had opened the door.

She was wearing jeans and a thin purple sweater that showed more of her breasts than it covered and her eyelashes were stuck together at the edges in little black clumps, like she'd been wearin' the same mascara for a couple of days. Her blue eyes were glassy and bright as the ice on the road I'd drove up on.

She swallowed and then she said "Lonny" like for a second she might've forgotten my name.

I'd planned this moment for so long, the first look at each other, then the hot frantic groping at each other's clothes, the wildfire kisses, the hardness of Julia's nipples and the wetness between her legs. Now the fantasies seemed as pointless and stupid as a teenage boy jerking off to the picture of a movie actress. I felt like I'd come to the door selling magazines and this lady was tryin' to figure out a nice way to send me on my way.

"What'sa matter? You ain't glad to see me? You got my letter, didn't you? You knew I was gettin' out?"

She nodded—yes, yes, *yes*—the whole time I was talking.

"You gonna keep me standin' here or you gonna ask me in?"

"Oh sorry. Come on in, honey." She stepped away from the door. Just that moment she'd been standing there snow had got in her hair. The flakes sparkled for an instant and then melted away, leaving damp little strands.

"You know how I am, Lonny. All scatterbrained. You caught me by surprise. I wasn't expectin' you. I thought you'd call first."

"I *did* call. About a fuckin' million times!"

"I musta been out."

"Where the hell at? Where the hell could you *be* at two in the goddamned morning?"

"That's really none—"

"Uncle Lonny!"

I heard a shriek and then fifty pounds of six-year-old leaped into my arms. I hugged him. "Hey, how's my cowboy? How's my man? You been takin' good care of your mama?"

He giggled and grinned. He was a pretty little kid. Dimples and peach-colored skin. Big blue eyes like his mama.

I tossed him up in the air. Caught him and tossed him again.

"Not too rough," Julia said.

"Do it again!" Andy shrieked.

We went into the living room. A fire was roaring, and I sat close beside it, thawin' my bones. Julia brought me coffee. Just coffee. I figured there weren't no use askin' for booze, she didn't drink anymore.

Julia sat down across from me on the futon. She made a nervous little gesture of tugging her sweater shut, but the fabric was wore out and the top of her big tits still showed.

"I'm so sorry about your mama," she said.

"She was a good woman."

Julia looked at the floor.

"I talked to her on the phone right before it happened. She said you'd been by with Andy. Two of you chatted awhile."

"Yeah."

"So close to her doin' what she did, I wonder what was it y'all talked about. She say anything, do anything, give you any idea what was wrong?"

"Not a thing, Lonny. She'd been drinkin', but nothin' unusual about that. She was all happy you were comin' home."

"Well, now that's funny. She was so happy I was comin' home, why you s'pose she'da called me up that same day that you and she visited, tried to talk me into stayin' there in jail. Hey, look at me, will you? The answer ain't there in the fire."

"I got no idea what was on your Mom's mind, Lonny. Maybe she'd decided what she was gonna do and didn't want you gettin' out and doin' somethin' crazy on account of it. Your mom wasn't well. She heard voices, you know."

"Yeah, well, guess what? I'm hearin' voices now, too. And it's tellin' me that somethin' ain't right here. You're not glad to see me. You act like I'm some poor relation come by for a loan. And you expect me to believe you and Delores visited just a few days before she killed herself, but nothing, *nothing*, seemed even the least bit wrong?"

"How would I know, Lonny? She was *drunk*."

"I'm drunk, too, so the fuck what?"

"Stop shouting. You're scaring Andy." I looked around and saw Andy had crept around to the door that led into the kitchen.

He was standing there, shifting from one foot to the other like he needed to pee, eyes as big and scared-looking as his mother's. I hated the look of fear on his face, but I couldn't get my voice to go lower. "What the hell is he scared of? What the hell are *you* scared of, Julia? Now I'm an ex-con, what is it, am I some kinda monster? I ain't good enough for you all of a sudden. Goddamn it, talk to me!"

"Lonny, you come here like this. Unexpected. Catch me by surprise. I *am* glad to see you. Honest, honey. You're like a brother to me."

"Like a brother?" I leaped up, grabbed her by the shoulders and shook her till her head rocked back and forth "What about the letters, Julia? What about the goddamn letters?"

"I *told* you things had changed, didn't I? I told you I found the Lord, that I saw the devil had been tempting me, that I'd been a lost sheep."

"And who am I now? The devil? Tempting you to unlock the goddamn holy padlock on your pussy? Is that it?"

"For God's sake, Lonny. Andy's right here."

"Then tell him to go to his room!"

"Andy, honey, you better do like Uncle Lonny says. Go on to your room." She tried to pull loose, but I held on. "What's wrong with you, Lonny? You let go of me."

"I'll let go when I'm good and ready. And I don't think I'm ready yet. Now tell me the truth. Why did Delores kill herself. She musta said something. You must know something."

"I don't know *anything*. Now you let me alone. I was happy for you to be free, but now I don't know. Maybe your mama was right. Maybe you're better off locked up."

I whacked her across the face with my open hand. She fell back into the chair which tilted and almost turned over with her, except I caught her arm, yanked her forward, and smacked her again.

"You don't want me to kiss you, maybe you want somethin' else. Maybe you want me to force you, so you can explain to Jesus that it wasn't your fault. He made me do it, Lord. He fucked me against my will. It wasn't my fault."

"Lonny, stop it!"

"What about the letters, Julia? What about how much you used to love me, how much you loved spreading your legs for me. You were never anything but a whore and now you think you're God's fucking gift. Well, you're not. But if you don't want to take responsibility for fucking me, then I'm gonna let you off the hook with God, 'cause I *am* gonna fuck you, Julia, whether you want it or not."

"Let go of me!"

I grabbed her and shoved her ahead of me into the kitchen, where the smell of pot roast was coming from and I took a little tour. Pot roast in the oven, candied yams and turnip greens cooking on the top.

"Who's the dinner for, Julia? Who're you cookin' dinner for? Who?"

Her eyes got huge with fear. She looked past me, over my shoulder and said, "No, no, oh no, please don't do that," and I thought she was talkin' to me until an arm 'bout as big around as a tree trunk clamped down around my neck and commenced to crushing my windpipe.

I saw stars and then whole constellations and the pain pulsed and danced like tiny spurs jabbing my brain.

Julia skedaddled out of the way. I grabbed the pan of boiling sweet potatoes and flung it backward over my head. There was a howl and then I could breathe again. All I knew, all I could think, was that whoever'd grabbed me was the son of a bitch who'd been fucking Julia. My hand went inside my jacket and came out with the gun, and I fired a bullet point blank at the man who'd been choking me. His face blew out the back of his head and most of it hit the refrigerator door, which was covered with photos of Andy and pictures he'd done.

My heart just about broke.

I looked at Julia, wanting her to tell me there was some mistake, that the man I'd just killed wasn't who I thought, but she just covered her eyes and moaned.

"Tommy? What the fuck? Tommy? Jesus Christ, Tommy, not you."

I looked at the gun in my hand, and I hurled the hateful thing across the kitchen. It slammed into a spice rack, which crashed to the floor, little bottles of this and that rolling everywhere.

"Oh, Jesus, Lord in Heaven, help us. Oh, Jesus."

Julia sank to her knees.

"You were fuckin' him. All the time I was in prison, all the time you'd conned me into believing you had something going with the Lord. It was all lies wasn't it? Then you found out I was gettin' out early and you panicked, didn't you? That's why you stopped taking my calls."

"I was afraid, Lonny. After Delores did what she did, I told Tommy I thought you'd go crazy. I asked him to help me."

"So that was why he wanted to go with me so bad? He wanted to keep an eye on me. Make sure I didn't hurt you. My best friend in the fucking world and *this* is how he repays me. You fucked him, didn't you? Tell me the truth!"

"We were friends, Lonny. That's all."

"You fucked him."

"No!"

"Dammit, Julia, tell me the truth!"

Andy poked his head in the doorway. "Honey, go to your room," Julia whispered, real calm and steady-like. I was impressed. She wasn't like Delores, who always shattered into fifty thousand pieces when the shit hit the fan.

Andy disappeared.

"That's good, son," I said. I turned to Julia. "Now I'm gonna fuck you, but later, you understand. First you better tell me what you know about Delores."

Julia shrugged and sat down at the kitchen table. Wasn't for Tommy's body leaking blood all over the tiles and the smell of pot roast turning to charcoal in the oven, you'da thought this was just an ordinary evening. I went over to the cabinets, opened them all up, rummaged around till I found a bottle of cooking sherry.

"This all you got to drink?"

"It's not meant for drinking. It'll make you sick."

"It'll make me a lot sicker if I don't drink it."

I tilted the bottle back, drank as much of that shit as I could stand. The ropes tethering me to my insides were dental floss thin. Crazy as it sounds, I knew I still had a chance. To wake up, I mean. But waking up to who I really was would mean I was crazy.

"Delores was worried about you gettin' out. She was afraid."

"Of what? Of me?"

"Of herself, I think. Her voices had been talkin' to her, she told me. Sayin' it was her fault you turned out the way you did. Weren't for her, she told me, you wouldn't be a alcoholic, wouldn'ta been to jail so many times."

"I take the blame for whatever I may have done. No reason for Delores to blame herself."

Julia didn't say anything, but something changed in her face, her eyes darting, mouth twisting at one corner, like the beginning of a smirk that fear snagged by the tail and yanked off her face, but not quite in time before I caught it.

"What did Delores tell you?"

"Nothin'. Nothin' more than what I said."

I sprang around the table and grabbed her, lifted her up by the elbows. "Stop lyin' to me, you fucking bitch! Fucking little nun can't let herself get fucked by anybody 'cept God and Tommy Rabbit. You're nothin' but the lyin' little gutterslut you always was. I never loved you, either. Those things I wrote in my letters, they was all lies. Just lies to try to get in your pants again once I got out. You think I'da ever married a lyin' little gutterslut like you? You think I'd stick my dick into the public *toilet?*"

She started to sob. "I did love you, Lonny. I *did*. And I was willing to try it again with you, until—"

"Until what? Till Mr. Tommy Fucking Gleason come on the scene?"

"It had nothin' to do with Tommy. I never loved him. Not like I loved you."

"Then what happened to that love? What the fuck happened?"

Her face crumpled up like used Kleenex. Like some kinda science fiction movie, where the beautiful woman suddenly turns into some slime monster.

"What happened? Delores *told* me. She was drunk, and she let it slip, and she *told* me. About what her and you've been doing since you were thirteen years old! That she couldn't stop and you couldn't stop, and all the time you and I were together, all that time, Lonny, you were with Delores, too. Your own mother! When she realized what she'd done, that everything I felt for you had changed because of what she'd told me, she got scared. Scared of what you'd do when you found out I knew. Guilt killed Delores. Guilt over what you and she *did*."

"That's a lie! That's a goddamn fucking lie!" I backhanded her and she slammed into the sink right at kidney level. I saw the pain in her face but the next blow—fist closed—wiped it off. Her eyes glazed and she sort of fell in slow motion, like a candle melting down, onto the floor.

Behind me the room exploded with a terrible roar. A bullet rocketed past my head and tore a hole the size of a basketball in the kitchen wall. Julia screamed.

I whirled around, thinking somehow Tommy had come back to life.

"Stop hurting my mother."

Andy stood there with my .38. It would've been funny, a little kid playin' stick 'em up, if the gun he was aiming weren't real.

I held my hands up. "Hey, chill out, little bro. You'll hurt somebody."

His little face closed up like a fist. "I hate you. You're mean. You shot Tommy."

Behind me I heard Julia scraping herself off the floor, getting to her knees. "Andy, honey, you give that to me. Give the gun to me, baby."

Andy's eyes darted to Julia. Then to me. Then to Julia. Me. Julia. Tears squeezed from his eyes.

"Why did you kill Uncle Tommy? Why did you hurt Mom?"

Julia started crawling across the floor toward him. Blood leaked from her nose and marked her progression across the tile.

"Give me the gun, Andy. Please."

"That's right. Give the gun to your mom."

As soon as I spoke, Andy gripped the gun harder and tilted it up toward my head.

"Just you shut up," said Julia. "Let me talk to my son."

"I hate you! I hate you!" screamed Andy.

Julia got to within a few feet of him. Stretched out her hand.

"Baby, it's okay now. Just give me the gun. Uncle Lonny and I are through fightin'. Nobody else will get hurt. I promise you."

"Don't be stupid, Andy," I said. "You can't shoot nobody."

The way he reacted to the sound of my voice, you'da thought I was spittin' poison. The barrel of the gun tilted up at my face again, and he stepped back from his mom, who was on her hands and knees crawling toward him. Crawling, I thought. She never did that for me. Never crawled on the floor with her ass in the air and her tits hanging down and her own blood makin' a trail.

Something angry and evil and old stirred up and wiggled inside me. Like some kinda worm that nests in your guts and stays quiet, biding its time, till suddenly it starts to look for a way out, through your skin, out your nose or your eye or your ear.

"You're just a kid. I ain't 'fraid of you. Why don't you go ahead an' shoot me?"

Julia said, "Oh Lonny, shut up," and Andy said, "Fuck you!"

"Fuck you, too," I said. "Go ahead an' shoot."

'Cause I'd realized all of a sudden that this was his moment, this was the moment that Andy, with a single decision, could change the whole course of his life. He could fire the gun and kill the bad man who'd beat up his mama and shot Uncle Tommy or he could put the gun down and spend the rest of his life dragging around the "what ifs" of that moment like a sack full of stones tied to his balls.

I envied him. In spite of the fact that it would cost me my life, a part of me hoped that he'd do the right thing.

"C'mon, you little shit. Shoot me."

"He's crazy, Andy. Don't listen to him."

Julia stretched out her hand.

Andy looked at me, at his mother, then back at me. His mouth started to quiver, and a part of me felt sick, 'cause I knew he was too young and too scared and he wouldn't go through with it. He gave Julia the gun.

"That's a good boy," she said.

"Yeah, Andy, that's a good boy," I said. I grabbed the gun away from Julia and shot her in the chest. Then in the face so I didn't have to see her expression. Then, as she lay on the floor, I kicked her legs open and fired into her pussy—her sweet, silk-lined pussy that I'd fucked so many times, but I fucked her this time with a bullet.

Andy musta gone into shock. He didn't make a sound. I picked him up and carried him to the closet, pushed a bureau up against it so he'd have to stay put.

"I'm sorry, bro," I said. "When you get older, if you want to come after me, if you spray my brains all over a wall, I'll understand and I'll forgive you. I swear I will."

Chapter Twelve

I figure I'll go visit MaryLynn. She's the redhead works in a Shop 'N' Save, lost her kids when she went to jail once for writing bad checks, likes some guy on *The Young and the Restless*, and has a tattoo of a unicorn jumping over a rainbow on her left shoulder blade.

Yeah, MaryLynn—why the hell not?

At Colorado Springs, I pull off the road and call the cops from an all-night diner, tell them I heard a child screamin' at Julia's address and maybe they better go have a look-see.

Then I head straight to a Liquor Mart and use the money I took out of Tommy's wallet to buy a bottle of Beam. 'Cause I got to stay drunk now. I don't dare sober up. I get sober, even for a few hours and think about what I just done, I'll never make it to see my new girlfriend. I'll go fuckin' crazy.

The first few twenty miles or so, Julia rides with me, sitting there in the passenger seat, pulling her top down, playing with her big tits. But then she starts to blur, her face fades into pale grey streaks, like rainwater on a dirty windshield. Finally, she ain't there at all.

Then Delores takes a turn, her mouth moving like she's trying to talk, trying to tell me something, but I can't hear her voice at all. The sweetest voice in the world, and now I can't even remember it.

The night closes in on me like a fist. I uncap the bottle and take a long gulp, then another one. I drink a third of the bottle, but something's wrong. It doesn't feel like it ought to. It doesn't feel like that moment of relief and pleasure and bliss when your dick first slides inside a warm, wet pussy or a hot, cum-thirsty throat.

It feels empty and sickening and old, and I feel sober as hell.

That scares me more than anything that's happened so far.

'Cause now I can *think*.

God, Delores, I'm so sorry it turned out like this. Julia and Tommy, I'm so fucking sorry.

I don't know what happened. If I could do it all over...if I could...

There's the faintest of tingling in my fingertips. I brace myself for the sensation of something inside me coming awake, of energy rising, of something greater than Lonny surging up through my spine, and I think: *God, the alcohol don't seem like it's working no more. Maybe I'm ready to try and get past my fear of You. To let go and open my heart and let You come in. Maybe I can do this for Delores and Julia and Tommy and everyone else that I've hurt. Maybe I won't have to kill nobody else.*

But as I keep driving, the tingling stops and my hands start to go numb.

And I realize it's only the cold.

☙

ABOUT THE AUTHOR

LUCY TAYLOR is the award-winning author of seven novels, five collections, and over a hundred short stories. Most recently, her work has appeared in her collection *Fatal Journeys* and in the anthologies *Fright Mare* ("Dead Messengers"), *Into Painfreak* ("He Who Whispers the Dead Back to Life"), *Peel Back the Skin* ("Moth Frenzy"), and at Tor.com ("Sweetlings," May 4, 2017). Several of her stories can also be found on the short fiction app Great Jones Street.

Upcoming work includes short stories in the anthologies *The Five Senses of Horror* ("In the Cave of the Delicate Singers"), *Edward Bryant Tribute Anthology* ("Blessed Be the Bound"), and *CEA Greatest Anthology Written* ("Fecundity"). A new edition of her Stoker-winning novel *The Safety of Unknown Cities*, illustrated by Glen Chadbourne and published by The Overlook Connection Press, will be out later this year.

Taylor lives in the high desert outside Santa Fe, New Mexico.

AVAILABLE BOOKS

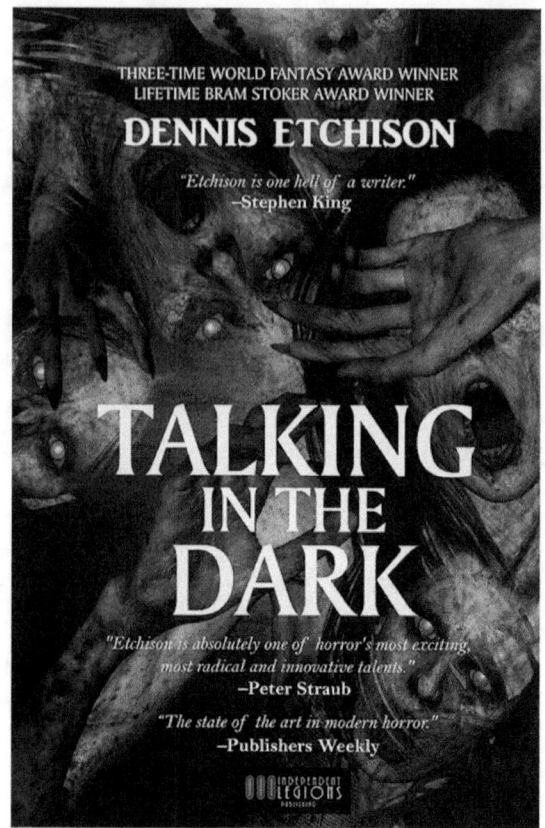

THREE-TIME WORLD FANTASY AWARD WINNER
LIFETIME BRAM STOKER AWARD WINNER

DENNIS ETCHISON

"Etchison is one hell of a writer."
–Stephen King

TALKING
IN THE
DARK

*"Etchison is absolutely one of horror's most exciting,
most radical and innovative talents."*
–Peter Straub

"The state of the art in modern horror."
–Publishers Weekly

INDEPENDENT LEGIONS PUBLISHING

TALKING IN THE DARK
by Dennis Etchison
Collection – **eBook Edition**
December 2017

THE LIVING AND THE DEAD
by Greg F. Gifune
Novel – **Paperback and eBook Edition**
December 2017

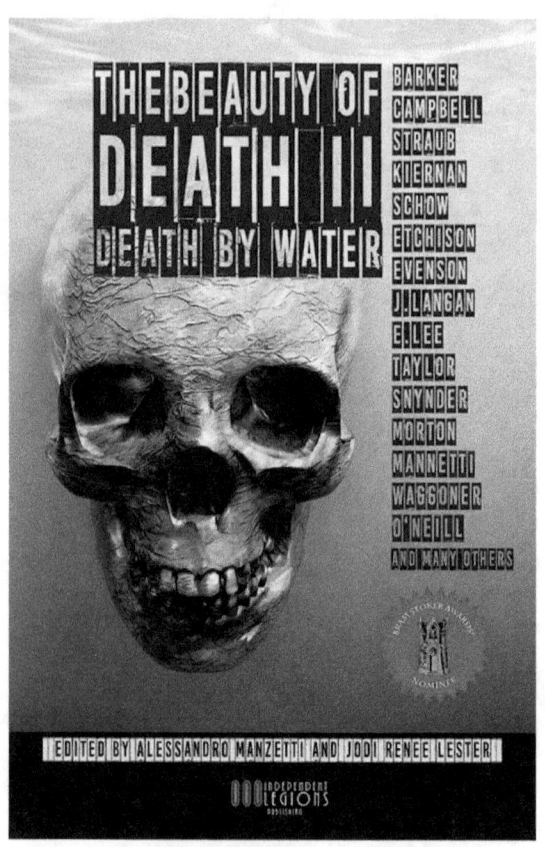

THE BEAUTY OF DEATH VOL. 2 - DEATH BY WATER
Edited by Alessandro Manzetti and Jodi Renée Lester
Anthology – **Paperback and eBook Edition**
November 2017

CHILDREN OF NO ONE
by Nicole Cushing
Novella – **Paperback and eBook Edition**
October 2017

DREAMS THE RAGMAN
by Dennis Etchison
Novella – **eBook Edition**
October 2017

THE RAIN DANCERS
by Greg F. Gifune
Novella – **eBook Edition**
September 2017

THE WISH MECHANICS
by Daniel Braum
Collection – **Paperback and eBook Edition**
July 2017

THE ONE THAT COMES BEFORE
by Livia Llewellyn
Novella – **Paperback and eBook Edition**
May 2017

SELECTED STORIES
by Nate Southard
Collection – **Paperback and eBook Edition**
April 2017

THE CARP-FACED BOY AND OTHER TALES
by Thersa Matsuura
Collection – **Paperback and eBook Edition**
February 2017

ALL–AMERICAN HORROR OF THE 21ST CENTURY
Edited by MortCastle
Anthology – **Paperback and eBook Edition**
November 2016

BENEATH THE NIGHT
by Greg F. Gifune
Novel & Novella – **Paperback Edition**
October 2016

THE BEAUTY OF DEATH VOL 1
Edited by Alessandro Manzetti
Anthology – **eBook Edition**
July 2016

DOCTOR BRITE
by Poppy Z. Brite
Collection – **eBook Edition**
January 2017

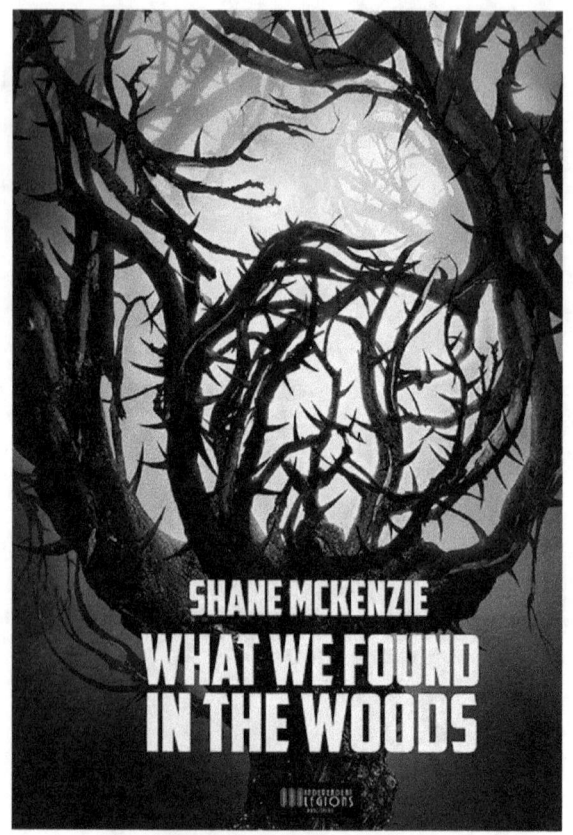

WHAT WE FOUND IN THE WOODS
by Shane McKenzie
Collection – **eBook Edition**
September 2016

USED STORIES
by Poppy Z. Brite
Collection – **eBook Edition**
June 2016

THE HORROR SHOW
by Poppy Z. Brite
Collection – **eBook Edition**
August 2016

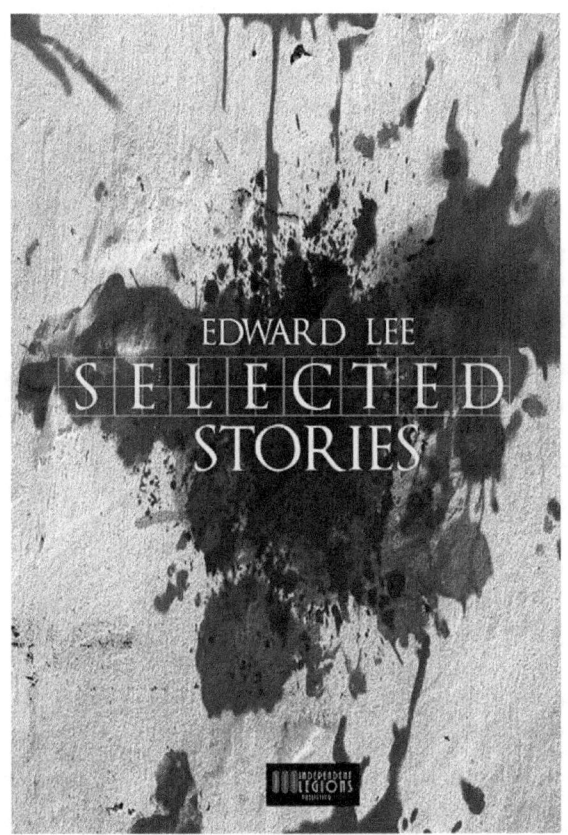

SELECTED STORIES
by Edward Lee
Collection – **eBook Edition**
July 2016

THE USHERS
by Edward Lee
Collection – **eBook Edition**
May 2016

THE CRYSTAL EMPIRE
by Poppy Z. Brite
Novella – **eBook Edition**
May 2016

SELECTED STORIES
by Poppy Z. Brite
Collection – **eBook Edition**
February 2016

THE HITCHHIKING EFFECT
by Gene O'Neill
Collection – **eBook Edition**
February 2016

SONGS FOR THE LOST
by Alexander Zelenyj
Collection – **eBook Edition**
April 2016

INDEPENDENT LEGIONS PUBLISHING

INDEPENDENT LEGIONS PUBLISHING
by Alessandro Manzetti
Via Virgilio, 10 - 34134 Trieste (Italy)
+39 040 9776602

www.independentlegions.com
www.facebook.com/independentlegions
independent.legions@aol.com

Books in Italian:
www.independentlegions.com/pubblicazioni.html

ASSOCIATION

SPECIALTY PRESS AWARD RECIPIENT